Will and The Whisp

Jessica,

Enjoy Reading,

Ron Markey

Will and The Whisp

Ross MacKay

ISBN: paperback 978-1-956183-81-8
Ebook 978-1-956183-55-9

Cover Design by Diana TC Triumph Covers

First Printing Edition 2022

Published by Creative James Media
Pasadena, MD

For Noah.

Chapter 1
The Night Chase

The Whisp hurtles down a side street and then spins to the left.

Faster and faster, as fast as she can.

She hears heavy boots on the damp cobbles and the howls and whoops behind her. A glance back shows some of the Hunters grasping electric spears, running them against the granite walls. The sparks crackle in the air as they singe the old stones black. The rain lashes down onto the old slate roofs making the whole city bristle with noise.

Amongst all this chaos, she keeps running, tries hard to concentrate on the sound that beckons. It's fragile, like fine thread unwinding from a spindle. She knows if she loses it, inside the noise of the chase, it might never be found again.

The sound is hope.

The Whisp propels herself forward. She has never heard the song of the Thresholds until this night. She didn't even exist when they were last open. But if a Threshold was open and singing to her, then there was a chance . . . A small chance, she might escape with her life.

1

The city is woven like a tightly gnarled knot through which she twists and turns, doubling back on herself when she comes across another squad of Hunters in the alleyway ahead of her. They are systematic, cutting off streets, encircling her, trying to pen her in. She works fast to plot a new route in her mind, turning towards the sound whenever she has the chance.

The Hunters are like a pack of wild dogs catching the scent of prey in their nostrils. They will not lose her. She is quicker than them, but they are relentless. And while she may be invisible, the lashing rain runs down her body, making her shimmer.

They are swooping upon her, again and again. Each trying their best to seize the Whisp in their talons. But agile and quick, she darts across a city square into another crumpled heap of side streets.

The Whisp tries to turn another corner but misjudges the pivot and crashes hard into a wooden door that rattles on its hinges. Trying to correct her balance, she slips as the wet gravel beneath her gives way. Landing in a heap, she looks up and notices a looming shadow in front of her.

The only humans ever out at this time of night are Hunters.

She scurries upwards, grabbing the nearby lamppost. The wet metal squeals with her grip—she freezes as he turns and smiles.

She knows what he sees: the raindrops are not falling through the air as they should but running down her transparent frame. The outline of her shape is like the film of a bubble, and he aims to burst her wide open.

The Hunter grips his stinger with both hands and thrusts it forward with force. There is a hellacious crack. With a flash, she is no longer invisible, appearing instead as a stark blue outline of a girl that shines bright in the night air.

The Whisp spasms with shock as the current jolts through her. The streetlamp that she has been holding onto goes out with a bang.

They are both startled as the glass of the lamp shatters and cascades down with the lashing rain. She recovers first, using the distraction to dart off in the other direction. From the corner of her eye, she sees that others have caught sight of her again and join the chase.

She runs as tiny bolts of power pulsate through her, tiny sparks snapping along the air, dashing down the empty road so fast that some of the shop shutters tremble in her wake.

The electricity zips and buzzes, and suddenly the Whisp loses all sense of the sound she had been chasing. She desperately tries to find it again, but she cannot stop to listen. Cannot take a moment's breath to focus on her surroundings.

The Hunters are too close. They bellow and bark as they pursue their prey. They brandish their stingers like tiny electric tongues lapping at the wet air, hoping to taste the Whisp once more.

She wishes she had never left her hiding place.

The sound is lost, and they almost have her captured.

All of her friends had disappeared, one by one. Caught by the Hunters and never seen again. She didn't know if she was the last spirit left, but she hadn't seen another Whisp or Ghast for days, possibly weeks. All the Whisp can do now is run, but she knows they will catch her too—it is inevitable.

The Hunters are so close she can feel the electricity as it jumps from their stingers, launching through the air towards her.

en, as she rounds another corner, the sound
.c more. The note, it is there again, louder than
ver, and it pulls her forward. She pushes towards it with a burst of energy so strong it creates a little space between herself and the Hunters.

Sprinting down a side street on the right, all the time following the sound, the Whisp finds herself in the vast openness of the university square. The sound has become rich and harmonic, like it is singing to her, willing her to keep running. The spindle threaded tone pulses, like a throbbing heartbeat.

The sound is emanating from a tall marble fountain that stands in the centre of the square.

As the Hunters emerge into the square they begin to fan out, cutting off as many exits as they can. They think they have her trapped.

They don't hear the sound. She knows they cannot hear what she is hearing. It must be a Threshold. This is her chance. She runs full tilt across the square, making for the fountain.

A ferocious Hunter hurls his stinger. It skids on the ground beside her as it lands. She notices another in the corner of her eye flying through the air and ducks just in time.

They hope to harpoon her like a prized beast—she runs for her life.

Making one last surge towards the tone, the Whisp dives headfirst into the ornate marble fountain.

She instantly regrets it as the first stinger plunges into the water.

She steels herself, expecting the pain of the electrified water to slice through her. But there is nothing. The stinger is in the water, the water vibrating around its horrific prongs. But it seems so far away.

The Whisp is deep in the water now, deeper than a fountain should go. She looks up at the world above, illuminated in the moonlight.

The world of Hunters and stingers and thrashing rain, the world that was so immediate and real and close only a second ago, is now a tiny fading dot. All she knows is that the sound, the alluring sound that had drawn her out of hiding now surrounds her, resonating through the water.

She is in a deep seam. It feels like a cavern at the bottom of the world; the edges of it close around her. The satisfying tone builds to a crescendo, and then with the slightest of breaths, she feels the world above her close, and below her, a new world rushes into existence—

She collapses into it.

Still in the water, but no longer in a fountain, the sound and the world the Whisp has lived in all her life disappears completely.

It was a Threshold. I have crossed over. I'm somewhere new.

She turns and turns, looking for an escape, but all she finds are walls of cold ceramic.

Turning for the third time she notices the small hole at the bottom. It's a pipe, and it too is filled with water. She begins to flow down it. At first, she feels relief at the opportunity to escape, but in a flash realises that the pipe is too small for her.

But she is running down it. Flowing. Pouring down the pipe. Her invisible form is now inside and part of the water. It is as if her whole body had dissolved into it like a teaspoon of sugar.

She was there only a moment ago, but now she is not.

The Whisp tries hard to unbind herself, to reform her shape, but it is impossible.

Perhaps the sound was a trap. Perhaps the Hunters

weren't chasing her. Perhaps they were herding her to the square, to the fountain.

Maybe they wanted her inside a Threshold with no way to escape. But why have they bound her to the water? What are they planning to do? Why would they push her through a Threshold in the first place? She had learned that the Hunters were locking the Thresholds. Why would they keep this one open?

Maybe it was luck, maybe she'd really escaped . . . But where was she? What world was she in? What kind of trap had her in its hold? Would they kill her? Was this where all the captured Whisps have been sent? Another world? A prison?

A thousand thoughts are cascading through her mind, all at once.

Whisps bind and unbind all the time, she reminds herself; it's what they were supposed to do.

Bind and unbind.

Bind and unbind.

She repeats this mantra over and over. It soothes her.

Bind and unbind.

When she was first whispered into existence, she bound to all kinds of things. Though, she had never bound with water before, but then again, she had never crossed a Threshold either.

It was a new experience, and for the moment, it was safer than being surrounded by fifty feral Hunters desperate to catch her.

She concentrates her mind, opens her awareness, and lets her consciousness move into all the particles of the water. Travelling through them, her mind navigates a vast maze of pipes, syphons, and cisterns. All at once, she is everywhere as the water runs through the system.

And still she sees nothing but ceramic and worn lead.

The smell of mildew and the sweet tang of urine lingers all around her. Her new prison would be unbearable if it were not for the noise.

Because from every corner she can hear children, laughing.

Chapter 2
Running Late

The classroom was a stark and austere place. The smartboard was streaked in dust and looked like it hadn't been used for a long time. Even the teacher's desk was bare except for a stack of neatly piled jotters under an antique paperweight.

It was a bright day, and a faint light was trying to pour in the windows, but the collection of half-broken blinds that hung at odd angles was doing its very best at blocking it out. It meant the room was filled with shafts of shadows that created irregular patterns on the walls and floor.

Will let the other students file in first so that he didn't need to introduce himself and ask which space was free. He slipped in and took the last seat available, drawing as little attention to himself as possible.

Will hadn't spotted the teacher, Mr. Anthony, but he was sure that anyone with a classroom this bare must be an authoritarian taskmaster.

"Time to begin, I suppose." A strained voice of an old man came from the back of the room. The students spun around, but there was no one there.

Mr. Anthony rose up from behind a desk with a stretch. To Will, he looked like a wolf keening at the moon as he cricked his neck. The whole class heard it crunch as he stretched out his arms. Had he been sleeping back there? Had he just woken up? Will couldn't be sure.

"The bookshelves in these classrooms are too bloody low. Who puts a bookshelf just above the skirting board? I had to bend like a contortionist to find the bloody thing."

The classroom giggled.

"I don't know what your all are laughing at. Old age and creaky knees will come to you all one day too."

At that, Will immediately warmed to Mr. Anthony. He wasn't like the classroom at all. He seemed jovial. He had a grey moustache that twitched at the edges as he talked. His bushy eyebrows followed the same suit.

"Still a bloody good read this book, so that's what we will do today, I think."

Mr. Anthony had made his way to the front of the class, ruffling a kid's hair as he went by.

The class giggled again.

Will saw the teacher's teeth were slightly yellowed, and there was a flash of a gold tooth at the back, so when he grinned, it really did seem to sparkle. He sat on his seat and pushed it with his weight, making it roll backwards. He put his feet up onto the desk and folded them over one another. It was only then Will noticed the teacher had no shoes on. He had two worn looking socks, thick woolly things that had seen better days. One had a hole in the big toe.

"Oh, don't mind the smell," Mr. Anthony jabbed. "I call it Eau de Hoof."

The classroom erupted in laughter and Will let himself join in with a chuckle. It seemed that everyone liked Mr. Anthony.

"So, class shall we begin?"

Not waiting for a response, Mr. Anthony opened his book and began to read from it.

It was a tome about the battles of World War One. Mr. Anthony read it like he was living through it. He made the words spring to life. Every so often, he would stop and skip back a few pages, muttering to them that he was trying to make sense of what he was reading. He was absorbed in every detail and seemed to relish in every twist and turn of the battles.

The class didn't jot down a note or answer a question, they just watched, enraptured by the teacher's performance. Will rested his chin in his hands and, like the rest of the class, he sat and listened.

Until, splodge, a red blot landed on his desk. Then another. Will instinctively brought his hand to his nose. When he looked at his fingers, he saw the blood trickling onto his palm.

He tilted his head back in the hope that the blood wouldn't run onto his shirt. The motion caught Mr. Anthony's attention amongst the stillness of the other students.

"New boy, what's the matter?"

Will didn't need to explain. As soon as he tilted his head down to answer, the blood ran off his chin and onto his shirt. It was dripping in thick heavy globules, sploshing around him. He heard the class react with "eww" or "gross."

Mr. Anthony seized command of the situation just by raising his finger, and the rest of the class fell silent. "Don't worry lad. A little bit of blood didn't harm anyone."

The history teacher picked up the telephone on the wall and began to dial. He twisted slightly to the side, murmured something into the phone, and then he hung up. "Mr. Scroggie is the caretaker. He will get all this cleaned up. The rest of you lot, let's call this the end of the lesson. Just don't let them know I let you out early," he said with a wink.

The rest of the class picked up their bags and shuffled out the door, being sure to give Will a wide berth.

This was not how he wanted his first day to go at all. He had worried over every inch of himself that morning. He had one aim for the day, and that was to enter his new school with a minimum of fuss. Before leaving that morning, he had checked himself over, each aspect of his appearance becoming a deliberate decision: bag on one shoulder; tie on, but top button undone; shirt untucked. He decided to let his belt a little loose, so his trousers didn't hold his waist to tight. It made his little round belly protrude, and he didn't like that. His hair was a little ruffled but not sticking up.

Sacha would have cultivated her look. Would have carefully composed each element, aiming for as high an impact as possible. But Will was nothing like his sister. He never dressed to impress. That was the last thing he wanted to do. He wanted to leave no impression at all.

But now, there he was, covered in blood. There was no chance of him blending in now.

Will sat frozen in his seat, unsure if he should try to leave like the rest of the class or wait for Mr. Scroggie to arrive.

"Prone to them, are you?" Mr. Anthony asked, trying to put Will at ease.

Will nodded.

"Stressful time, being the new boy."

Will nodded again and was pleased that Mr. Anthony's attempts at conversation was then disrupted by a faint rap at the door.

"That will be Mr. Scroggie," Mr. Anthony said, before the door opened.

The caretaker's large figure loomed in the doorway, ducking his head slightly as he entered.

"The boy here—wait, what's your name?" Mr. Anthony turned his attention to Will.

"Will Devine," Will answered, his voice sounding squeaky as he pinched the bridge of his nose trying to stem the blood as it continued to trickle.

Mr. Anthony nodded, turning back to face the doorway where the caretaker waited. "William has a nosebleed. We'll need a mop before the next lesson."

Mr. Scroggie gave an almost timid nod.

"Also, the boy will need a new shirt. Take him to the lost and found," Mr. Anthony commanded.

Mr. Scroggie chewed at his lip then grunted, arching his head at Will as if to say "follow me" before he started walking.

Hesitantly, Will followed behind, still tilting his head to the ceiling. The faint taste of blood was now in the back of his mouth and his eyes were stinging with tears.

When they arrived at his office, Mr. Scroggie took out a card and held it to the key panel—the door bleeped open. "Wait 'ere." He headed into the dark room, slamming the door behind him.

A moment later, the door opened up, and an arm thrust out a wad of paper towels. Will took them and muttered a "thanks" as the door slammed again.

When the door opened a second time, Mr. Scroggie was holding out a large white t-shirt. Taking the shirt, Will noticed the grey hairs on the man's hands ran all the way down to his knuckles.

"Will that do?"

"It might be a bit . . . big," Will said around the paper towels, trying not to sound ungrateful.

Mr. Scroggie stared at Will with his sharp judging eyes before crumpling the t-shirt up in his hands and stepping back. "Look fir y'rself then."

"Uhh…" Will slinked closer when Mr. Scroggie held the door open wider, motioning Will forward. Up close, Will could see how much tension the man held in his body. Even his veins seemed brittle and course. The man's breath wheezed in and out impatiently.

Hurriedly Will scrambled through the large cardboard box that had been pulled down to the floor, finding a jumper to pull over his shirt.

"Whit's y'er next class?"

"Biology. Mrs. Duncan's," Will replied, stuffing the bloodied paper towels into his trouser pocket before pulling on the jumper.

"First floor." Mr. Scroggie snorted, holding the door open for Will to slip past.

Will stepped outside and the door slammed closed behind him just as the bell rung to switch classes.

Running late, Will checked the classroom's number against his timetable, opened the door and slipped inside. Sniggers accompanied his arrival. Embarrassed, he stood still, waiting to be told where to sit.

"And this class is—" Mrs. Duncan stopped, her finger pointing at one of the dog-eared posters that hung on the wall by Will's head. She bounded over to him, her tight blond curls bouncing as she moved.

"Ah, the fresh blood has arrived," she declared with a

sense of mischievousness. "William Devine, or so it says on my list."

Will nodded.

"Well Willy, come in and take a seat. There's one spare beside Gabrielle there."

Will heard the titter amongst some of the boys sitting at the back of the class. His cheeks flushed scarlet. He heard some whisper "Willy" as he headed towards his seat.

The class was laid out with big, long wooden benches each with two tall stools apiece. Brightly coloured posters explaining things like photosynthesis and pollination hung on the walls. A row of shelves surrounded the classroom, each displaying an odd menagerie of items. The common items of any biology class were there: a plastic anatomical heart, a collection of pots filled with earth but no sign of a plant, and an old-looking microscope. There was a skeleton in the corner with a red clown wig on his skull, a football scarf for the Worldmouth Wanderers that was pinned like bunting, and a little stuffed tartan sock inside a cage labelled 'RARE SPECIES: HAGGIS.' Mrs. Duncan had a peculiar sense of humour; it seemed.

Will clambered up onto the stool beside Gabrielle who looked at him like he was a specimen, gawking through her spectacles.

"Hello, I'm Gabrielle Roland Crowsdale. You can call me Gaby. Are you the same age as us? You seem small. Some schools let you skip a year. Are you super intelligent?"

Will blinked at her. "I—"

"Are you—" Gaby started.

"Shhhh now, Gaby. You will have the chance to gossip with your new pal later," Mrs. Duncan interrupted, calmly.

With a sigh, Gaby turned away and Will tried to focus on the lesson.

Mrs. Duncan strode up and down the classroom as she talked. She took each of the students in, being sure to look them in the eye and give them a beaming smile—Will already disliked her. She was likely one of those teachers that would declare learning was fun and insist on making each of them answer out loud in class.

She was talking to the class about symbiosis. It meant animals living together and working together for mutual benefit. She gave examples of crocodiles letting birds clean their teeth and insects that helped flowers spread their seeds. Will had never heard of the word before but tried his best to spell it out in his notes. S-IM-BY-O-SIS.

Once she had settled the class to work on an assignment, Mrs. Duncan came over to Will's desk. "Welcome to biology or as I like to call it 'plants, people, and everything in between.' I will be the captain of Class 2B. Steering us onto new unchartered territories. Now, first things first." She paused to smile. "Lesson numero uno, Mr. Devine. I am Mrs. Duncan. With one 'd,' two vowels, a 'c' and a couple of 'n's.' You can guess the order." She winked and Will wanted to roll his eyes.

"More like Dunkin Donuts," a voice whispered from behind them.

Gaby gasped; someone laughed.

Mrs. Duncan's eyes darted to the culprit; Will couldn't help back glance over his shoulder to see who had spoken.

"Whispering voice could be better. Dunkin Donuts, hmm? Not the most original but you are off the mark. Usually, I don't discover my nickname until after Christmas. Now, the rulebook says name-calling is not tolerated. Strictly speaking, I should send you straight to the year head. But we don't want to do that, do we?"

The boy looked sheepish and quickly shook his head. Beside him, another boy looked away.

"Here's the deal I'm going to offer." She eyed the room, each student now focused on what she was about to say. "Anyone with a nickname for me, feel free to use it, but I get to give one back. Deal?"

The boy didn't know how to answer and got confused. First, he nodded, then he shook his head.

"Or do we want to go to year head?"

This time the boy shook his head.

"Good. So, I get to give a nickname back," Mrs. Duncan said causing Gaby to giggle.

Will shifted in his seat, putting his head down.

"Let me think." Mrs. Duncan tapped her finger on her chin, "Stephen, how about Urchin? Sea urchin." She hummed. "Now, why would I call him that . . . Class, any guesses?"

Gaby's hand shot up. "Because of his hair. Sea urchins are all spiky."

Stephen frowned.

"Got it in one, girl! Now for your laughing friend, Danny. Maybe a sea cucumber? Yes, Urchin and Cucumber, sea creatures of the murky depths." The biology teacher eyed the room again. The class shifted uneasily in their seats. "Anything else? Any more names for me? Chunky Dunky? Duncasurous Rex?" At their silence, Mrs. Duncan sighed. "No? Ok, let's continue. Who's finished reading page forty-six of the textbook?"

The class remained quiet for the rest of the lesson. Except for Gaby who still seemed fascinated with Will.

"Did you do biology at your last school? I'm pretty good. If you're stuck just copy me. I don't mind," she whispered.

Will tried hard to concentrate on his textbook and ignore her, but she was persistent.

"You can't copy for tests or quizzes, of course, but I

don't mind textbook stuff. My handwriting is very legible. I'm left-handed, so it sometimes smudges. Just ask if you can't read it."

Will whispered back, curtly, "I'm fine."

He thought this had ended the matter, but only a minute later, Gaby broke the silence.

"What other classes are you in? I have French next. What do you have?"

Will's heart sunk. He had French too. He didn't want to do another class with Gaby. Chances were, he would be stuck with her again. "French," he admitted.

Gaby's eyes lit up. "Cool. You can copy me there, too. My best subject is French. Most people in this school only speak one language. But I'm already bi-lingual. I know sign language too. So, technically French is my third language. I'd like to speak at least five by the time I finish university. My mum says I speak too fast in every language. Even my signs are lightning quick. If you want me to slow down, just say. I won't be offended, I promise."

Will considered asking Gaby to be quiet because he wanted to concentrate, but he didn't think he would be able to interrupt her long enough.

Gaby looked like she did everything at 100 miles an hour. Her frizzy black hair shot off in all directions, and her cardigan was buttoned up wrong so that one buttonhole was skipped, making the whole thing sit squint on her body. Her eyes continually skirted around the room, and even as she talked, she nibbled the top of her pen like a hamster. The hand that held her pen was smudged with wet ink, and so was her jotter.

She was a calamitous jumble of energy. Will was worried at any second that she might just explode with a new idea and send his neatly arranged belongings across the floor.

The more she talked, the more exasperated he became. He noticed that there was rarely a question amongst all of her fast-moving words. When there was a question, she took the raise of his eyebrow, pursing of lips or intake of breath as an answer. She inferred everything from those little gestures and thought that even without Will uttering a word, they were already becoming firm friends. Will tried twice to protest but was quickly learning that Gaby was not the listening type.

He exhaled with relief when the school bell rang, then winced when Gaby said, "I have a spare seat beside me in French. It can be yours, no problem! But I can't have lunch with you. Band practice."

Mrs. Duncan grabbed a giant mug emblazoned with 'Putting the TEA in teacher' written across it and headed for the door. She stopped long enough to say, "Last one to leave, turn off the lights!"

After she left, the class began to pack up their stuff and file out one by one. The newly nicknamed Urchin and Cucumber sauntered over towards Gaby and Will.

"You ever call me a sea urchin again, and my cousin will mess you up, got it?"

Gaby stood up from her stool and jutted out her chin. "Leave me alone, Stephen."

"Or what? You going to tell that fat bitch, Duncan?" Danny challenged.

Stephen cackled at her glare. He slowly picked up each of the items Gaby still had on the desk. One by one he dropped them to the floor: her pencil case, her jotter, each loose pen and pencil. Running out of items, he reached under the desk and plucked up Gaby's bag. He unzipped it and proceeded to tip every item out.

Will tried to keep his head down as he packed his own bag quickly. He felt uncomfortable; from the corner of his eye he could see Gaby was welling up. For the briefest of moments, he imagined standing up to the bullies and telling them to back off, but he knew that would be a terrible misstep for his first day at school. He noticed everyone else had already left—no one was sticking up to these two. Will packed his bag and tried to make his exit, ignoring the whole situation. Only he found himself face to face with Danny who was now between him and the door,

"Going somewhere, Tubby?" Danny spat.

Will felt his insides curdle. This was the last thing he wanted. How had he become a target so quickly? He hadn't even done anything.

He tried to sidestep Danny, but the path between the row of desks was narrow, and Danny easily blocked him.

Stephen's sharp sneering features shifted focus too, snapping towards Will.

"Awww. Gaby's finally got a friend, Little Willy." Stephen wiggled his pinkie at Will so that he knew exactly what he meant by the word little.

Danny guffawed, "Ha! Little Willy!"

Will felt his face becoming red and he blurted out, "She's not my friend. I don't even like her."

"Even the tubby boys don't fancy Gobby Gaby," mused Stephen, smiling.

Danny laughed before beginning to kick some of Gaby's items around the classroom.

Will lifted his head. He felt sick in his stomach, seeing how crestfallen Gaby looked. He knew he shouldn't have said what he did, but he didn't want any more trouble. He headed for the door and almost bumped into Mrs. Duncan.

"Just fetching the cafetière. Honestly, I would forget my head . . ." Mrs. Duncan trailed off. "What's going on?"

Stephen shrugged. "We were just playing."

"Lies! They stole the stuff out of my bag and kicked it everywhere!"

At Gaby's outburst, Mrs. Duncan looked to Will. "Did you witness this, William?"

Will kept his eyes down but gave a slow nod.

Mrs. Duncan's face went scarlet before she bellowed, "Stephen McFall, Daniel Stobbie pick all of this up and hand it back this instant. Then I would like you to wait behind, please."

Will didn't look up as he slipped out of the room.

For the rest of the day, he felt guilty. Even though he had told the truth, he should have done more, he thought. He should have helped Gaby, but he wanted so badly to keep his head down. He thought about finding Gaby to say sorry, to tell her he wanted to be friends, but he wasn't sure if she would accept it.

Chapter 3
The Binding

Will's first few days at the secondary school passed by and he began to settle.

At lunchtime, Will would queue in the canteen with his head down. He took his tray of food into the playground because he had found a hole in the schoolyard fence. It meant he could creep out and sit at the park. He didn't have any friends, so no one noticed that he was gone.

During one lunch period, he thought about joining a club, but that would mean introducing himself. That would mean knocking on a door and saying hello and asking to join in, and he couldn't do that. So here he was, on a park bench sharing his lunch with the seagulls and that was the best place he had found so far.

Soon he would have to find somewhere warmer to sit, but for the time being he would just zip up his jacket.

He watched the last leaves floating to the ground, adding to the crisp pillows of gold and red, leaving the tree bare. They looked like skeletal hands, Will thought, rupturing the earth, grasping at the dying sunlight. When he was alone, his mind often wandered to the thought of death. It had become such a big part of his life over the last few years, that he hardly noticed his mind drift towards it.

He occasionally wondered if Sacha had the same thoughts. Maybe, he thought, but maybe she is too busy with her new friends to let her thoughts wander back to the past like he did.

The seagulls squawked like they were trying to distract him, he smiled and tossed them a few crumbs from his sandwich. They were greedy and noisy, but they never called him names or laughed at him.

While he picked at the bottom of a packet of crisps, he remembered his old friends from his last school teasing him with horror stories about Worldmouth Academy. Things they had heard from a cousin once or from a friend of a friend.

Rumours had flown, and of course, Will worried about each of them, but now he realised almost none of them were true. No one had been hung up on the basketball hoop by their underwear. None of the teachers handed out five thousand-word essays as homework due the very next day. No one had stolen anyone's lunch money. It was all just myths and make-believe.

Until it wasn't.

It was a hot sticky day when it happened. The sun seemed to beam at full strength, and it felt like everything was sweating.

He was in history and Mr. Anthony grumbled, again, about the broken blinds and his inability to open the windows.

"Damn heat," he said, wiping his brow with a

handkerchief. He placed both fists onto his desk and watched the class file in. He looked withered. Will had noticed that over the last few weeks that Mr. Anthony's fantastic story sessions had dwindled and now they spent most classes in complete silence answering questions from a textbook.

"Where did we finish off last lesson?" he asked, barely lifting his head from his desk.

"Page fifty," someone behind Will answered.

"Then turn to page fifty-one."

The class let out a mutual groan, and Mr. Anthony looked up, his moustache twitched as his jaw clenched. "Page fifty-one."

The class got to work.

Mr. Anthony had aged in the short time Will had known him. He now had sunken cheeks and an ashen face. Even his moustache seemed more faded. All of the charisma he had from that first lesson had melted away. The history teacher looked old and vulnerable.

There was an uneasy atmosphere in his room now like the air had a weight to it.

About half-way through the class, the tension burst inside Will. His hand shot up as the first trickle of blood seeped out. He was already pinching his nose and tilting his head back to stop the blood from dripping onto his page.

Mr. Anthony just sat at his desk, twiddling his paperweight between his fingers, looking into space. When Will coughed to get his attention, Mr. Anthony looked as if he had stirred from a deep sleep. And instead of speaking, he waved his hand for Will to leave.

Will hurried down three flights of stairs. There were toilets on the second floor, but they never had any tissue paper or hand towels. He thought the toilets on the ground floor in the old block would be fully stocked and he could deal with the nosebleed in peace.

He instantly regretted his choice when the three boys turned to stare at him as he entered. One was playing with a lighter, one was perched upon a sink, and the biggest of the three, was on his tiptoes blowing cigarette smoke out of the thin rectangular windows at the very top of the toilet walls.

Will held his breath.

"Hey butter ball, did someone deck you?" asked the boy on the sink. His hair was shaved short. His eyes were piercing. He looked exactly like a vulture.

They all seemed like vultures to Will. They were circling around him, sensing dead meat.

Will gave a short nod and headed straight for the closest urinal.

The boy leapt down off the sink and blocked his path.

The one with the lighter gave a dirty grin. "What's the problem, Porker, your nose got a period?" He cackled. "Did you hear what I said to him, I said about nose periods!"

The last boy, the smoker, spoke, "Hey, Maccy, isn't that the new girl, Sacha's, little brother?"

Maccy, the head vulture, lazily placed his arm over Will's shoulders. "Oh, so your Sacha's little brother?" Maccy gestured to the smoker, "did you know that my pal Stobo here has a little brother too?"

Will tried to shake his head, no, while not letting the blood pour down his top.

"Yeah, you might look like a little fatso, loser kid, but, in fact, you are a huge bully. Aren't you?"

Will tried to hold back the tears welling up in his eyes. He felt trapped, like a mouse being batted by a cat. He thought about running out the door but knew he would never make it.

"Well, aren't you, little bully boy?"

Maccy was waiting for an answer. The other two moved so they were perched behind Maccy's shoulders, peering at Will.

At Will's silence, Maccy sighed. "You see Sacha's little brother was the freak that got Stephen and Danny detention on his first day of school."

Stobo grunted. "That was him?"

"Yeah, not a little cute pudding now, eh?" Maccy prodded at Will's belly with one outstretched finger. "You. Are. A. Bully."

Will was terrified; he saw the resemblance now. Stobo was clearly Danny's big brother and Maccy must have been related to Stephen McFall. They were the older, more vicious versions of Urchin and Cucumber.

"My little brother cried so much that night," Stobo said. "He said he got detention for no reason."

Maccy's pencil-thin lips drew into a smile when Will shuddered. "You made little Danny Stobbie cry … You're a little shit, aren't you? You know where shits go, don't you?"

Will's eyes widened. He knew what they were thinking, and there was no escape.

Stobo suddenly laughed with glee and scooped Will up in his arms.

The smoker crowed, "Let's teach him a lesson!" He pushed past Maccy and threw the butt of his rolled fag into the cubicle, pulling the toilet's handle.

Will wriggled as Stobo grabbed his body, turning him upside down. Maccy squeezed Will's legs together with a vice-like grip.

"Shit head, shit head, shit head!" the smoker chanted.

Will struggled with all his might—he was trapped.

The water swirled with the flush. The smell reeked as he got closer. He squirmed then gagged as his head went into the toilet.

The water rushed around him, flooding up his nose. Blood mixed into the water, thin ribbons of red churning around the bowl. He closed his eyes tight.

He felt like he was being pulled down like there was a huge weight sucking him deep into the toilet bowl. He held his breath, trying not to swallow. The swirl whipped more water over his face, and he gurgled.

When they pulled him out, he heard their furious laughter. He began gulping for fresh air. His tears, mixed in with the toilet water, slowly dripped onto his jumper.

"Leave my cousin alone, fat boy," Maccy yelled as he threw the door to the boy's toilet open. The others followed him out, and the door swung on its hinges, squeaking like it too had been through something terrible.

Will slumped back against the cubicle's door. The water was weighing on him, constricting around him. It hurt to breathe. He brushed his nose with his sleeve and fresh blood smeared on his jumper.

He didn't go back to class. He couldn't. He was hurt, and he was embarrassed, and most of all, he was wet.

Will didn't bother collecting his bag from the classroom —he just left. Slipping out one of the school's many side doors, one whose electronic locks had been broken, something he discovered one afternoon when he slipped away for lunch.

He headed through the school grounds and out the front gate.

Slowly he made his way home. The blood eventually congealed and crusted around his nostril. His eyes welled up, and tears dropped from his face, but he didn't sob.

He didn't make a sound.

Will bent down to reach the spare key under the mat and let himself in. After a half-hour walk in the blazing sun, he was still nowhere near dry. In fact, it felt worse. His whole body was covered in a dampness like when he'd wake up from a nightmare and was embalmed in a cold sweat.

When he got into the house, he ran straight into the bathroom and stripped off his clothes. He left them in a heap on the floor beside his shoes.

Jumping in the shower, he tried to wash. He wanted to wash every part of himself. He felt grimy as if he was rusting. He wanted to scrub at the rust and become shiny again. Not shiny and new, but shiny and old. He wanted things to go back to the way they had been.

He wanted to wash away his nosebleeds, wash away Stephen and Danny, wash away going to the toilet, wash away Gaby, and wash away moving here.

He wanted to wash away everything since his mum got sick.

He wanted to wash his life right back to nothing.

Skin feeling raw, he rinsed his body with the showerhead then lathered himself in body lotion. He smelled the mint of the shower gel mixing with the steam in the air. He often used his dad's body lotion when he wanted to feel a little bigger, a little more mature. But it wasn't working. He should have felt fresh again, but it was like there were two kinds of water. There was the water that ran off his body and down the drain and another heavier water that had seeped into him. He felt the weight of it in his body still. He felt sodden.

Will reached for the tap and turned the water off. It went from a consistent pour to an intermittent drip. He stood for a second with his eyes closed. He breathed deep breaths. The vapour of the mint tingled inside his nose.

Pushing back the shower curtain, he clambered over the side of the bathtub. The effort to do even these small motions felt strenuous. He lifted his towel and dried himself down, slowly. Then he tried to shake himself like a wet dog. Then he ran the towel over himself a second and then a third. But it was no use. He felt it all over him.

It was holding on to him, refusing to let go.

Will ran stark naked up the stairs and into his room. He looked in the mirror and saw nothing different. But he knew that he felt different.

As he stood looking at himself naked, he heard something speak—

Let me go.

It wasn't his voice. It was a girl.

Let me go, the voice demanded. It was scared but defiant.

Will gripped the sides of the mirror and leaned in. "What?"

Let go.

The voice was coming from inside him.

But it wasn't his.

You can't trap me here. This is imprisonment!

Will opened his mouth wide in the mirror and looked inside. He wasn't sure what he was looking for. He didn't see anything. Just in case, he looked in his nostrils, too. Still nothing. He stuck a finger in his ear and shoogled it. He wasn't sure what he expected to find.

He felt the voice, felt fear and rage bubbling from some deep place inside. It was like a feeling or a thought that had been lodged into his mind by accident. Another voice shouldn't be in there. But it was.

He heard it once more.

Please don't hurt me, it quivered.

He looked at himself in the mirror, he was still completely naked. He wondered how he could hurt anything.

"Hello?"

There was no response to his whisper. He started to wonder if he had imagined it. Like when you see a shadow in the dark and convince yourself someone else is in the room. But when the light comes on it is only the way a jacket is hanging. Maybe it was some acoustic trick. Maybe it was a distant bird call or a squeak in the radiator.

Maybe it was nothing.

"Hello," he tried once more, "anyone there?"

He felt ridiculous as he tried to listen for a reply. No wonder the other kids picked on him . . . He was a weirdo.

Chapter 4
The Candlelit Council

The Gatekeeper tried to pull at a loose thread on her tunic. It had been years since she had to dig out her old military garb and it had not aged well. She had been waiting for over an hour and was getting anxious.

A huge fresco was over her head: naked muscular men wrestling with wild animals. She thought it was rather vulgar even in such a grand hallway. The hallway itself was magnificent and designed to impose on any visitors but the torchlight was dying away as the night dragged on, making the place rather gloomy. The torches arranged on marble plinths were carefully positioned so that the statues that lined the walls would have cast up imposing shadows earlier in the evening. The marble statues depicted legendary heroes of ancient battles. Every one of them captured in their vigorous youth.

Not a room for an old, retired Gatekeeper, she thought to herself. *What am I doing here?*

She imagined how loud the place must get when there was a council meeting and the space was filled with every state elder, and their advisers, jostling for prominence. Now, it was deathly silent except for the click of the heels of some sleepy guard walking across the plateau on his nightly patrol. The marble of the floor was pot marked and was the only hint of imperfection, in the palace grounds. But of course, the statesmen would never see that, walking as they did on their rolled-out carpets.

The Gatekeeper wondered if this is what her old job used to be like in the ancient days, when the only doors in the world were big wooden ones. Would she have spent her days sitting outside stuffy meetings, just waiting for the door to open and the carpet to roll? Her job had been much more complex than that, guarding Thresholds, making sure they were never crossed by humans or spirits. Now though, with all the Thresholds locked, she had settled into the life of a veteran.

She never imagined having to come back to the Republican Palace.

Nevertheless, here she was, having been rudely awakened and almost dragged from her home by two brutish Hunters who refused to answer her questions. Now she was waiting for whatever it was that awaited her behind the closed door in front of her.

"Well then, what is it to be? Are you being hung or beheaded?" A loud voice bellowed across the hallway.

The Gatekeeper looked up and offered a strained smile. "Officer Otho. What is going on here?" She pushed down her panic.

"It's Lieutenant Otho, old crone. I'm in charge of all of the Hunters inside the capital now."

"Well, bravo boy. But I'm a veteran and that demands respect. Madam Gatekeeper still outranks a Lieutenant."

"You mean to say the Council didn't strip you of your

title when you were being sentenced? I hardly believe that."

Otho moved, towering over the Gatekeeper, with his hands on his waist and his legs wide apart. He was trying to look imposing, but the Gatekeeper was unimpressed.

"Otho, you bucket-head, you are going to have to explain yourself. I haven't been sentenced by anyone."

Otho gave a booming laugh. "Ahh, even better, you are still waiting. I get to break the news myself. Behind this door is the full Republican Council, I imagine they are debating the exact punishment for your treasonous crimes. As soon as I found you had left a Threshold open, I reported to the Council immediately. You are done for, traitor."

The Gatekeeper remained calm. "I can assure you," she said, "the Thresholds I guarded are sealed shut, I locked them all myself."

"Well then, where is my Whisp? You tell me, where did my Whisp go?" Otho barked.

Otho always was a foolish thug, or so she believed. One of her worst students. This was just his style; he would stab anyone in the back to cover up his own mess. He had lost a Whisp on a hunt and was looking for someone to blame. She would relish picking apart whatever snivelling lie he has told. He would be the one the Council would be beheading, not her.

"I will give you one chance, for old times' sake, *Officer* Otho. Are you sure your lost Whisp went through one of *my* Thresholds?"

"The marble fountain. Threshold 216—to the Realm of Gaia, known as Earth. It had been *supposedly* closed by the Gatekeeper to Gaia . . . which is you. I looked it up in the old charts. It's all in my report. The Council was impressed with how thorough I was. They know exactly what has happened."

The Gatekeeper scoffed. "With the rag-tag bunch you call Hunters now, who knows what happened? I've seen your team all whipped up into a frenzy, wildly jabbing their little sticks around hoping to electrify something. Not like it was in my day, we had to be cunning and skilful. We had to seek them out with only our wits. The Whisps in my day would have trembled at the sight of me. These young Whisps must laugh at you, Otho. I'm not surprised you were unable to find it, it's very hard to hunt something which is almost completely invisible, without the proper discipline. It probably just snuck out from under your noses."

Otho bristled. "My team are the very best there is, Madam Gatekeeper. Just look at my tally. Don't forget who trained me. I know their movements and their tricks just as well as you did. The Whisp isn't hiding, it isn't slinking in the shadows. I would have seen it slip away." He grunted. "No, the Whisp has vanished. Like they used to do, years ago, before the realm was sealed off."

The Gatekeeper pinched the bridge of her nose and sighed. "And so now, in front of the King, in front of the Council of the True Republic, in these hallowed halls, you have accused me of leaving one of my Thresholds open. Is that correct, Lieutenant Otho?"

Otho jutted out his chin and clasped his hands behind his back in a bid to look authoritative. "I only reported what happened, Madam Gatekeeper."

"You are a snivelling little rat. I can still take you in my jaws and shake. Don't you think the Council will want to know how their *best* lieutenant has only just realised one of the Thresholds was left open? If I forgot to close it, then it has been open for *years*. Who knows how many Whisps you've helped escape?"

Otho shifted a little on his feet and the Gatekeeper hid a smirk.

"I suggest you go in there and alter your report. Some of the other retired Gatekeepers might be easier to accuse. They might see a commanding lieutenant. All I see is the student with a nervous shuffle."

Otho made to knock on the door, but before he could, it creaked open, and an official-looking man greeted them. "The Council are ready for you now, Madam Gatekeeper."

"Formal title. Very respectful," she said flashing a look at Otho.

As she stepped into the room, Otho tried to follow but the footman placed up an open palm. "Just the Gatekeeper for the moment. They asked for you to wait outside." He gestured at the seat the Gatekeeper had just vacated.

The Gatekeeper gave a vicious smile before the door closed on her student's face.

The Gatekeeper was surprised to find that the door did not lead directly to the Council's chamber. Instead, she found herself in a long grand corridor. If the entrance hall was magnificent, the corridor was sublime. The dazzling white of the marble walls shimmered under torches that lit the path. Every so often, a large painting of some decorated hero of the Republic splashed vivid colour along the way. They looked splendid and regal.

She felt a little foolish in her tunic. It didn't sit comfortably on her body anymore and it was in a style they no longer used. The simplicity of it didn't fit in somewhere so grand.

Even the footman, who was in front of her, seemed sleek and efficient. He was in a fine black suit that was bordered with a decorative blue meander. His tie was also bright blue. He wore insignia on his right lapel. Every minute detail was carefully crafted to delineate his role. He looked modern and ancient at the same time. The very definition of the Republic's manifesto: *Reaching to the wisdom of the ancestors to create knowledge for the future.*

She had been so confident with Otho. So brazen. But as she followed the footman down the corridor, she realised that it had all been for show. She was still in trouble. Even if Otho was going to be punished, it didn't for one second mean she would be let off. The Council would be as happy to lop two heads off as they would with one.

Surely, the Council in their wisdom would not sentence her for a crime she didn't commit? She had, most definitely, sealed that specific Threshold shut. She remembered. It was the last one she closed before she relinquished her Threshold key to the Council for safekeeping. Wasn't it? Or was it the second last?

She shrunk into herself; doubt growing.

The pictures seemed to get bigger and grander the further they went along the corridor. She felt their eyes observing her like she was nothing more than a minuscule beetle scurrying across the hall's carpet.

"This corridor goes on forever, doesn't it?" She tried, wanting to strike up a conversation with the footman. She hoped to get some clue as to what mood the King and his Council might be in.

But all he gave was a polite nod and they continued along the corridor in silence.

When they reached the end of the corridor, he opened another door and motioned for her to go through first.

She stepped through and entered into darkness.

The Gatekeeper assumed the chamber was vast because echoing from above her head she heard the roof's glass panels trembling from a rainstorm. It created a cacophony of noise that along with some flickering candlelight, gave the room the feeling of immense pressure. It was as if the darkness was slowly choking out the light. Even the biggest candles only managed to illuminate the room in a smear of smoggy grey.

Through the haze, she made out the shape of a large table which she approached slowly. Around the table, candles were arranged so that the faces of each state elder could be picked out.

All their eyes sparkled with malicious glee in the orange glow.

A different footman approached her and placed a candle in her hand. He lit it with a match and then nimbly slinked back into the shadows.

"Hold the candle to your face, so we can see you better," a voice commanded.

She did as was instructed, tensing.

Another voice, this one quivering with age, spoke next. "Do you know why you were sent for?"

"The Lieutenant Otho's report. It is full of lies," she answered, her eyes searching for the face that asked the question.

The first voice snarled, "The report is truthful. I have decreed it so."

Only then did she notice the voice came from the unmistakable face of the Thinking King. He looked just like he did on all the newly printed coins.

"It's impossible," she rebutted. "The Thresholds to

Gaia are locked; I locked them myself. No human, no spirit, no creature can cross over."

He lolloped forward off his seat, his jowls quivering. "Are you defying my decree? Are you questioning the Council?"

"I'm sorry great . . ." She quickly thought how best to address him. ". . . Leader." The Gatekeeper stepped back from the table and bowed deeply.

The woman who sat next to the King placed a gentle hand upon his arm to calm him. "The Gatekeeper is not defying us." She paused. "Please, I summoned her for a reason."

The woman, who the Gatekeeper suspected must be Queen Agrippina, rose from her chair and disappeared into the shadow of the room. The Gatekeeper followed her movement by observing the head of every statesman as it turned when she walked by. One by one their gaze fell on the Queen as she rounded the table. She was sleek, slipping in and out of the candlelight, like silk weaving across a tapestry.

"Do you know what this is?" The Queen emerged beside the Gatekeeper, her face illuminated by the light the Gatekeeper held, and placed a contraption on the table.

The Gatekeeper studied it closely: it was made of glass and about the size of a wine goblet. On the bottom was a strange array of silver gears. They cricked together and caused the glass shell to pivot on an axis. The inside glowed with a phosphorous light.

"Fascinating, isn't it? It's for divination."

"It's mesmerising," the Gatekeeper agreed.

"With this device, if you can read it properly, you can tell which realm any person or spirit might be at any one time. It was used when the Thresholds were open to round up any rebels trying to escape us. When I read Otho's report, I did a little investigation myself."

She leaned into the Gatekeeper and whispered, "Watch." Turning the dials on the bottom of the device, the glass spun on the axis. The phosphorous light concentrated into a pinprick so hot it pierced the glass.

The whole room was focussed on the Queen.

"Do you know where this is?" she asked

The Gatekeeper's eyes widened. Each gear represented a constellation of stars: the North Star, Great Bear, Plowman, and Orion's Belt. It was her world, Gaia, or Earth as they called it. The world whose Thresholds she had guarded for years.

"Please." The Gatekeeper turned to the Queen "I swear to you that—"

"Hush," said the Queen. "If I thought for a second you would defy the Republic and open a Threshold, I'd have strangled you myself."

An old man, one of the only ones around the table who didn't seem to be beguiled by the Queen, spoke with a lilting voice, almost singing every word.

"This is all wonderfully theatrical, Agrippina, but didn't we already establish where the Whisp was? The King decreed it."

Agrippina turned to address the elder statesman. "You've missed the point, Elder Cato. I wasn't looking for the Whisp. I was looking for the missing General."

The Council gasped almost in unison.

Cato's thick grey eyebrows raised with a twitch. "Your little device has *found* the General of the Orbis Alius, in another realm?"

The Queen ignored the question, shunning Cato in favour of addressing the Gatekeeper. "The General of the Orbis Alius is a traitor. He went missing at the time of our

King's coronation a couple of months back and stole a Threshold key from the palace. We don't know his plans, but he has opened a Threshold and is luring Whisps to the realm you protected."

"I promise you, I had nothing to do with this." The Gatekeeper whimpered. "I've never even met the General."

"You are not a suspect," the Queen replied. "You are our lead investigator. You were stationed in Gaia for years and know the world inside out." The Queen paused and her eyes narrowed very slightly. "Take this as a little test. Go into your world, arrest the General, lock your Threshold, and bring us back that Whisp. It shouldn't be too hard. There are no other Whisps or Ghasts in the world, according to your reports."

"We don't need a spy," Cato muttered. "Let's just lock the Threshold and let the Whisp roam free in the other realm. Good riddance. We don't need it. We have enough Whisps locked in our Pandora jars for centuries." He shrugged. "As for the General, what damage can he do? The only person who knows he disappeared outside this Council is this old woman." He regarded the Gatekeeper with disdain. "Besides, do we really think such a delicate . . . old thing can capture the General? Let's just choke her and be done with the whole affair."

The King nodded. "Yes, yes, bring me her neck, I want to do it myself." He stretched out his hands and wiggled his stumpy fingers, like a toddler demanding his rattle.

"The Thinking King needs to think!" snapped the Queen. She took a deep breath. "My husband, your Majesty, if the General has a key, as soon as we lock the Threshold shut, he might open it again. Right now, we are a step ahead of him. He doesn't yet know we have discovered his whereabouts." She sighed, motioning towards the Gatekeeper. "She's a veteran soldier. She can handle herself—no matter how *delicate* she looks." She glanced at Cato, unimpressed. "I would wager she can still break your neck like a twig."

The King rocked back into his chair and pulled at his beard.

The Queen added, "And she knows the other world's customs, so she can slip through unnoticed."

Cato leaned forward. "If the General is in another realm, maybe he doesn't want to rebel. Maybe he wants to conquer this other world. Why provoke him? Let's strangle the woman and lock the Threshold."

The Queen rubbed at her eyes. "The General of the Orbis Alius learns the secrets of soul binding and then disappears. Now a Threshold is open and a Whisp is gone. Don't you realise how powerful that Whisp is? Do you know the damage it would cause if it fell into the General's hands? Or are you conspiring against us too?"

"Are you accusing me of treachery?" Cato snapped, rising to his feet. "I am the King's oldest advisor. As if I would conspire with the General . . . I hate the man."

"That means nothing Cato. You have always slithered and schemed with anyone who might give you a morsel of power."

The rest of the Council began to descend into chaos with each of the elder's accusing one another. The Gatekeeper took a step backwards, trying to retreat from the chaos. She sensed danger, right now they were arguing amongst themselves, but at any moment one of the statesmen might lash out towards her and she would be finished.

The ruckus grew to a deafening peak before the King shouted, "Enough!" At their silence, he folded his arms. "I shall pass a decree. Bring me some inspiration."

A footman brought forward a large clay jar which the King grasped with both hands. He reached into the neck of the vessel, removed the stopper, giving it to the footman, and placed his face in the jar as if he was breathing in a hot vapour. When his head emerged, he blinked and readjusted to the light of the room. The footman replaced the stopper and whisked the jar away immediately.

"Bring me back my Whisp, old Gatekeeper. That is the decree of the Council."

The Gatekeeper bowed deeply. At that moment she felt she wanted to bless the world for her salvation. She knew how close she had been to death.

"Bring back the General's head as well if you find it," Cato said wearily, "preferably on a plate."

The King clapped his hands together and shouted to the footmen in the shadows, "Bring in the Lieutenant. I would like to strangle someone before breakfast."

At that the Queen motioned for a footman, sending a smile towards the Gatekeeper. "Come, there are some things you will need for the journey."

Chapter 5
Telling Lies

L*et me out of here.*
    Will screwed up his eyes and pressed his head against his hands. His body had been chaotic recently. Teachers at school would talk about it but they would use terms like 'transitioning to adulthood' and 'becoming sexually aware,' so no one really knew what they were trying to say. The bits that Will had gleaned from TV, books, and watching Sacha morph into an acne-ridden devil sister, were enough for him to realise that this wasn't normal. No one anywhere had said you would get an extra thought in your head. An extra voice.

Let me out!

"Go away!" Will shouted.

"Will, is that you? Who are you talking too?" Sacha shouted through the wall from her bedroom next to his.

"No one. Don't come in. I'm naked."

"Okay. Chill. I wasn't coming in. How did you get home so fast? You weren't on the bus."

"Ummmm." He paused. "P.E. was my last class and they let us go home early as long as we jogged."

He heard her snort. "Sure. Don't worry I won't tell Dad you skipped school. He will freak out. But if you get caught you are going to need a *way* better excuse than that."

Before he could reply, Sacha's music went on and Will deflated in relief that the conversation was over.

Will closed his eyes and pleaded, *Please leave me alone.*

I can't. I'm bound to you. Unbind me! Now!

He thought again silently and deliberately, *Can you read my thoughts?*

I'm a Whisp, of course, I can.

What is a Whisp?

It's a, well, it's a … what I am.

I don't know what that is, thought Will, frustrated. *Are you a virus or some kind of brain disease?*

No, replied the Whisp. *A Whisp is a fleeting feather of a thing. It is supposed to trace upon your soul and then in a moment be gone. It is the whisper in your ear, the sparkle in your eye. It is the moment you yell 'eureka!' and leap from the bathtub. A Whisp is that tiny spark before your bright flash of brilliance.* There was a pause before the Whisp added, *That is what a Whisp is. That is what I should be.*

But you're not? Will asked in his thoughts.

No, I'm not. I'm stuck. Tethered like a kite twisted in the branches of a dead tree.

What are you stuck to?

You, you idiot. You are the dead tree! The Whisp was growing impatient. *I'm bound to you.*

Will growled, *Well I don't want to be bound to anything. Thank you very much. I just need to be left alone. Thanks for coming and saying hello. But you can definitely go. Now!*

Arrrgh! the Whisp screamed in frustration. It vibrated through Will's bones and made his spine shiver.

Don't scream, that hurts!

Well, stop being such a slow little mugwart. I want to leave. I would love to jump out of your stupid body and never hear your annoying wobbly voice again, but I can't. I'm stuck. I crossed a Threshold and was bound to the water in that plumbing system, and then you stuck your head in the toilet, and now, I'm bound to you.

I didn't stick my head in the toilet. Someone pushed it in, Will replied as he began to get himself dressed. Whatever it was inside his mind, he didn't like that he was having the conversation in the nude.

Who was that? Maybe they know what happened. Maybe they bound us together as some kind of punishment.

I don't think so. I think all they thought they were doing was flushing my head down the toilet.

The Whisp fired back, *Well someone must know what happened. Whisps aren't supposed to bind like this. The only way this could happen is if someone meant to bind us. Who bound us?*

I don't know who bound us. I don't know what that means. I don't know what's happening here. All of this is completely barmy. I know you say you're stuck but you're just going to have to unstick yourself. This is my body and I want you out of it. Will paused, rubbing his forehead in frustration. *I thought you said you can read my thoughts; can't you tell that I don't know what is going on?* Will pulled his t-shirt over his head and collapsed back into his bed, looking up at the ceiling.

You are just so—

It was only at that moment that the Whisp realised how much she had been fighting. How much she had been trying to unbind, to block him out. All she wanted was to get as far away as possible.

I . . . She stopped her reply and flowed into Will, entering his mind to discover what he knew. As soon as she did, she realised Will was even more frightened than she was.

He was not her imprisoner after all.

I need to find who bound me to you. I need to find them and get them to undo it. Or someone else, someone who can sever the link. Is that even possible? There needs to be a way . . . I can't . . . I have to — The Whisp's voice was like a cornered animal. It was lashing out, trying to fend off the danger that it felt.

"Stop," Will breathed aloud. He felt the voice inside him bristle with nerves. His hairs stood on end. His heart began to race.

Then a shout came from downstairs, and it distracted them both: "Will! Tea's ready!"

Who's that? Are they in charge?

Will shouted back, "Coming!" He quickly sat up and looked at himself in the mirror once more, relieved there was no obvious sign of this 'Whisp' in his body.

Stopping at the door he thought to the Whisp, *Stay quiet. Please. We will have to figure this all out later.*

Downstairs, Dad presented some chips and a bowl of tomato sauce when Will walked into the kitchen. "I forgot to defrost the steak pie," he said, apologetically.

Sacha pushed past Will to take a seat at the table. "It's fine, I'm going out in fifteen minutes anyway. Some of the girls from school invited me to the cinema."

"Ah, boy's night it is then. There's a pool table in the hotel I drive past to get to work. We haven't played since that caravan holiday, fancy a game?" Dad looked expectantly at him.

"I can't. I've got homework," Will said, only half lying and trying to mask his panic. He did have homework, but since he had left his bag at school, he was just going to have to face that problem tomorrow. He had bigger things on his mind right now.

"Oh, okay." Will's dad dipped another chip into the bowl of sauce, shrugging. "No problem. I should crack on with painting the stairway."

Do you always tell lies? the Whisp asked, with a touch of judgement.

Will reached for a chip, ignoring the voice. Just as he bit down on the chip, his dad started a new conversation.

"How was school?"

"Pretty uneventful for me." Sacha smiled, "How bout you, Will?"

Will gave his sister a kick under the table as he frowned at her. She kicked him back and continued to smile.

"Well, Will, how was it?" His dad said, unaware of Will and Sacha's secret exchange.

Tell them the truth. Maybe your dad can help. Maybe Sacha has heard something at school about me.

Will gulped down another chip. "Just the usual classes. I really do have a lot of homework though. Can I take dinner upstairs?"

His dad sighed, "I suppose so."

Will scooped some chips onto his plate and headed back for his room.

The Whisp pleaded, *Don't leave. Maybe your father can help.*

Will kept quiet as he dashed up the stairs. If he told the truth, if he blurted it out, then he would have to tell them some kids flushed his head down the toilet. He would have to explain that he left school in the afternoon, and no one must have even noticed that he had vanished because no one had called his dad or came looking for him.

For the rest of the evening, Will and the Whisp went back and forth, learning all they could from each other but still being unable to figure out their situation.

Eventually, as the night drew on, the Whisp became

exasperated. *If we can't go to the school tonight, then you really should tell your dad. Someone needs to do something!*

Will scoffed. "You can scream in there all you want but I've realised something—right now the only one who can hear you is me. I'm in charge. If you ever want to get free, then you're going to have to work with me. Because this is my body and I decide where it goes and what it does, and you just have to come with it." In anger, he had spoken the words out loud.

The Whisp was quiet; Will felt it retreat.

Fine, the Whisp said. *What's your plan?*

Will hadn't thought that far ahead.

Noticing his hesitation, the Whisp asked, *Can I suggest something, please?*

Will thought it was being overly courteous and wondered if he sensed sarcasm. *Okay.*

We need to go back to where we became intertwined. We need to go and investigate those toilets. That's where the Threshold was, in the water system.

What's a Threshold? asked Will.

You really don't know anything . . . The Whisp sighed. *A Threshold is a gateway. It's like a little slip in a curtain that lets you glide from one place to another.*

Like a wormhole? Will questioned. He had learnt about wormholes in a science magazine. They let you jump through space. In theory, you can go from one galaxy to another in a nanosecond.

Yes, said the Whisp learning about wormholes in that exact moment by reading Will's mind. *Exactly like a wormhole. Only imagine if instead of going from one part of space to another it went to somewhere else entirely.*

So, you are from another world. Will paused and thought to himself, *maybe it's an alien.*

No, I'm not an alien, and I'm not an IT either, stop thinking like that . . . I'm a Whisp. A girl Whisp. Don't you have Whisps in your world?

I don't think so. I don't know, replied Will. He wasn't very sure at all, maybe everyone had these Whisps. What if everyone had them and he was so dumb he never realised he had one till now? Or what if he was the only one in the world that had one? He didn't know which was worse.

You're scared of me, aren't you?

Will realised this thing could feel his feelings. He didn't bother to reply, it already knew he was terrified.

I'm not bad . . . I won't-I'm scared too, she said, quietly.

Will felt tension ooze out of him. Was it his tension or the Whisp's? He couldn't tell, but he felt his muscles relax with the revelation.

I don't know what has happened. I don't know why I'm stuck with you. I thought you had imprisoned me.

Will heard a sense of pity in the Whisp's voice and closed his eyes. *I didn't imprison you.*

I know that now. The Whisp fell silent. Maybe she had been too harsh. This boy, who was not her captor, had got caught up in something all by accident. He didn't mean to bind with her. She listened for a reply but all she felt was his exhaustion.

Will? She tried, speaking his name for the first time.

As his muscles started to relax, she felt their heaviness. She felt the weariness of his mind as it tried to stay alert. He was carrying a burden, not just the confusion over her presence, but something even deeper than that. She felt it inside him now, a fresh wound upon his soul. One of deep humiliation. He had been mortified, not because he had a Whisp attached to him, but because some older boys had stuck his head down a toilet. The wound was raw and continued to eat away at him.

She had distracted him from it, but it had not gone

away. She knew the sleep would be restless. She knew that the image of those boys would taunt him in his dreams.

The Whisp realised she should push him no further. Tomorrow, they would solve their binding. Tomorrow they would talk. Tomorrow they would find a solution.

She settled and thought to herself, *Be kinder, Whisp. Be kinder.*

Chapter 6
The Ghast and The Gatekeeper

After the Gatekeeper was escorted from the Council meeting, and given supplies from the Queen, she went straight to work. She took herself around the city examining all the old Thresholds she had sealed shut long ago. Of the fifty that she had been in charge of, most were still closed but four had been opened. Each of the opened Thresholds led to the same place, Worldmouth. It was a dull little do-nothing town in a do-nothing country, that she remembered well.

If the General was a nefarious traitor, why would Worldmouth feature in his schemes? The Gatekeeper had grown to hate the world she had guarded, and she despised Worldmouth the most. It was a town filled with stubby little grey buildings that barely stood out against the drab grey skyline. And it stunk. She remembered the smell, vividly. A burning noxious odour that belched from their vehicles. The thought of having to go back there made her skin crawl.

Armed with a small torchlight, she made her way across the city towards the eastern wall to avoid detection.

If someone saw her, and realized the Thresholds were open, panic would ensue, and the Council wouldn't be pleased.

While it had been decades since she had been there, and even though it was dark, it wasn't hard to find her way. Soon the wall towered above her dominating the horizon. She felt her way around its edge trying to find the steps of the stairway that was hewn out of the stonework.

The Gatekeeper took her time climbing the stairs. She remembered how in her youth she would dart up and down these stairs on an almost daily basis. Now she ached; an old war wound, a deep scar in her leg, burned with every step. Early in her career, she had scoffed at the numerous requests by others to fit a handrail on these stairs. Oh, how foolish she had been—look at her now. Stifling a cry of pain, her hands grasped at the stones, feeling for anything that might give her stability.

It was an effort, but finally she reached the top of the city walls. She paused to breathe in the air—it was fresh from the night's early storm; only a faint breeze was left behind.

And below the city slept.

It was an impressive city, full of marble and mud. She wished she had time to see the sunrise. The Council palace would radiate in faint greys and whites. The slate roofs of the poor district would glisten. In the early morning darkness, the palace and roofs were like an expansive ocean of shadow, with the occasional marble mansion floating like a little island of opulence. They had built this. Not the spirits. Not the Whisps nor the Ghasts. Them, human beings.

We can do anything, she thought. *If I had my way, I wouldn't just trap the spirits, I would kill them completely.*

The Gatekeeper reached into her rucksack. A key to

open the Threshold had been given to her by the Queen along with a set of clothes in the fashion of Gaia—she hoped it hadn't changed too much since she had sealed the Thresholds shut. Also in her rucksack were her notebooks full of all the odd eccentric customs she had discovered from her time on Earth and two Pandora jars. One jar was to trap the Whisp; the other a precautionary spare.

She must not let the Council down . . . If she did, the Queen wouldn't need to strangle her, she would do it herself. The shame of letting down the True Republic would be too much to handle.

Hugging her rucksack to her chest, with her other hand she held the Threshold key out in front of her. She stepped to the edge, looked down, and flung herself off the wall.

She fell through the air at great speed, hurtling towards the ground. She kept the key outstretched in her hand.

For a split-second she worried she had miscalculated. That she would die.

Suddenly the key burned white-hot and with a flash it ripped at the sky. The Gatekeeper tumbled through the hole and she found herself inside a cramped little chamber.

It's always much lower than she expected. It didn't matter how many times she had crossed over; it always gave her that rush of adrenalin. The fear of death would always surge through her veins, making her blood sing.

Now, here she was, in a crumpled heap in another world.

These Thresholds must have been tampered with. The sky Threshold used to lead her straight into her old apartment, but instead she was inside some wooden box. She felt around until she found a slight gap in which she squeezed her brittle finger through to slide one of the sides of the box open. Pausing to listen, she emerged into darkness. She noticed, first, the wide windows and moved to pull at a broken blind. Outside, she peered onto her old realm.

It was the early morning, and still, some hours until the sun would come up and the people of Gaia would begin their daily business.

At least she had some time to investigate. With the Thresholds changed, her job was that much harder now. Whatever memory she had of where the old Thresholds were situated had become completely useless. The Thresholds could open up anywhere. The route she had planned in her head no longer helped her. She would need to find her bearings before she even began to try and outsmart a Whisp.

She rummaged in her rucksack and found a torch. She clicked it on, and it whirred into life.

The room was grim-looking, full of uncomfortable-looking seats and small little desks, all in tight rows facing away from her. It reminded her of one of the sweatshops where the prisoners worked during the old wars. She flicked at a lid of one of the desks and looked inside, it was scratched with graffiti and hard little lumps of white gum were packed into the corners. Glancing over her shoulder she realized she had not been in a box after all, but a cupboard that was along the wall.

Yet there was no obvious clue as to where exactly she was, or why the General would have hidden a Threshold to another realm in the back of a cupboard. Since she knew that the Whisp had crossed through the water Threshold, that's what she would try to find first.

She began to remove the change of clothes from her bag and placed them neatly on a desk beside her. She would change, so that, if for any reason she was spotted, her old tunic wouldn't make her stand out. In this world, the fashion for white tunics had vanished thousands of years ago in the time of Alexander the Great.

The Gatekeeper hated the fashion of this world. It was stiff and uncomfortable. Layer upon layer, of stuffy fabrics. She buttoned up the blue blouse then put on the bright red cardigan. It was garish to adorn yourself with so many colours. She wasn't a jester. She grimaced as she put her feet into thick nylon tights and then over that a heavy woollen skirt. Finally, she slipped her feet into brown loafers that were scuffed along the toes. It was revolting to imagine having to wear this all the time.

"How do these people even move in all of this?" she asked to herself as she gathered her tunic into the rucksack and headed for the exit.

She turned to close the door behind her when her torchlight poured across the whole room and landed upon the figure slumped on the floor, behind a large desk.

The Gatekeeper gasped in fright. She hadn't expected someone might have been in the room with her. Peering closer, she saw that his chair was lying on its side a few feet away from him. His body curled up into a tight little ball. His knees were against his stomach and his arms were crossed on his chest like he had been rocking himself to sleep.

Was he—

She crept closer and used her torch to prod at him . . . There was no reaction. She bent down with a groan and grabbed a tuft of his grey hair and pulled it back, lifting the head. She moved the torch to get a full look and winced. The light reflected off the whites of his wide-open eyes. Eyes that stared into blank space and did not react.

The man was dead.

She felt his skin, finding it was still warm. He must

have only died that night. She turned his face towards the light to get a good look at him.

The Gatekeeper recognised the face immediately, his paintings had adorned the old military headquarters for years. It was the General of Orbis Alius, General Anthony. The missing General she had been sent to arrest. What happened? What was his plan? It must have gone wrong somehow. This had all gotten more complicated. Now, not only did she have to catch a Whisp, she now had to solve a murder.

Maybe the two were linked . . . The Queen had mentioned before that the General had just learnt the secrets of binding. Would he have tried to bind with a Whisp? Maybe it had bound with him. Maybe it was still stuck inside . . .

She took out one of the Pandora jars and reached for the stopper about a quarter of the way down in the narrow neck that she carefully teased out with her fingers. From there she heaved the General's body over on the floor, his face looking up to the roof. Pulling his jaw open with her thumb, with her other hand she reached for the jar. Without hesitation, she shoved the open mouth of the clay jar into his mouth so that his lips formed a seal around the rim. She pushed it deep into the mouth—if he wasn't already dead, he would have choked.

It was an awful sight: the dead man spread eagle with a ceramic jar sprouting out of his mouth.

The body began to twitch.

She held the jar with one hand and waited. The body writhed and twisted. It shuddered. It convulsed. A bulging mass rose from the stomach. His skin stretched as it moved up through his body. It travelled up through the chest and into the throat.

Once the jar began to tremble, the Gatekeeper

grabbed it with both hands and wrenched it from his mouth.

An ear-piercing scream shot out of the jar, and it shook violently in her hands. She quickly grabbed the stopper and thrust it inside sealing the jar shut.

"A Ghast!"

The spirit she had caught was not a Whisp at all. She would recognise that scream anywhere. It had haunted her nightmares, ever since she was a child. It was why she joined the army of the True Republic as a teenager. She had seen the havoc a Ghast could wreak—her mother never recovered. She would also remember that scream as it left her mother's corpse.

Of course, it was a Ghast. Which explained now why the General is dead. The Ghast must have been feeding on his soul. It ate his soul alive and left him a corpse, just like what happened to her mother. From years of battling these monsters, she knew that a Ghast will linger in the body, long after death, like a bear falling into a deep and satisfying sleep after mauling a deer. The General must have opened the Thresholds, but, surely, he would never have intended to bind with a Ghast. What had happened? Perhaps he told someone in this world about Whisps and Ghasts? Had he been betrayed?

She was more confused now than when she arrived and needed to investigate. She would trace the General's steps, finding every Threshold he had opened, looking for the Whisp. If she couldn't find it, she would just have to ask every single wretched person she found until she did.

Chapter 7
A Death in the Academy

Will awoke the next day and the first thing he felt was the Whisp, still inside his mind, wriggling with impatience. She was ready to get back to the school and investigate.

Will set about his day with his usual routines trying to keep things as normal as possible, only speaking to the Whisp when he had to. *Yes, he was going as fast as he can* or *no, he won't change his mind about telling his dad anything.*

He heard the argument between his dad and his sister that had now become a daily ritual in the new house.

"You're not wearing that to school."

"Stop stifling me, Dad! I have rights."

He used it as an alarm clock.

Stomp. Stomp.

SLAM.

I wish I had bound to your sister she seems fierce, the Whisp commented.

Yeah, well tough luck for both of us then. You're stuck with me. Before she got the chance to reply, Will rushed out the door and jumped in the car so his dad could give him a lift to school. It would get him there before the bus, which would hopefully give him time to investigate.

He sat in the front seat as his dad tuned on the radio. He liked a station called *Hits of the 80s* that would blare out old pop numbers. Every so often the song would be interrupted by another channel that gave traffic updates.

When the updates began, his dad would swear under his breath if a so-and-so junction was backed up. If the traffic report was particularly bad, then chaos would unfold. Will would get an apology from his dad who would have to spend the rest of the drive speaking to various members of his office rearranging meetings.

Today was one of those chaotic days.

Will would usually use those car journeys to ponder the day ahead. He would run through his timetable and plan the best route between classes. Once he had finished that, he would let his mind wander to silly things like whether he was too old to have a conker collection or if he should collect them for another year. He wondered how his old classmates were getting on and whether any of them would be brave enough to dive off the tallest diving board this term. He liked this time with his thoughts, but today he had company.

Are most people like you, or are you particularly weird?

I think you are the weirdest thing about me, Will replied, trying not to look too cross so his dad wouldn't get suspicious.

I've just never been with someone when they slept before. Does everyone dream like you? It started with you digging a hole in the ground, said the Whisp. *Then you found this wooden chest and you kick through it—stomp a hole right in the middle of it. The wood is all rotten and it collapses straight away.*

You fall right through it and land into a room which is just filled with flowers. The flowers are blossoming in all these amazingly bright colours, and they are all over the floor and on the walls and a table. You just start ripping them up, attacking them like a wild boar. Tearing through them until you get to the table and then you get even more ferocious, clawing at the flowers with your hands and even your teeth.

Will tensed, keeping his gaze straight ahead.

Once the table is cleared of the flowers, you realise it is actually a bed and it is covered with a white sheet and there is someone underneath it. You can see their outline in the fabric. You get a big smile on your face, and you pull the fabric away because you've found what you're looking for.

But then you realise that all that under the sheet is just a pile of clothes. Perfectly folded shirts and trousers and things. And you look so sad. Then this hand, like a gnarled, dead hand bursts through the clothes and reaches for you ...

And then—then you woke up.

Will stayed silent; he hadn't realised he was still having those nightmares.

The Whisp crowed in excitement, *It was so weird! Like being told a story that didn't make any sense. What do you think would have happened next?*

I don't know I can't remember it, Will thought, trying his hardest to shield his emotions from the intruder in his head.

I know, but what do you THINK happened next?

I don't know, Will snapped back.

Shall I tell you what I think might happen? Not waiting for his response, the Whisp continued. *The gnarled hand belongs to some kind of undead monster who grabs you and—*

"SHUT UP!" Will yelled, out loud.

His dad looked at him with shock. "Will—"

A voice through the car sound system comes through, "Charlie was that you?"

"Uhhh . . . no, sorry, Sandra." Will's dad glances at

him in concern. "Listen, I will call you right back." He jabs his finger at his phone screen and the call disconnects. "What are you playing at Will? That was my boss!"

"Sorry, Dad . . . I was . . . uhh . . . remembering a bad dream." Will looked down at his bag and began fiddling with the zip between his fingers.

His dad pulled the car off to the side of the road and turned to look at Will. "Nightmares? I get them too sometimes." He paused, sighing. "Listen, let's definitely grab that game of pool tonight. Just me and you, yeah?"

Will nodded and scratched behind his ear. His dad gave a warm smile, that made Will feel a little guilty for not agreeing to the pool game sooner.

They drove the last few minutes of the journey in silence.

Even the Whisp didn't utter another word.

Something she had said about that dream had scared him. She was trying to make him laugh. She hadn't meant to frighten him. But he didn't want her to know—

"Here we are!"

The car pulled up at the school entrance and Will unbuckled his seatbelt.

The phone began to ring again as Will got out of the car. His dad hit the button to answer, and Will mouthed "sorry" before he closed the car door. His dad gave him a forgiving look, as they exchanged waves before he drove off, already deep in conversation with another colleague

The Whisp sighed. *I'm sorry for going on about the dream and for making you shout.*

Will didn't respond. He turned and marched towards the school. He wanted the Whisp out of him as soon as possible.

The Whisp took in everything Will's eyes could see, looking for any kind of clue. She noticed how old and worn the school looked. She felt Will shiver a little with the draught that blew down the corridor. The giant mosaics that hung on the walls, reminded her of artwork back in her own world. But the coloured little tiles did not look nearly as good in the hall's fluorescent glare as they did in the ancient buildings of home.

Then she spotted them, old pipes that snaked across the ceiling. Big round tubes of red-painted clay.

Were those pipes my prison? Are they my chance of escape? The Threshold must be somewhere in the sewage system.

Will let her ramble as he weaved through the crowd of students, into the quieter part of the school. The ground floor toilets were secluded, located at the beginning of a little dead-end corridor. There weren't any classrooms down that hallway, just some changing rooms that were now used for storage. Chairs lined the walls at points, likely stashed in the hallway and forgotten about long ago. He found the place one rainy afternoon when the park was not an option. He wanted to find a quiet spot to hideaway in peace. That was why Will had liked these toilets, they were more private. He imagined that was why the older boys liked them too. No sharp-nosed teachers wandering around to sniff the second-hand smoke.

When Will and the Whisp rounded the last corner to the toilets, Will noticed that the lights in that part of the corridor were all switched off. It made the place feel eerie. It was only in the darkness that the usual quiet of the corridor felt menacing.

Perfect place to catch me, the Whisp commented. *You can hide all kinds of nefarious goings-on in this school, can't you?'*

Will shivered. He hadn't considered until that moment that maybe someone had meant to capture the Whisp. What would they make of Will dabbling in their plans?

Come on, quickly before anyone sees us, said the Whisp encouragingly, sensing Will's fear.

Alright, alright, I'm going, Will thought.

Will approached the door and in the darkness, he saw a sign:

OUT OF USE.
PLEASE USE MAIN CONCOURSE TOILETS.

—MR. SCROGGIE

He pushed at the door—it had been locked.

Whose Mr. Scroggie? asked the Whisp. *Do you think maybe he knows about me? Do you think Mr. Scroggie might be the—*

Will cut her off with a groan. *Maybe, I mean, the toilets were working yesterday.* He shoved hard at the door, trying the lock a second time.

"They're out of order, Will."

Will startled, his whole body jolted in fright as he swung around; Gaby was already laughing.

"Hahaha. You pooped your pants. It's just me."

"What do you want?" Will growled. "Were you following me?"

"Yes," replied Gaby confidently. "I thought you might want your bag back. You left it in history. I took it to your next class but you weren't there so I thought I would just keep it and not say anything." Her eyes narrowed. "I didn't want you to get into trouble for skipping school. But if I knew you were just going to be all mad and stuff, I wouldn't have bothered." She threw the bag at his feet and turned away.

Will snatched his bag, calling out, "Gaby, sorry." He came to stand beside her. "Thanks for taking my bag."

"You know, I don't need to be nice to you," Gaby said with superiority in her voice.

"I know," Will conceded.

"I am being nice to you because no one else has been."

She was right. She was the only classmate that had shown him any kindness since he arrived in this place.

"I'm sorry, I just got a fright and then you laughed at me. That's all."

"It's okay. Where did you go yesterday?"

"Ummmm . . . doctor's appointment."

Stop lying, the Whisp jabbed. *She is trying to help.*

Will wondered if Gaby had sensed the Whisp because she immediately followed up with, "Stop lying Will. Your nose was bleeding and then you just vanished."

"I'm not lying," Will snapped. "You shouldn't be so nosey."

Gaby stopped in her tracks and placed her hands on her hips. "William Devine, you have an attitude problem." She huffed. "You know what? You can sit by yourself at the special assembly." Gaby stormed down the corridor and before Will apologised again, she added, "and don't follow me."

Just so you know, I'm on her side, said the Whisp

I know, thought Will quietly. *Now shut up.*

Will didn't want to follow Gaby. He wanted her to storm off down the corridor so he could be left alone to figure this all out. But he realised he didn't have a choice. The toilet door was locked, and he couldn't get in. He didn't have any other plan than to go to the special assembly.

"Gaby, wait. What special assembly?"

———

The vast assembly hall was packed with people. Every class was there seated in a neat row facing the stage. There was an incredible din of chatter that echoed up into the high ceiling. Will saw the teachers lined up at the sides, the students in rows in front of them. It didn't look like anything had started yet. He still had time to creep in and find his seat without much notice.

As he made his way down the aisle, there was the familiar shrill ring of the electronic bell through overhead speakers. The place went silent, and Will realised he was the only student still standing. He kept his head down and hurried to find a seat by his class sign. He was in class 2B, near the front.

The headteacher, Ms. Sharpe, took her place at the lectern just as he sat down. Her hands gripped the podium sides like talons and her waspish eyes skirted around the room waiting for complete silence. Her pursed lips looked poised, ready to dress down anyone who would step out of order.

Will noticed that the seats on the stage were not just filled with the year heads. Police officers were sitting there too. There were three of them sitting together, all upright and with their hats on their laps, as if posing for a photograph. Only there wasn't a single smile on the whole stage. Everyone looked sombre.

"We gather here on a very sad occasion," Ms. Sharpe began. She remained aloof, not giving away too much emotion in her voice. "Mr. Anthony, from the Social Sciences Department, unfortunately, passed away last night."

As soon as Ms. Sharpe said this, Will felt the temperature drop. There were some gasps, more than one "oh my God," and from an older kid a "holy shit." The teachers tried to hush their respective classes but not with very strict tones; sympathy clear on their faces.

"I realise this may come as a blow to you all," Ms. Sharpe continued. "As you can imagine it has come as a very big blow to us, too. You have lost a teacher. But the staff have lost a friend. Be caring to everyone you see today. If I hear of a single student using this as an opportunity to act out of line or behave irresponsibly, I will not hold back. Please do not let me down." Her eyes flashed across the room and Will had noticed they were bearing down upon the vultures from the bathroom, obviously well-known troublemakers.

Ms. Sharpe cleared her throat, regaining her composure. "Mr. Anthony had only been with Worldmouth Academy for a short time, but in that time, he made a big impression on us all. He will be sadly missed. I believe it is only fitting that we take a minute of silence to remember him on this hard day."

The school pupils stood and bowed their heads. Will did too. He felt the shoulders of the boy beside him trembling and wondered how many of the kids in school had felt the looming shadow of death in their life. Since Will had felt it already, he wondered if that was why he felt so unmoved by the situation. He reminded himself that he barely knew the man. Still, what he did know, he liked. Mr. Anthony had entertained him and stood up for him.

But Will felt nothing.

With his head still bowed, he peeked out of his half-closed eyes and picked out his sister a few rows back. She stood there, expression blank as well. But, he reminded himself, she wasn't taking history this semester, she didn't know the man.

Who was Mr. Anthony? the Whisp asked.

We're supposed to be silent right now.

Yeah, well no one else can hear me so it isn't a problem.

Will bit back a groan. *It is for me.*

Just tell me who he is and then, maybe, I can be silent for him, too.

He was my history teacher.

The Whisp paused for the briefest of moments—*Do you think he knew about my world?*

What? No. Now please, stay silent.

"Ok you may take your seats," Ms. Sharpe interrupted before the Whisp replied. "I'm now going to hand over the lectern to Police Inspector Dougal McNamara, from the—"

I'm just saying its suspicious. I arrive in this world, into this school, into some kind of trap, and on the very same night, a teacher dies.

Well, I won't know anything about it if you don't shut up. We might miss some important information. Will knew the Whisp was right, but if that was the case then maybe the police might say something vital. Maybe they knew exactly what has happened. Maybe they knew how to get rid of a Whisp.

Maybe.

The Inspector was a short man with tufty brown hair. He stood with his hands in his pockets and his shirt untucked, at the side of the lectern. Just by looking at him, Will could tell he was one of those adults who hadn't really spoken to teenagers, ever, and he wasn't sure how to begin.

"You see the thing . . . the thing is . . . this is a properly delicate situation we have here. Ideally, we want to be in and out of your hair as quick as we can. We want to let your schooling continue as normally as possible. We don't want to deprive you of classes or for some of you rapscallions, your detentions."

He looked out to the crowd with a smile expecting a laugh, but none came. The students were still mostly shocked and upset. Realising he had read the room wrong; he cleared his throat and shifted his balance. "What I want to say is, to get you back to normal as quickly as possible, we would appreciate that you follow our orders. Now, I'm going to level with you, Mr. Anthony's body was discovered only this morning, in his classroom."

Will tensed, suspicion growing.

The Whisp started, *This can't be a coincidence, this has to be connected. Do you think that he . . .?*

"Obviously that classroom and surrounding corridor are off limits so we can investigate. If you see the blue and white police tape up that means back up, do not pass go, and do not collect £200. Catching my drift?"

The pupils stared at the Inspector blankly. Will wasn't sure if his question had been rhetorical or if he expected a response. Some heads around him nodded but that was it. Inspector McNamara turned to look at his officers who smiled reassuringly, one motioning him to continue.

"Aye, so police tape means do not cross. Clear? Good, aye. Now, last night was a busy night in the school we had —" He was interrupted as one of the officers handed him a clipboard. "We had badminton, drama, chess, debating society, movie club and the, what does that say, the grime club? What's that?" He turned to his officer who shrugged. "Well, we had a whole bunch of after school activity going on. If anyone saw Mr. Anthony after his last class or has any information at all then come see me or any of my officers here straight away. Understand?"

Again, some heads nodded. Most just stared.

"Now, just to reassure you, the death does not seem suspicious. It just needs some further investigation. We need all the help we can get with that because, the fates have conspired against your janny here, who had the unfortunate position of discovering Mr. Anthony and then discovering his whole CCTV system has been kablamoed for months."

The Inspector gestured towards the back corner where Mr. Scroggie was leaning on an old mop. Mr. Scroggie grunted in response.

So that's Scroggie, said the Whisp. *He looks scary.*

He is, thought Will remembering his first nosebleed.

"Aye, that's me about done. Anything else, team?" the Inspector asked his officers. One pointed from underneath her folded arms trying to make her gesture as subtle as possible but everyone in the school saw. She was pointing to a woman who sat apart from them on the corner of the stage.

As the school's eyes fell upon the woman, she gave a wry smirk. Her wrinkles made her nose scrunch up and her eyebrows arched apologetically as if to say, 'Oh don't worry about little old me.'

"Oh, of course, Mrs. Porter." The Inspector cringed. "Sorry there, Mrs. Porter. I'd forget my head if it wisnae screwed on." He looked around at the students. "This is Mrs. Porter who has gladly volunteered her services at this time for you all to, well chat and stuff like that. Oh, now what's the name of it, forgive me, what's the right title for the job you do?"

Mrs. Porter gave a rusty cackle, that sounded like coins rattling inside a tin, and smiled. "Well, why don't I introduce myself? You've been working hard all morning, Inspector McNamara" Will had expected her voice to be soft and quiet, but it was gruff and flavoured with a strange accent. She croaked a little as she spoke.

"Of course, take it away." McNamara bobbed his head in deference and took his seat.

Mrs. Porter looked unusual on the stage. A little round pair of spectacles sat on the bridge of her nose and her thick skirt looked like a blanket around her lap. She would have looked more at home in a children's picture book, if it wasn't for the fact she sat completely upright and alert the whole time.

"I'm Mrs. Porter and I'm a bereavement counsellor. That means—"

Ms. Sharpe interjected, "Speak a little slower and louder please, Mrs. Porter. Or perhaps you would prefer a microphone? You mustn't be used to addressing crowds."

"Oh no," the counsellor chuckled, "I'd be no good with all that technology. No, I'll just use my lungs." She looked at the first row of students in front of her. "Now can you all hear?"

The students nodded.

"Good. I am here because, as we all know, this will be a very difficult time for everyone. People can react in all sorts of ways to grief and that is ok. That is what I'm here for." She smiled. "I am here to listen and will have a short one to one chat with every one of you. I will start today, going year by year to see how you are each coping. Then, if we need to do anything more together, we can take it from there. How does that sound?"

Ms. Sharpe didn't wait for the school to respond, she stood and began speaking before she even reached the lectern: "For the police to fully undertake their investigations there will be no clubs or after school detentions running for the next week." There was a murmur amongst the older years, that had her frowning. "And if I hear as much as a squeak of celebration about that, your detention will become a full-blown suspension. Have I made myself clear?"

The hall fell silent.

"In honour of Mr. Anthony, who was fascinated with the Second World War, I'm going to close today's assembly with a quote he would have liked—'let's keep calm and carry on.'"

The Whisp groaned. *Well, that didn't give us any clues . . . Now what?*

Chapter 8
Take Over

Will's first class of the day was maths. He had his textbook and jotter open, but he wasn't concentrating on anything numerical. Instead, Will spent the session arguing with the Whisp. From the very outset, he had been incredibly unsettled by her. He viewed her as a trespasser in his body. She had lodged herself into his mind, whether she meant to or not, and he did not like how she would intrude on him constantly with her own ideas and opinions.

He thought it would be much more polite for her to stay quiet while he sorted the whole mess out. She, on the other hand, thought that Will wasn't giving *their* problem, adequate attention. She wanted to skip class altogether and go kick the boy's toilet door in. To her, Will's usual routine didn't matter. Will argued back that the police were in the school and kicking a door down even on a normal day would get him into quite a lot of trouble. And today, if he was caught . . . well, Ms. Sharpe would be apoplectic.

This argument had been bouncing back and forth for a while until Will tried to once again ignore the Whisp, and pretend she wasn't there. He stared hard at the first question on top of the page.

'If Jeremy boarded a train heading south at 10.24 travelling at thirty miles per—'

The Whisp started twisting and turning.

Stop it! he snapped. The dizziness he felt grew worse. Up until this point, he had imagined the Whisp as a shape inside him. Filling him up, wearing his body like a suit. Now, he wondered if he had it all wrong. Maybe she was a tiny little thing, lodged up in his brain, like a virus. Was she making him feel all these sensations just by prodding at the right nerve ending?

Of course, as he pondered this, the Whisp heard. And it gave her an idea, which in turn Will heard her think. He immediately began to try and fight it.

The Whisp had never tried this before since she had never been in a body for long enough to need to. But here she was, stuck, with an unwilling and unhelpful host so it was worth giving it a try. She concentrated hard and tried to feel her way into Will. Just like before with the water.

She begins whispering her mantra, *Whisp's bind and unbind, bind and unbind, bind and unbind.* She does not fight with Will's body. She does not wriggle or squirm, trying to free herself. Instead, she relaxes. She feels herself run through him, become part of him.

Will feels it. It's like a rush. It tingles his body. It makes his senses alert. Everything feels vivid for a moment. He looks at the question he'd been trying to work on and instantaneously knew the answer to write down. He knows it is correct, just by glancing. It's like he's been awoken from some giant slumber and now the world feels alive and full of possibility.

For the first time, Will feels the power of the Whisp. She is inspiration. Inventive. Creative and beautiful.

She feels her consciousness move through his body. She lets the pulse of his blood become her rhythm. The electricity of his nerves, her melody. She harmonises with every ounce of him. She feels the complexity of a human, every organ working together at once. She marvels at this magnificent machine that she has become part of and then—

She snatches control of it.

Will can feel it instantly. His mind recedes inwards. He is weightless. For a second, he worries that he has become paralysed but then he notices, no, he is not paralysed. His body is moving. But he is not making it move. He watches as his hand folds a sheet of jotter paper over and then presses down as the other hand tears along the seam. He is not doing this. He is not making this happen.

She is.

Hey, stop that! he commands, trying to wrestle control back.

This body is just a vessel you know. Either one of us can be the captain, the Whisp whispers.

Will feels nothing but panic.

The Whisp knew what she said wasn't strictly true, but she enjoyed the chance to goad him. She is a fleeting visitor while Will has lived in this body all his life. She has to concentrate hard to keep every element of it working; Will can do this unconsciously. He doesn't need to think about breathing or digesting but the Whisp is using all her power to keep him functioning.

She knows he is going to get control again soon. Once Will realises how powerful he is inside his own body he will gain the upper hand. But right now, Will is still panicking and it gives her just enough time to work.

She thinks hard—Will's hand takes his pencil, and she makes it write. It's not as neat as when Will does it. She can't completely control the body, so the motion is very jerky. This makes the writing on the torn piece of paper look like it's been scratched into stone with a knife. But it is legible: *'GABY, MeeT AT CLosED TOILET, LuNCH. WANT TeLL U SOMETHING.'*

The Whisp keeps concentrating, trying to get the two arms to work together again to fold the paper. She tries to get Will's eyes to look at the paper, but she overthinks it and makes them look in different directions before everything goes blurry. Will sucks in a breath. She realized then that she's been putting far too much effort into breathing. So, now, Will is cross-eyed and panting heavily.

It's no wonder then that this ludicrous display attracted the attention of the teacher, Mrs. Hewlett. She snatches the note from Will's malfunctioning hands. This moment of distraction startles the Whisp and in a whoosh, Will's mind rushes back to gain control of his body. He takes a large gulp of breath as everything returns to normal. It takes him a second to recompose and realise everyone is laughing at him.

In the time it took for him to take his body back, to uncross his eyes and relax his breathing, Mrs. Hewlett had read the note out loud to the entire class.

Will's mouth opened as if he was about to speak but he realised he had no excuse that explained what just happened. So, instead, he just stared at Mrs. Hewlett, like an animal in the crosshair of a gun.

"Really," she said peering down at him with her two beady eyes. "I would have hoped you would have picked a more romantic spot than the toilets for a rendezvous. And I have to say, your handwriting is atrocious. I would avoid this one at all costs, Miss Crowsdale."

Will looked at Gaby who was sitting on the other side of the classroom. She was avoiding eye contact and pulling at some of the loose wiggles of hair to shield her face. Will felt his face flush and he looked down at his desk.

The Whisp had never felt shame before, she didn't like it. *I had to do something. I didn't mean to . . .* But the Whisp let the apology fade away, she knew Will did not want to hear another word from her.

Stephen and Danny began to make loud smooching noises and the rest of the class brayed with more laughter.

Mrs. Hewlett, realising she was losing control of the situation, grabbed a long metre ruler from her desk and thwacked it on another pupil's desk.

"Silence! I can't believe you are all laughing like hyenas on today of all days," she said.

Immediately, Will felt a venomous disgust towards her. He didn't like her using Mr. Anthony's death as a method for crowd control.

What a hypocrite, the Whisp muttered. *She started all that laughter by reading the note.*

You started it by writing the damn thing, Will retorted. *Never take over my body like that again.*

I had no other choice. You can't keep ignoring me, Will. I need to get out of here. I need to get home. You have got to try to fix this.

The toilets are locked, replied Will. *We can't break into them; I've already told you that. What more do you want me to do? I've run out of ideas.'*

I know, that's why we need help. That's why we need to tell Gaby.

When the lunch bell rang, Will made his way straight to the corridor where the boy's toilets were situated. He decided to skip lunch entirely. He wanted to make sure he was there if Gaby did show up.

As he walked, he tried to rehearse a possible conversation through in his mind, but he couldn't think of a way where the truth didn't sound stupid.

The Whisp remained quiet, realising that if she pushed Will again, he might give up on telling Gaby anything. The Whisp had liked Gaby since she first observed her that morning. She seemed trustworthy and fearless—and she helped Will keep a secret before, looking after his bag, telling no one he had disappeared.

"Why are you trying to humiliate me, Will Devine? And why do you like hanging out in this creepy corridor so much," Gaby said, rounding the corner, with her fists clenched at her sides.

"Gaby, I didn't write that note," Will replied quickly.

"You are lying, again. Mrs. Hewlitt caught you writing it."

"I know, but I promise it wasn't me. Gaby, I have something inside me that can control things. I know it sounds strange, but it took over my—"

"William Devine, I don't have time for your ridiculous games."

Will thought about giving up, but he had to tell her something, and right now there wasn't anything that explained the note . . . except the truth.

"It's not a game. I promise," Will said. "It wants me to tell you all about it. It's like it's another person that has become trapped inside my body. I know it sounds crazy but it's true. We need to get it out of me. But we don't know how to do that. It thought you could help."

Gaby looked at Will and began to smile. Will thought she was going to burst out laughing at him at any moment, but she didn't.

"I knew this place was haunted."

Will was taken aback, sputtering, "Y-you b-believe me-e?"

"Are you lying?"

He shook his head.

"Then I believe you. Why wouldn't I? You were acting really weird in class. There has to be some explanation." She paused. "Hmm. I think we need to perform an exorcism."

"What's an exorcism?"

"It's a thing that priests do to get demons or ghosts out of someone's body. It's a ritual with crosses and prayers and things. It's super scary," said Gaby with a wild excitement in her eyes.

"You think it might be a demon?" asked Will.

"No, it's not a demon," said Gaby shaking her head. "It's a ghost."

The Whisp had not liked the direction the conversation was heading in. *I'm not a demon or a ghost*, she muttered. *I'm a Whisp.*

Gaby continued, "You've been possessed by the ghost of Mr. Anthony."

"I don't think it's Mr. Anthony," replied Will. "She has a girl's voice for a start, and she acts totally different."

"Well, then what is she? Do you think someone else has died here? Maybe she's a pupil from long ago and maybe Mr. Anthony's death has awoken her. Maybe she's looking to take him to the other side, and she thought it would be nicer to stay and do some haunting and scare the new boy. Maybe she's a poltergeist and Mr. Anthony caught her, and it gave him a huge fright and that's how he died. My great auntie died of a heart attack when her smoke alarm went off. Maybe it was like that. Like the ghost did something and scared Mr. Anthony and now she is in trouble for killing someone. She didn't want to go back to the underworld and be punished . . . that's where ghosts go once they're dead, the underworld . . ." Gaby would have carried on rambling if Will didn't grab her shoulders, giving her a little shake.

Tell her I'm nothing like a ghost. I'm not dead for a start.

"She's not a ghost," Will interjected. "She says she's a Whisp."

At Gaby's silence, Will realised she was studying him and took a step back. He hated the feeling of being watched and it was even worse when he thought he was being examined.

"Can I talk to her?"

Yes, let me talk to Gaby, said the Whisp, excited. *You're not explaining this situation at all well.*

Will didn't like this idea one bit. He definitely did not want to give up control of his body again. "Why don't I just tell you what she's saying?" suggested Will.

Gaby nodded, intrigued to hear more.

Hello Gaby, we need your help. We need someone a bit braver than Will to solve our problem

"She says, Hello Gaby."

"I say hello back. Please tell the Whisp I'm very pleased to meet her. I've never met a Whisp before."

"She can hear what you are saying, you just can't hear her. I know it's confusing."

Tell her it's nice to meet her too. I think she looks really pretty. She has nice hair.

Will scrunched up his face and shook his head. "I'm not saying that."

Okay . . . then tell her she needs to break the toilet door down because you're too scared.

"No! I'm not saying that either."

Gaby sighed. "Will if I'm going to help, we need to

work together. I need to know exactly what Whisp is saying."

Will crossed his arms and scowled. "She's being mean. I'm not saying it out loud."

"Fine," said Gaby reaching into her bag. She produced a notebook and a pen with a furry top that she offered to Will. "If you're not going to tell me what she said, then ask her to write it down, like before."

"No way!" said Will. "When that happened, she took over my whole body. She just stole it from me. That's not happening again."

Please, the Whisp said. *I will only use the wrist and the hand. I won't take over anything else. I promise.*

"Fine."

Gaby grinned just as Will felt his hand become numb. It jerked and twisted until it got the pen within its grasp.

You need to look at the paper, Will, otherwise, I can't see it.

Will turned his head. It was so weird to see his hand again act independently from him.

It scribbled at the paper—

NEED TO GO bACK TO WERE WILL BONdEd TO ME. BOY TOILET.

"These toilets?" Gaby asked, reading the note.

"Yes," Will confirmed. "The Whisp thinks there might be a solution in there. But I keep telling her the toilets are locked."

"Then we need to break in," said Gaby with infectious excitement in her eyes.

YES!

"No," Will responded. "There's police everywhere, we can't just kick a door in. We would get in so much trouble."

"Then we use a key," Gaby suggested, looking smug. "Mr. Scroggie has all the keys for the old part of the school in his office. I'm supposed to go to Bridge Club tonight, so

Mum won't expect me back till late. We should sneak into the office and get the key and have a look in the toilet. I've never been in a boy's toilet before."

"No way," Will retorted. "You heard what that policeman said about parts of the school being off-limits."

"This is serious, Will. This poor Whisp needs our help."

"Poor Whisp! I'm the one stuck with her!"

"Exactly, if you want to go back to normal, we need to do something."

PLEASE! wrote the Whisp.

Will huffed. "Fine. I will text Dad and tell him I'm going to stay over at a friend's house, and we will break-in at the end of the day."

"We can hide in the library. Mr. Gelliway always leaves early so he can get out of the staff car park area first."

The Whisp wrote *THANK YOU* on the pad and Gaby smiled.

"You're welcome."

Suddenly annoyed, Will took his arm back into his control and snapped the notepad shut thrusting it back into Gaby's hands.

We are breaking into the toilets. Happy now? he thought to the Whisp.

The 'thank you' was for you both. I know you're both being really brave. We will fix this. I promise.

English was one of the few classes Will didn't have with Gaby and so while the rest of the class was chattering happily as they worked, he gazed out the window.

There was a hazy sun fighting to break through from the clouds. Birds chirped on the school wall and the traffic was beginning to build, as it always did, towards the end of the school day. The nearby nursery building had already finished for the day, and small toddlers were waddling along with their parents.

Will thought it was funny how everything was so different for him, but the world carried on exactly the same. It hadn't noticed—he felt comfort in that.

He imagined himself melting away and he liked the idea. He wondered if he would like to be a Whisp, invisible and fleeting. He wouldn't need to worry about dressing the right way or saying the right thing. He couldn't be picked on if he couldn't be seen, or so he thought. It must be nice to just jump in and jump out of people's lives so quickly no one even notices. It must be nice to not worry about friends or family. He couldn't get hurt anymore or let down. He wouldn't have to deal with anyone else's emotions when all he wanted to do was shut himself away and not talk to the world.

Nope, thought the Whisp, interrupting Will's thoughts. *You are wrong. Being a Whisp is hard. Always on the move, never feeling settled. It must be nice to be you, a person, with a family that knows you and comforts you. Shares in your successes and your worries. It must be nice to have someone that sees you and sees the effort you put into the world and smiles. Being a Whisp isn't an easy life.*

They didn't talk about it further. They didn't need to. They were becoming more attuned to each other.

Will wondered how powerful the Whisp was. The surge of power he felt when she took over his body was immense. How is there so much power in his body? How is something invisible that strong? But then he thought, a strong wind can uproot a forest and a great idea can change the world. Still, it was incredible to think that inside him there was a strength. Even if it wasn't his.

Caught in this fugue of thoughts, it took him a minute to realise someone was calling his name.

"William Devine next, please. Is William Devine in this class? William Devine?"

It was the bereavement counsellor, Mrs. Porter. Slowly, Will raised his hand and she made a 'come, come' gesture with her hand.

"Take your bag. You're the last one of the day. The bell might ring before we finish," said Mrs. Porter using her other hand, which was clasping a walking stick, to point into the hallway.

"We're just in a wee office down the corridor. It's actually the printing room but it'll do fine," she said to Will as he joined her at the door. "You walk ahead. You'll be here all day if you keep up with my pace."

He hadn't noticed Mrs. Porter's stick on the stage at the assembly. It made her seem even older since she hobbled slowly. He decided it was more polite to walk with her.

Besides, the slower he took to get there the less time they would have to *talk*. He hated to '*talk.*' The *talk* was where the counsellor would tilt their head and give him a sympathetic smile then suggest things like 'going for a walk' or 'seeing your friends,' which only makes them feel better, and not him. That was what Mrs. Porter was here for, to have the *talk* with the kids that had never heard it before.

Will had hundreds of them by now. Almost every adult he knew tried to have that *talk* at one point or another with him.

When he opened the door to the printing room and let her in first, she smiled and said, "What lovely manners. Respect for your elders, I like that"

"I—" Whatever he had been about to reply faded as he took in the mess that was the printing room. There was a small desk set up with a chair on either side and papers scattered everywhere. Each desk had their own scribbled notes titled with a name at the top. Mrs. Porter looked so well put together that Will hadn't for a second suspected she would be messy. But in the space of a day, she had transformed the printing room into a giant wastepaper basket.

Someone must have rearranged the room because the printer had been unplugged and shoved up against the back wall. School textbooks were piled on either side of the printer. They had been fashioned into two plinths and adorning each stack were what looked like two small blue and white funeral urns.

"They're vases. Just to make the place a little more homely," said Mrs. Porter, spying Will, looking at them.

"I will get some flowers for them; maybe tomorrow. Seems like I will be here a while. I was hoping to get through half the school today and I'm only on D's." She sighed and went towards the desk on the left. "Never mind. All worthwhile. Take a seat."

Will plumped himself into the chair nearest the door and took a deep breath.

"I gather you haven't been at the school very long," Mrs. Porter started, reaching for a piece of paper.

Will nodded without making eye contact.

"I'm new here, too, just arrived in the town. How are you settling in?" Mrs. Porter asked.

"Fine."

"It's okay if you're not, Will. Anything you say here is strictly private."

"I know," Will muttered, shifting uneasily in his chair. "I've been to a bereavement counsellor before."

"Oh. When was that?"

"A few months ago." Will paused for just a moment, before recomposing himself. "I'm fine now."

"I'm sorry to hear that. Was it someone close?"

Will didn't answer but the Whisp felt memories of his mother rush through his mind. Felt him fight them back. *Will* . . .

Mrs. Porter honed in. "A parent, by any chance? I lost my mother when I was young. Grief can be a very painful thing," she said, scribbling a note on a loose sheet of paper.

"It was my mum. At the start of the year." Will swallowed. "But I'm fine."

"That's three times you've used that word—'fine.' I'm glad things are 'fine' but are you OK?" Mrs. Porter looked up from her paper and directly at Will.

He shifted, looking down to the floor. "What's the difference?"

"Well, that's a good question. You can be fine and not be happy." She paused. "I suppose I meant to ask are you happy?"

Will nodded. The Whisp squirmed inside him, knowing he lied.

I think this woman is trying to help you, Will.

"I don't really like it here," Will replied to Mrs. Porter. "We moved here because Dad found the memories hard. He changed his job and we moved to a new house. It was going to make everything better—or so he said. But now we're here and it's not changed anything cause it's all still the same really. Same plates and bowls we ate from. Same smell on the towels. Same TV we laughed at. Same everything . . . just different. Different cause Mum's gone. Moving hasn't changed anything."

Will had never said that to anyone. He was surprised how quickly Mrs. Porter had opened him up. No one else had listened to him recently, not properly. It felt good to have someone sit with him, if only for a moment.

"Grief can be a funny thing, can't it?" Mrs. Porter said sympathetically. "You know, I like to think of grief like a parasite. Do you know what a parasite is?"

"A sort of insect," Will offered with a shrug.

"A parasite is a thing that lives inside you and feeds off you. It takes away your nourishment and your energy and uses it all for itself. It crashes into your life uninvited and then expects all of your attention. That's how Mr. Anthony died. A parasite ate away at his soul until it became too much for him. It's very sad, isn't it?"

"Yes," agreed Will, taken aback by the information.

"You are going to hear a lot of people try to dart around the subject and not talk to you like a grown-up. But I'm not going to do that." She peered at him closely. "I think you know what pain feels like. You're old enough to understand some people just can't survive it. It's not a choice when you die like that. You don't give up hope. It's wrestled away from you."

Will listened closely, understanding everything she was saying; it felt true to him. He had felt that deep aching pain.

"Now, I've been very honest with you. I want you to be honest with me." She waited till they made eye contact before continuing. "Do you have a parasite within you?"

Will stilled as the Whisp whispered, *It's ok. You can tell her.*

"No," Will said out loud.

"No?" Mrs. Porter replied. "None at all?"

He shook his head.

The Whisp tried hard to search Will's mind. She could find no sense in his answer. *Will, you can tell her.*

"Well then looks like we're done. I can't treat you if you're cured," she said, returning to her scribbled notes. "But please come back at any time if you feel different or if you notice anyone acting oddly. Grief is a funny thing. It can strike people in many different ways. And if there is anything amiss, I really want to know about it."

Will picked up his bag and made to leave. "Thank you."

As he closed the door to the print room the Whisp said, *You should have said something about me. Mrs. Porter could have helped.*

No, she couldn't, thought Will. *You don't get it. I'm a kid whose mum died and now their teacher is dead. If I start talking about hearing voices and losing control of my body, there will be evaluations and doctor's appointments and all kinds of things. None of which will get you actually out of my head. No one will believe me.*

Gaby believed you, replied the Whisp.

Gaby's a nutcase. She thinks you're a ghost. You don't know this world. Things like you don't exist here.

Before Will got back to the class, the shrill ring of the end of school bell rattled down the corridor.

Anyway, we don't need Mrs. Porter. We have a plan, Will reminded her. *Time to go hide.*

Chapter 9
The Glass Key

Will found Gaby between two of the tall bookshelves at the back of the library, her legs resting on one of the shelves while her back leaned against the other. She held a book close to her face and was muttering as she read.

"Where have you been?" she asked, not shifting her gaze from the book. "You've taken ages."

"Sorry," said Will. "I had to text Dad and wait for his reply before I could put my bag back in my locker."

"I just skipped my last lesson and came here early. Thought it would be a good chance for some research. Look at this." Gaby thrust the book she had been reading into Will's hands. The front cover read *Myths and Folklore, an Encyclopaedia*.

"It has a whole section in it about Whisps."

"Really?" Will asked, hurriedly flipping through the pages. He felt the Whisp's own excitement; it made his heart rate quicken. Will leafed past chimera, giants, and kelpies, only glancing at each image, not stopping long enough to take anything in.

"Well, it doesn't call them Whisps—they are spirits. So, 'S' for spirits. It says there have always been tales of spirits in every culture." Gaby snatched the book back and found the right page. "The Arabs called them Djinn and kept them in lamps. The Ancient Greeks called them Daemons. The Shinto people of Japan called them Kami and the Dutch called them Wittewijven. They've also been called Fairies and Angels and all sorts of things. The Ancient Romans called them Genii and that's where the word 'genius' comes from." Gaby tapped the book page, thoughtfully. "She must be clever. Does she make you feel smarter?"

Will ignored the question. "Does it say anything about them becoming trapped in human bodies? Or how to free them?"

"No, nothing. I checked it twice just to be sure. But listen to this, it says here that they are always considered powerful and that there are many stories of people trying to catch them. And also, that sometimes people will even kill to get their hands on one!" Gaby exclaimed in a loud whisper

"So?"

"Well, a Whisp arrives and the next day a teacher is dead. Don't you think that seems suspicious? What if Mr. Anthony was murdered?"

"You think Mr. Anthony was murdered? Who would want to kill him?"

"I don't know," Gaby said, "but it can't just be a coincidence."

Will gulped. Gaby might be right and if she was, this whole thing had become a lot more dangerous. Sneaking around after school suddenly felt life-threatening.

The Whisp felt his fear and tried to calm him. *It's ok. I'm sure once we get to the toilets it will all make much more sense.*

Will didn't feel so sure. What if they got there and realised there weren't any clues or answers? What if it was just the old stinking toilets where the vultures went to smoke and there was nothing that suggested it might contain a doorway to another world or Whisps or anything? What if all of this sneaking around didn't help them at all?

But they had to try something, and he felt a little less scared knowing Gaby was there beside him. She had closed the book, placing it back onto the shelf, and made her way to the edge of the room.

"Listen, no footsteps in the hallway. Sounds like the school's quiet now. Everyone must have left. We need to get the keys from Mr. Scroggie's office. He hangs them on a hook on the back of the door," said Gaby, as she began to sneak around the shelves.

Will followed her, stooping down as they crept so that no one would spot them from the library windows. They snuck up to the library door and Gaby teased it open, just enough to peek out. She held her eye up to the crack in the door and looked down the corridor.

"Okay, lights are still on."

"And?"

Gaby moved back to look at him. "Mr. Scroggie is still doing his final rounds. Once he comes back, he will turn the lights off and leave, that's when we go and grab the keys. Just need to wait until the corridor goes dark."

Will crouched with Gaby beside the door and waited. The longer the silence dragged on, the more Will's breathing picked up. It reminded him of quiet hospital corridors, waiting, endlessly waiting, until he was allowed to see his mum.

I'm sorry about your . . . But before the Whisp could finish, Will cut it off with a grunt. He scrunched his eyes closed and pushed his fists to his head. He didn't want anyone seeing those memories. He had opened himself up to Mrs. Porter and he had regretted it all afternoon. He didn't want the Whisp to see any more. He tried hard to make his mind go blank. Pushing his fists into his temples.

"We are going to get her out of you. I promise."

He unclenched his fists and looked over to Gaby. Her smile tried to reassure him, but he knew she was nervous too. She didn't need to be here, but she was.

When Will text his dad earlier in the day, his dad had seemed overjoyed that Will was going to postpone the pool game to hang out with a friend instead. Will hadn't realised, until that moment, that his dad knew how lonely he had been. And although he might have lied about what they were doing, Will had made a friend.

The Whisp agreed, *She's a good friend to both of us.*

And then they heard a voice. They held their breaths and listened.

"Now you're absolutely sure Mr. Scroggie? Not a trace of CCTV? Not even a smidge of footage? Not a morsel? Every single camera wiped seems impossible." Inspector McNamara's voice boomed down the corridor.

"I didnae say they were wiped. I said they didnae work. Did your officer say that I wiped them? Cause that's a lie—"

"No, no, no. She didn't report that. Just my clumsy wording. I'm not insinuating anything untoward here. Just wouldn't be doing my job if I didn't double-check." The Inspector paused. "It's just weird that every single one of them was faulty."

"Well, it is weird. No other explanation though. I only ever check them if there's been some vandalism. They were probably broken for a long time . . . It's no ma fault."

"Of course. Not your fault at all, Mr. Scroggie. It's just

all very mysterious. Anything else mysterious ever happen here?" The Inspector almost whispered the last question, conspiratorially.

Gaby silently mouthed the word "mysterious" back to Will. Both of them had their ears against the door, but they didn't need to. The police inspector's voice boomed down the corridor, and Mr. Scroggie was almost beside them, leaning against the wall on the other side of the door.

"I dunno. Always been normal since I've been here."

"Well, aye, I'm sure it's just a faulty system." The Inspector cleared his throat. "It all looks pretty straightforward—tragic but straightforward. Of course, the classroom remains out of bounds until we do the post-mortem. Then I can hand it back to your dutiful care. No problemo."

"OK," Mr. Scroggie said, his tone gruff. Even from behind the door, it was obvious to Will and Gaby that he wanted rid of the police inspector.

"Well, I think that's me finished for the day. I'll be off," said Inspector McNamara. "Do I need to hand back the swipe card?"

"Put it in the red basket at reception."

"Or shall I just keep it? I suppose I will need it again tomor—"

"Red basket," Mr. Scroggie interrupted, raising his voice.

Gaby and Will exchanged a look, Gaby had only ever heard Mr. Scroggie use that tone with litter dropping students, never another adult.

"Red basket it is then. Shall I wait for you?"

"No. I need to buzz you out," Mr. Scroggie snapped. "That's the rules. No exceptions."

"Righto, it's just, well I mean, strictly by police rules, I shouldn't leave the scene unattended with a civilian."

"Did you turn off the lights when you left Mr. Anthony's classroom?"

"Oh-of course. Do my bit to save the planet. Always hit the switch. I'm an eco nut, I even—"

"If the lights are off. I won't go near it," Mr. Scroogie barked. "I'll buzz you out then I'll leave and be right behind you."

"Well . . . ummm . . . okay . . . I suppose the whole school, isn't the crime scene. And the CCTV's working now?"

"It's working. That's what I said in my interview earlier."

"Ok, well then I suppose no reason for me to hang around."

"Right," Mr. Scroggie agreed. "I'll buzz you out."

Will and Gaby heard McNamara sigh and mutter, "What a misery guts."

Mr. Scroggie wanted rid of those police officers. And he was the one who locked the toilets where I was trapped. And all the CCTV is gone. Which he's in control of, the Whisp commented.

Will scoffed. *Mr. Scroggie is certainly grumpy and scary, and definitely a misery guts. But that doesn't mean he is a murderer.*

But Gaby, who hadn't heard the Whisp's thought, was thinking the same. "You don't think Mr. Scroggie did—?"

"I think—" Will suddenly stopped and put his hand over her mouth. "Shhh."

Looking out they watched Mr. Scroggie closing the door to his office, his footsteps moving up the corridor away from them.

"He's not turned off the corridor lights," Gaby noted.

"What does that mean?" Will asked.

"Doesn't matter, now's our chance," Gaby whispered ignoring the question. She pulled the door open and began to crawl along the corridor, scurrying up to the janitor's

office. She reached up and pulled the door handle gently—
the little lights beside the door flashed red.

"It's locked . . . I'm such an idiot, I forgot about the
swipe cards." Gaby looked crestfallen but Will was already
moving past her on the way up the corridor.

"Follow me," he whispered, and Gaby obliged.

Brilliant idea, Will, quick thinking, said the Whisp, reading
his thoughts.

Will headed down the corridor and into the small glass-
fronted reception. Sitting atop of the red basket was the
visitor's swipe card with Inspector McNamara written on
its sticky label. Will grabbed the card and flashed Gaby a
smile. "It says, *access all areas.* Let's get to the toilets."

"Not so fast, Will. The swipe card is only for the new
building, the other parts of the school still have old
fashioned keys," Gaby pointed out. "Still, this will get us
into Mr. Scroggie's office where all the old keys are kept."

They scuttled back the way they came and held
Inspector McNamara's card to the keypad. It bleeped
green and with a slight shove, Gaby was inside the office.
With Will following her, she headed to where the keys
usually hung.

"They're not there," she mouthed to Will as he hovered
in the doorway.

While Gaby began searching for the keys, Will looked
to the far wall, noticing a small stack of TV monitors that
showed the footage of all the cameras dotted around the
school. Will caught the image of a tall man prowling the
school corridors and froze. He watched closely as Mr.
Scroggie was picked up camera by camera, heading further
and further into the school.

The Whisp's thoughts began to whirr. *Mr. Scroggie said he
would be right behind Inspector McNamara, but he isn't leaving at
all. He lied to the police. We need to follow him!*

Will didn't like the idea of following but the Whisp insisted.

"The Whisp thinks Mr. Scroggie might have had something to do with all this," Will said, turning to Gaby. "She thinks we should follow him. I think this is already risky enough." He frowned. "What do you think?"

Gaby was already creeping out the door. "Let's trust the Whisp. Remember the ancient Romans called her a genius. Can't get into the toilets without those keys anyway." She motioned for him to follow then started down the corridor.

I like her, the Whisp said, as Will chased after her.

Mr. Scroggie must have been turning the lights off as he went because as Will and Gaby followed, the corridors ahead plunged into darkness. The corridors seemed even bigger in the silence of the early evening. Will had never been in the school when it was this empty. It was stark, reminding him once again of nights alone walking the hospital corridors as his mum slept. Nights where he would look in on all those sleepy wards, full of suffering souls.

The silence now made his hair stand on end.

Gaby and Will moved quickly until they got close enough that they could hear Scroggie's footsteps just ahead of them. They hung back at a corner and peeked around just in time to see two double doors swing on their hinges. They rattled loudly as they hit the door frame. The sound echoed through the hall.

Gaby whispered to Will, "He's going up the stairs."

Will pulled her back when she went to follow. "Give it a minute. Let's not get too close."

They pressed the key card to the panel beside the stairwell doors and it beeped. They pushed them open just enough to slip through and quietly pushed the door close behind them.

Will looked up. The stairs wound up four flights, in the darkness it looked like they spiralled on forever.

Holding his breath, Will froze and gripped the banister. Only one flight above was Mr. Scroggie's hand—Will heard him wheeze. He was right above them now.

Gaby gulped.

The hand disappeared into the shadow, but they could still hear Mr. Scroggie's wheezing as he climbed. Gaby waited until he was a little higher, then she scurried up the stairs. She got to the first landing and craned her neck upwards.

Gaby held up two fingers to Will and pointed up: second floor. They began to clamber up the next set of stairs.

The Whisp whispered in Will's head, *Second floor . . . Isn't that . . .?*

"Mr. Anthony's classroom," Will answered out loud.

Gaby turned to look at him. "You don't think he . . .?"

"I don't know," Will whispered back. "We need to keep following."

They climbed to the second floor and Will slowly held the swipe card to the reader. It gave a little bleep and Will pushed one of the doors slightly open. It creaked noisily.

Mr. Scroggie coughed. It sounded harsh and painful.

Will used the noise of the cough as cover, to close the door back over. He held his breath. Gaby moved closer, her shoulder brushing his as they listened.

Mr. Scroggie coughed once more before his footsteps returned. It sounded like he was still moving away from Will and Gaby.

Will sighed in relief. He unlocked the doors again and this time pushed on the second door that glided open more smoothly.

Gaby stuck her head up and down the corridor. "Coast is clear."

They slowly moved down the corridor following it to the very end where it turned sharply right. There was no other way for Mr. Scroggie to have gone, but the rest of the corridor had been crossed shut with police tape.

Gaby took Will by the hand and ducked under the tape. Slowly they edged down the corridor until they reached Mr. Anthony's classroom. The door had also been plastered in police tape with a large no entry sign attached. But the door was very much open, and Will looked inside. Mr. Scroggie was lurking in the shadows.

His bear-like figure was hunched at Mr. Anthony's desk. He was carefully removing a set of gloves from his inner pocket.

"Wait is he——"

"Ssh," Will whispered.

Mr. Scroggie began to slide the desk drawers open. He would stop and reach into each drawer, carefully sifting through it before moving to another one.

"Oh, Marcus, y'flaming idiot. Did you want me to get in trouble? What did you do with that key?"

Mr. Scroggie left the desk and headed towards the cupboards at the back of the room, opening them and shuffling through the books stored there.

"Where did you leave it, eh? Where did you leave it?" Mr. Scroggie muttered to himself as he bumped into one of the student's chairs nearly knocking it over.

"Can't see a damn thing in here. Come on Marcus where did you put it? Make it easier for your old pal, Scroggie."

Gaby took the chance while Mr. Scroggie was at the back of the classroom to dart past the doorway. She moved down the corridor and into the open classroom next door.

Will sighed at Gaby beckoning him to follow. He peeked into Mr. Anthony's room and saw Mr. Scroggie rummaging now in the tall filing cabinet at the back of the classroom. Since the janitor's back was turned, Will took the chance and dashed for Gaby.

When he made it inside the classroom, Gaby quickly closed the door behind them and whispered, "This is serious. Mr. Scroggie shouldn't be in there. He is up to no good."

"I know that," Will said. "And who's Marcus?"

"That was Mr. Anthony's first name. He must be looking for a key that Mr. Anthony left behind when he died. The police must not have found it." She hummed. "Maybe it proves that Mr. Scroggie killed Mr. Anthony."

"How can a key prove that?"

"I dunno—shhh," Gaby said holding her finger up against Will's lips. "Sounds like Mr. Scroggie's leaving."

"Can't see a damn thing!" Mr. Scroggie said.

They peeked out the classroom door to see him striding back down the corridor to the stairway.

"What do we do now?" Gaby asked when the janitor was out of sight.

"Doesn't sound like he found his key. Maybe we should go look for it?" Will suggested.

"You mean go into the classroom? That's the crime scene!" Gaby exclaimed, surprised at Will's boldness.

"We've already come this far. If this key does prove that Mr. Scroggie is a murderer or if it has anything to do with my Whisp, then I think we should try and find it before Scroggie gets his dirty, big hands on it."

Before Gaby had the chance to agree, or disagree, Will left the classroom they were in and slid the door open, heading right into Mr. Anthony's classroom.

"If the key is here," Gaby started, "it can't be anywhere Mr. Scroggie already looked."

Unless, the Whisp commented, *it didn't look like one of Mr. Scroggie's kind of keys at all! Will, take a look at the desk!*

Will realised that the Whisp had spotted something out of the corner of his eye and turned to focus on it.

It sat proudly on top of the desk and there wasn't a chance Mr. Scroggie wouldn't have seen it. But it didn't look like any key Will had ever seen. It was more like an elaborate ornament, about the size of a Rubik's cube. It was made of fine threads of coloured glass; its thin pipes melted from red to blue to green. As Will looked at it, he made out shapes inside shapes, a thin glass pyramid inside a thin glass cube inside even more shapes. It was intricate and immensely beautiful. The Whisp had immediately recognised it as something from her world. He reached to grab it.

Gaby gasped. "Don't touch anything, Will. Your fingerprints!"

Will turned to Gaby and shrugged. "But it's the key."

"Have you lost your mind? That's just Mr. Anthony's paperweight. Come on we don't have time to waste."

"Gaby, this is it. The Whisp says this is a key from her world. A key for opening Thresholds."

Gaby's eyes shone with amazement. "Mr. Scroggie must have killed Mr. Anthony to get it! We need to get out of here before he finds us."

He opened the door to Mr. Anthony's classroom and peered out into the corridor. "The coast is clear—wait!" Will saw a small spot of light on the floor which became a bright full beam as it rounded the corner.

"He's come back with a torch! Hide!" Will whispered, backing into the classroom.

Mr. Scroggie's footsteps were thudding along the

corridor; soon they saw the torchlight swinging from side to side with every step he took.

Will and Gaby fell to the floor, crawling between the legs of the chairs and the desks until they found the back wall. Gaby felt for the edge of the cupboard door with her fingertips and slid it open just enough for Will and her to crawl inside. It was a small tight space and there was barely enough room for them both between the dusty piles of books.

Mr. Scroggie entered the classroom just as Will slid the door shut.

We're safe. We just need to keep quiet. The Whisp tried to reassure Will, feeling his shallow breaths.

They listened to the janitor mutter to himself unintelligently as he headed back to the desk to recheck the drawers. Mr. Scroggie was careful not to let any light spill out of the window, covering the torch with his hand as he searched. This created a chilling effect for them as they watched out of the cupboard's keyhole. A small drawer or bookshelf would suddenly become illuminated, lighting Mr. Scroggie's rough face as he stared inside before the whole room would again plunge into darkness.

Light dotted around the classroom. Sometimes closer. Sometimes further away. Until eventually the light returned, and Gaby looked out to see Mr. Scroggie back at the classroom door. Gaby breathed a sigh of relief when his hand moved towards the doorknob.

"Is he——" Will started in a whisper.

"Got ya," Mr. Scroggie crowed. He reached for the hook on the back of the door.

"What's happening?" Will asked.

Gaby whispered, "He wasn't looking for the paperweight. We made a mistake. He was looking for a key card."

Will heard Gaby but didn't pay her much attention now. He, and the Whisp, were distracted.

As soon as the cupboard door opened, the Whisp heard the same pure tone that led her to the fountain, singing to her. When she told Will this, he admitted he heard nothing, but then the Threshold key started to throb in his hand. Soon one of the glass shapes began to pulsate with light. Will used both his hands to try to contain it, scared that the light might spill from the cracks in the cupboard door.

It's working, said the Whisp. *Look.*

Will felt it before he could see it. At the back of the cupboard, the air ripped and there was a slight breeze that brushed across his face. He could smell the dewy air of a cold night sky as it filled his lungs. It wasn't the stagnant air of a stuffy cupboard full of books anymore.

Turning, Will blinked at the rip now located at the back of the cupboard. Where he should only see the dark mahogany of the back wall, there was a section of starlit sky—big enough to crawl right through.

The breeze rushed into the cupboard and made the door rattle slightly. Mr. Scroggie's torch spun, and Gaby gasped, pulling back from the keyhole. Mr. Scroggie began to march towards the cupboard, his torchlight growing more intense with every step.

"Our chance to escape," Will said, tugging at Gaby's jumper to look.

But just as Gaby turned, Mr. Scroggie approached the door. He fumbled trying to slide it open. The door shook a little as he wrestled with it.

Will froze with fright.

Gaby noticed the Threshold then gave Will a push and turned away—

Will plummeted into the night sky. As he fell, the glass

orb in his hand shone white-hot and the hole in the air sealed itself instantly.

Mr. Scroggie hurled the cupboard door open and shone his torch inside. Gabrielle Crowsdale sat crossed legged looking up at him, like an expectant puppy.

"What on earth you doing in there? What was all that noise"

"What noise?" replied Gaby trying her best to make it seem like it was the most normal thing in the world to be a stowaway in a dead man's book cupboard.

Chapter 10
The Other World

Will tried to grab Gaby's hand and pull her through too, but as soon as he was shoved, he lost all balance completely.

And now he fell. His limbs tangled as his body tumbled through the night sky. He landed on the ground with an almighty thud and a billow of dust. He coughed, as the particles got caught in his lungs. Then he groaned as he felt pain in his abdomen.

You're okay, you are going to have some bad bruises, but I don't think anything's broken, reassured the Whisp, internally scanning for injuries.

Will winced as he clambered to his feet and looked up; the hole in the sky was gone. *We need to get back there. We need to open the Threshold again.*

That might be a problem, the Whisp murmured. *Look.*

Will opened his hand, noticing tiny cuts had already started bleeding and the crimson red was mingled with shards of glass.

The Threshold key was shattered completely.

"We can fix it. We need to fix it and get back. Mr.

Scroggie's got Gaby. We need to stop him—" He wanted to say, "from killing her," but he choked on the words.

We can't. It's broken, Will.

Will reached into his pocket. *Will my phone still work here? I'm calling my dad. He will know what to do.* He saw the screen was cracked and the buttons were unresponsive. *It's smashed too. Do you have phones here? I think I can remember his number.*

Will we need to go hide right now, the Whisp urged. She knew how much trouble Gaby was in, but she also knew how much trouble they were in, too.

Hide? We can't hide. We need to find someone to help us. He started to shout for help. But he choked again, this time though it was the Whisp's fault. She held his tongue tightly, not letting it move.

What are you doing? he cried in his thoughts. *Let me go!*

You can't, Will, we are in big trouble.

Will wished that he could reach inside and grab the Whisp. He wanted to shake her and make her come to her senses. "Gaby is going to be murdered!" he shouted out loud.

And so will we if you don't shut up!

She rushed through him, with a surge that made his chest throb.

"Urgh," Will groaned, "tell me what is going on."

It's night-time, in this world, and there's a curfew. It's a law, no one is allowed out at night except the Hunters. If they catch me—

"People are hunting for you?"

Yes, the Republic has an army of Hunters, the Whisp said. *They've been catching Whisps for years. We're powerful. The Republic want to control that power.*

"Yeah, cause you're SOOOO powerful!" Will shot back, anger in his voice. He didn't care that he was still speaking out loud. "So powerful that you had to get two kids to help you do everything. And so far, the only help you've given is screaming in my mind."

Will's body was trembling with an anger. "Telling us that Scroggie was looking for the Threshold key when he wasn't. It was the key card he wanted! Do you realise the danger we put ourselves in for you? Gaby might be dead right now—killed! And now I'm trapped here in another world with no way back. And all you want to do is hide!"

The Whisp didn't know how to respond. She knew she didn't have time to explain right now.

"I don't see why I should do anything for you," Will continued. "I should just wait here or shout for a Hunter to come. Explain to them I've caught a big powerful Whisp. If only they can pull it out of me and send me back home. Then I'll be rid of you and all of this danger. I'm sure the Hunters will be quite happy to help. Maybe I'll get a big fat reward for having put up with a criminal who tried to steal my body."

The Whisp was terrified. She tried to spin inside of Will hoping to spur him into action. She managed to tense his muscles before jerking his leg forward. Seconds later she felt his fury.

"Leave me alone!"

The Whisp felt every ear of every Hunter being pricked by Will's shout. She sensed all their hungry eyes spin onto their location. Hunters were prowling all over the city. *They might come from anywhere.* Again, she tried to take over Will's body to make him run but she felt him fighting her. He refused to budge.

NO, WILL PLEASE! PLEASE! THEY WILL KILL ME, she shouted inside his mind.

Will didn't even flinch.

WILL! she screamed. *I'M SORRY! PLEASE DON'T LET THEM CATCH ME!*

The howls of the Hunters rang through the night sky. They were out for blood. Will noticed the fizz of electric blue as the first Hunter emerged on the horizon. The stinger he held promised terrible violence even from a distance. Locking eyes with him, the Hunter bounded towards Will like a wild cat. There was a power and athleticism in his stride. Another soon followed and then another from a nearby rooftop.

Will felt the Whisp scream with sheer terror in his head—

He ran.

His feet scrambled to find grip on the soft gravel, and almost fell. He propelled himself forward as fast as his legs would allow, but the Hunters spotted his movement and began to chase him.

Will ran along the course of the wall until the Whisp yelled, *Left!*

Without thinking, Will twisted his body and pivoted down a tight side street. He entered at such a ferocious speed that he clattered against one wall and then the other.

Faster, the Whisp yelled, and Will tried to force his legs to move quicker. The hiss of the stingers zipped through the air as the Hunters turned onto the same street.

The Whisp yelled more commands: *right now, through the arch, right again*.

Will ran, weaving and dashing and darting but he did not lose the Hunters. He heard their snarls right behind him.

"Got you, you little barbarian!" one yelled as he hurled himself down from the rooftop.

In a moment of pure reflex, Will dove forward skidding along the ground and the Hunter missed him by inches. He reached out to grab Will's leg, but Will managed to stamp the hand into the ground, hard.

The Hunter howled; Will rushed to his feet and took off again.

Back up is arriving, the Whisp muttered.

They both heard the howls of more Hunters only a few streets away

We're in big trouble. She fought hard to shield her fear from Will, urging him forward. *Run, Will, run!*

Will tried to gulp air into his lungs. His cheeks reddened, and he felt his legs ache with hot pain. But still, he ran. He knew it was their only option.

Running and running and—

Will's body crumpled, a single-arm grabbed him hurling him to the ground. The huge hand clasped him by the collar and dragged his body into the shadow of the alleyway from which it had emerged. He tried to fight against it, but the hand had an iron grip. His body scraped along the ground, and he felt his trousers snag and rip on loose stones.

We're caught, said the Whisp cowering at the back of Will's consciousness. *I'm so sorry.*

"I'm not catching you. I'm saving you," a raspish voice replied. It sounded inhuman. Mechanical.

He can hear you? Will thought to the Whisp.

"I can hear everything," the voice said. "I cannot drag you further. Move quickly."

The cold iron fingers that had so tightly held Will's collar began to ease. The arms let off a piston-like hiss as they pulled away from Will. Will twisted to see his captor and realised that the figure was completely metal. He saw its hulking iron legs clunk forward as gears whirred where its pelvis should be.

The figure bent over and pulled at the bars of a drain cover. The drain cover split open and the cobbles of the street parted ways with it, revealing a set of steps heading underground.

The secret cellars, said the Whisp in awe. *I thought these were just myths.*

The figure held the doors open. "Hurry."

Will stepped down, realising the passageway was no bigger than him. His elbows brushed against either side as he took a few more steps. The figure closed the cobbled doorway behind him, and Will stilled. He felt trapped, now plunged into complete darkness.

Will heard the giant machine man whirring above his head as its huge body began to clunk back down the alley. Will wondered for as second if he had been tricked, then he heard the blood-curdling whoops of the Hunters.

The automaton has hidden us, the Whisp said.

Why? Will asked, but before an answer came, one of the Hunters spoke from above.

"Well, what do we have here? What's a rust bucket like you doing out past the curfew?"

"Have you been hiding scared little boys, mech man?" asked another.

The automaton said nothing.

Will heard a sickening snap of electricity then the sound of metal clattering to the ground.

"Awake now?" a Hunter barked. "Where's the boy?"

Again silence.

Another hiss of electricity sliced the air.

In the darkness, Will could smell the electricity as it burnt and singed the mechanical man. He heard the metal grind and groan as the hunters began to rip at the wounded automaton. It sounded like they were shredding his limbs apart, with clunks and crashes as each bit of metal was ripped from him and thrown to the ground.

Will felt a slow drip from the drain run into his hair.

The smell reminded him of his dad putting petrol into his car.

It's his oil, their killing him, the Whisp said, Will could almost hear tears in her voice.

We need to do something, he pleaded.

We can't. If we go up there, they will kill us.

Will knew the Whisp was right. And yet the sounds from above sent a chill streaking down his spine. He felt small, helpless against the terrible violence of the Hunters. *Animals,* he thought, *vultures.* And for a moment, only a moment, he remembered being held down into the toilet, gurgling with pain.

We have to keep going before they find us.

Unable to argue with that, Will shuffled slowly down the steps, feeling his way along the cold stone walls. The lower he got, the smaller the corridor became until eventually he was completely bent over, easing his way forward.

The secret cellars are supposed to be a web of passageways that connect the ancient caves underneath the city. When the Republic started to hunt the Whisps, it was said that these tunnels were made to hide us. But when the Thresholds were discovered the Whisps travelled between the worlds to hide and the caves were abandoned. Then the Republic started to close the Thresholds and a whole bunch of Whisps tried to find the passageways again. But none of us found a single passageway. We thought the whole thing must have been made up. I would never have thought that an automaton would know about it.

O-tom-a-ton, Will sounded the word out in his head. *Is that what he was called? The one that saved us?*

There are lots of them. They're all called automatons. I don't know if he had his own name. They're mechanical machines powered by ether oil. It's the same material that is used to make Threshold keys. The Republic used them as soldiers during the war. Now, they're mostly sold by merchants and used as servants in pubs and at the docks—places where there's lots of heavy lifting. I don't know why that one helped us.

There was a lot Will didn't know about this world and he knew that if he was ever going to get back to his world, he would need to trust the Whisp. It was his only way out.

"I'm sorry," he whispered in the darkness. "I should have run when you wanted me to."

She didn't reply. She didn't need to. He knew how sorry she felt too, for everything.

Will continued forward in the darkness. The further he went, the smaller the hole became, and soon he was down on his hands and knees. He knew that they were going down, deeper underground. He suspected he must have been at least 10 metres below the street by now, if not more. He worried that the walls would become so tight, he would get stuck down there. Or that the tunnel might go on forever, and he would never find an exit. Or that he would hit a few forked paths and get himself lost. Or that—

Will, it's ok. Look. Ahead of us, said the Whisp with hope in her voice.

He saw light in the distance. He crawled towards it, and it grew in intensity. The passageway began to widen again, and the walls became illuminated in the flickering light as he got closer. He noticed on the stone, marks of paint and chalk: letters, in blood red and ghostly whites.

They are all names, said the Whisp.

Will stood up fully as they came to a great open doorway. A fire flickered from inside.

Where are we? Will asked the Whisp.

I don't know, she replied.

Hesitantly, Will stepped into the cavern where the hearth in the centre burned brightly. He looked up and saw all of the smoke curling towards a small aperture. It was high in the ceiling—a drain cover, he realized. They were deep, deep underground.

"You made it. I am gratified to see you again," said a raspish voice as an automaton stepped to greet them.

Will recognised the voice immediately and the whirr of the cogs and gears. The automaton looked just as it did when they had crawled into the drain. It stood in the firelight without a scratch on it.

"But we . . . we thought . . . The Hunters didn't kill you?" Will sputtered.

"Confusing, ain't it?" came another voice from the corner. "I said to him, you just stay quiet and let me do the explainirations. Then y'can use say yer hellos. But let me go first. That's what I says to him but he don't listen nothing. He has tin ears."

Will turned to see a grubby looking man poking at the fire. The man continued. "You had a morsel to eat yet? Cooking a couple of grub rodents if yer wanting some." He reached his stick outwards to Will who saw there were a couple of rat-like creatures on the end of it, both burnt through.

"I'm ok, thank you," said Will, shaking his head.

"Suits yerself," said the grubby man before he took a bite, staring at Will. "Yer stayin here now. So's you got to go write yer name up."

"Oh, I don't think I'm staying." Will paused. "But I'm Will." He outstretched his hand to the man to shake.

"Nope, nope, nope. No names down 'ere. You ain't Will and I ain't no one either. Names left at the door. That's why they're there. It's the rules. I says no handshakes either—overly familiar. I's don't want to know you and you's defernately don't want to knows me."

Will turned his attention to the automaton. "Thank you for saving us. We thought you had died."

"You are correct. The machine above did not survive. But do not mourn. When the Hunters attacked, I moved out of that machine and took up residency in this new one."

"Are you a Whisp?" asked Will.

"Bah ha!" blurted the grubby man. "A Whisp. They ain'ts been around for years. Old tin ears aint a nice old Whisp! Hes a grubby little soul muncher, aint you?"

"A what?" Will asked.

"I am a Ghast," explained the automaton.

The Whisp gasped. *Will, we need to get out of here. A Ghast is a terrible thing.*

He felt her begin to panic once more.

"You confuse me, child," said the automaton. "Don't you know you have been bound to a Ghast?"

"I've been bound to a Whisp," Will said a little defiantly.

"That's where you's got it all confusiled." The grubby man waved his dirty finger at Will. "It can't be a Whisp, now can it? A Whisp doesn't bind to you. It bounces and skips from one person to the next. You's got yerself a Ghast inside you. Old tin ears sense-nd it. He says he's out patrolling, and he hears a Hunters' chase, and he spots you and he hears the spirit inside you. And he knows it's a Ghast inside you on account of it being bound to you. So, he saves you, to save his fellow Ghast. He ain't bothered about saving yer life one bit. He just wants to save his Ghast friend."

At Will's silence, the grubby man continued. "And anyways, I knows a Ghast when I see it. A Ghast is a wretched pain inside your soul. A Ghast will chew on yer life till you got no choice but to croak yer last breath.

That's what you got; I can see it in those eyes. You's got the touch of a dark pain in yer soul. You aint got no Whisp."

Don't listen to them Will, I'm not causing you pain, the Whisp said. *There is a pain but it's something else. It's not me.*

"I know my Whisp. She's not a liar. I'm bound to her," Will said, crossing his arms high up on his chest.

"Well, well, well." The grubby man got up to his feet and began to hop around the fire. "La di da, in the presence of a wonderful Whisp then are we? Why's don't you's prove it? A Whisp's s'posed to give you bright ideas. That's what they say ain't it. A Whisp lands on you and eureka! A flash of brilliance. So, what's yer bright idea. How you going to escape?"

"Escape?" Will began to panic.

"Ba ha ha!" The grubby man's croaky laugh echoed in the cavern. "Yers Ghast has got you all confusiled with its lies, ain't it? You's don't even know what's happenin ere, do yi?"

Will noticed the automaton move behind him, blocking the entranceway—he was trapped.

Quickly, grab a branch from the fire!

But before Will made a move, he felt the iron grip of two huge metallic arms wrap around him, pinning him tightly to the automaton's chest. He kicked wildly but the automaton only squeezed harder.

The automaton spoke directly to the Whisp this time: "Stop helping the human. You can feast on him here. This place is our haven."

The grubby man huffed. "Let me do the explainirations tin ears, this Ghast and his boy still ain't getting it."

"I's had a Ghast come and try and get me once. But before it got its talons in, I notices it. I's a happy man ye see. So, I feels the pain of a Ghast right away. And I says to it, I'm a powerful man. I's work on the black market. And I's can get you anything yi's want. Anywhere in the city. Ye's let me go and I can give you a safe place where no Republic Hunters going to trap you in a jar. And I can get you souls, lots of them."

The grubby man pauses. A glint in his eyes. "And the Ghast says no. But I bargains and I bargains and I does a deals. Ye get me off right now and I feed the whole gang of ye. I give a space for the Ghast and all his Ghast friends. So, I takes them down 'ere; I lure. I lure rich men and school children, old widows and aristocrats. I lure anyones I can down here and the Ghasts can chew on them till they're dead. Then I's eats the body and gets them another. It's a system we gots going. They eats what they want and they stay away from me."

The names, the Whisp whispered, horrified.

"That's why I don't want no names. Don't taste as good if you knows the person. But I ain't evil. I knows people has their families and some folks are fond of each other, so you's can choose to write yer name up if you want, like's a little memory-al. For y'er sacrifice."

The grubby man waved a piece of chalk at Will, offering him to take it.

Will turned his head in disgust. The automaton's grip tightened, making it harder for him to wriggle at all.

"Don't blames me! I don't want you 'ere. Yer Ghast is just another mouth to feed once yer dead. I gets one of them once in a while to go into one of those machines and patrol the streets. Make sure the secret cellars stay secret. But old tin ears goes patrolling and instead finds you. He wants yer Ghast to be safe and kept out of the Republican pandora jars. So now's yer 'ere. I aint got no choice." The grubby man shrugged. "Cause now ye's know the cellars. So, you got to go to the crypt with the rest of 'em. Where your Ghast can chew on ye in peace."

"But I don't have a Ghast! I have a Whisp!" Will shouted.

"Ba ha ha. Ye's believe what's yi want. Makes no difference. Yer's know the cellars. I can't let you out. Yer goin' in the crypt."

Will tried to wriggle his way free. His fingers clasping at the iron body hoping he could find a cog to pull out or twist. But in response, the arms squeezed harder. The more Will fought the harder the arms squeezed until the world became darker, the air leaving his lungs.

The Whisp began to shout, *Will! Will! Will!*

His body grew limp; light fading.

Will!

The Whisp's shouts sounded like they were coming from a thousand miles away.

Don't—

Will heard her cry out before the world went dark.

Chapter 11
A New Decree

P hilo supped at his cup of hot cocoa then slammed it to the table with a thud.

"Was this really necessary? What is so pressing? My entire household was awoken, and I was dragged to this Council chamber and now I find you are the only one here." Philo's neck tensed as he spoke. Distrust had been running high between Council members ever since the General disappeared and he eyed the whole situation with ferocious suspicion.

Cato lifted his weary head from his hands and gave a faint smile.

"Don't look at me. I'm in the same ship as you. I've been waiting here for half an hour. I was just about to drift off in my chair when you burst in all noise and bluster."

"You mean to say, you've been here for half an hour and haven't even found out the purpose of the meeting? What if we have been accused?" Philo asked, incredulously.

Cato rested his head back into his hand and yawned. "We will hear soon enough what the matter is. Why waste away my energy? Besides, I don't have anything to be afraid of . . .Do you?"

Philo looked at Cato with disgust. "You're a pathetic creature sometimes. You really are." At Cato's shrug, he opened the door to the Council chamber and roared down the hall, "Guard!"

Cato groaned at the noise as he stretched his arms and gave his head a shake.

Philo was cursing at the guard when Cato came over to address them. "I assume he told you what you wanted to hear then? Are we doomed?"

Philo turned to Cato, snapping, "This ingrate says he doesn't have the slightest clue why we were summoned."

"And you thought he would?" Cato chuckled. "Really, Philo . . . and you call yourself a member of the Republican Council. A philosopher with the duty to give wise guidance to the King. Sometimes I think you have all the wit of a dung beetle." Cato dismissed the guard with a wave of the hand all the while staring at Philo.

Philo's nostrils flared. Cato always made sly digs at him, but this was a direct insult and in front of an inferior as well. "I summoned you; I dismiss you!" Philo roared and the guard turned on the spot.

"Sir?" The guard was unsure of whether to stay or go and decided his best move would be to make a low bow of apology to both of the Council Elders.

"Good," Philo snapped. "Now you can get out of my sight."

The guard turned on his heel and headed quickly down the corridor.

"Happy with your little display of power, Philo?" Cato asked with a wry smile.

"If you ever insinuate that I am a dung beetle ever

again, I will strip out your guts and hang them like bunting from the palace windows, old man!"

Cato was not at all shaken by the threat. He tsked. "Come, come, Philo. All I was trying to say was that if we have been summoned in the middle of the night, the matter is clearly confidential. How was a lowly guard to know why we've been called?"

"I'm beginning to suspect you summoned me yourself," Philo spat, "as part of one of your misguided political manoeuvrings."

"Hardly," Cato said with another cat-like stretch. "I prefer to manoeuvre quickly. You would never keep up."

Philo took a deep breath, ready to launch a furious tirade at his fellow Council member when the King's chamber door opened. Both Cato and Philo looked on in alarm as they noticed the full retinue of the other Council members with the King. They all filed in and took their seats.

Cato sidled up to the King's side and spoke, "Sire, I did not know we had been summoned to your chambers. I would have come straight away."

"Hush now, Cato," the Queen scolded, arm in arm with the King. "You and Philo haven't missed any official business. The other members of the Council know just as little as you do.'"

Cato grimaced. He hated Agrippina for embarrassing him, but he hated the prospect that he might be in trouble even more. When he played matchmaker between her and the King, he thought she would be a useful pawn for him to play with. But now she had grown into quite a powerful player in her own right and in sharing a bed with the King every night, she was able to persuade him of a great many things.

Philo, embarrassed but not as sly as Cato and without

his sleep, became even more brusque. "Was the Council meeting the King without me and Cato? It is strictly forbidden in the laws of the Republic for the King to meet without full Council. I demand an explanation!"

"Ah now see Cato, you should take a leaf out of Philo's books." Agrippina was trying and succeeding to ruffle the old man's ego. "Why cut with a sharp tongue when you can hit something right on the head with a big blunt brick?"

The Council members laughed with the Queen. Philo and Cato looked on in horror, being the subjects of such ridicule. Cato had been out of the King's favour ever since the General absconded. The King had blamed Cato for supporting the General in his experiments. Agrippina knew this and had decided it was better to dispatch of the old man than to help him.

What better way to diminish me, Cato thought, *than to pair me with Philo and make me the butt of a joke. If I'm not careful the Queen might finish me off tonight completely.*

The Thinking King bellowed across the chamber, "Settle down. Settle down. Dear Cato and Philo, we would never think of meeting without you. You've got this all wrong. Take your seat gentlemen and let me explain."

Cato and Philo looked like two churlish children who had been told to finish their meals before getting up from the table. They both took their seats but made sure to display that they were in a terrible huff. Philo sat with his arms crossed and Cato refused to make eye contact with any other member of the Council.

"I have received a report from Lieutenant Otho's replacement. I summoned the Council and sent for you both. The other Council members happened to already be in my chambers for the Queen's birthday dinner."

Philo's voice raised to a squeak as he said, "Birthday

dinner?"

"Yes," the Queen said with an accusatory tone. "Invites were sent over a month ago. Do you not read your Council correspondence?"

"O-Of course, I read all official documents. Must have slipped my mind. Apologies and happy birthday, your Grace."

Agrippina smiled with fake appreciation then turned to Cato. "And your excuse?"

Cato thought quickly. The Queen had outwitted him. Everyone knew Philo didn't read his documents, he gave that job to one of his servants. If Agrippina had missed him off the list, he would never realise. No, Philo was just a fall guy in this little plot and the servant at home would take a beating because of it.

Cato read his documents assiduously and knew that he had not received an invite. Did he claim, like Philo, that he had forgotten all about it and make it appear like he doesn't read his documents with due attention or . . . He wasn't sure what the Queen wanted. She likely wanted everyone on the Council to think he is growing slow in his old age. On the other hand, if he claimed the truth, that no invite was ever sent, he risked angering the King by accusing the Queen of playing petty games. Which she, of course, was.

He felt trapped.

"Happy Birthday, your Grace," he said, with a slight bow. "The great Thinking King mentioned a report from the head of the Hunters, I believe. Has he failed us? Lieutenant Sulla, was that his name? Otho's replacement. I was worried about this. The Queen recommended him, if I remember correctly."

Cleverly played, he thought to himself, no excuse needed since he diverted the King back to the task at hand.

At Cato's words, the King gestured to one of the guards who hurried out of the door and came back with the new Lieutenant. The man knelt and bowed his head as a mark of respect. When he removed his helmet, Cato took note of his tight blond curls, and muscular shoulders. Young and probably hungry, he thought. He'd need to watch him.

"Go on," said the King, "tell us what you saw."

The Lieutenant rose to his feet and began to address the chamber. "My Hunters are currently pursuing a boy across the city. At this moment he is evading us, but I have my best men scouring the city looking for him."

Philo scoffed. "You got me out of bed to tell me your men are playing a game of chase with a child?"

The King pointed his stubby finger across the table. "Lieutenant Sulla didn't get you out of bed, Philo. I did. And we wouldn't have had to wake you at all if you had remembered my wife's birthday. Let my man finish his report!"

Philo gave another small bow of apology.

The King nodded for Sulla to continue.

"The boy is not an ordinary subject of the city. One of my Hunters reports that he fell out of the sky. As if from nowhere. And multiple Hunters who gave chase have provided me with witness reports—his dress is not of this world."

"He is possibly a child from Gaia," Agrippina theorized. "The world where we sent the Gatekeeper to only yesterday. The world where our own General disappeared to. The world where the last Whisp is in hiding."

Cato saw his chance to strike and pounced: "More Thresholds have been opened. This man is as bad as Otho. He needs your punishment."

"Aren't you following, dear Cato?" Agrippina replied. "The Lieutenant hasn't opened the Thresholds. It was the General and his co-conspirators."

"Co-conspirators?" Cato looked the Queen directly in the eye, daring her to make her accusation.

"Well, I don't think the General would have acted alone. He isn't a brave man."

"Ahh, I see. No evidence at all then. All we have here is some leaky Thresholds and hearsay. The General has been gone for months and we haven't seen as much as a finger raised against our King. Yet all the Queen has talked about is coups and conspiracies. This is paranoia, your Majesty."

The Queen glared. "When the Gatekeeper returns with our General in shackles, we shall know everything."

"And in the meantime, our glorious city will just sit with who-knows-how-many-Thresholds open, ready for who-knows-what to fall out of the sky waiting for the old battle-axe to return who-knows-when. This sounds like a tremendous plan." Cato emphasised every word to make sure his disdain was noted.

"It *is* what the King decreed," Agrippina replied.

"She's right I did decree it," the King remarked.

"Then make a new decree," Cato fired back.

"A new decree?" The King tugged on his beard and arched his eyebrow.

"Destroy the Thresholds." Cato sat back in his chair to let the full weight of his suggestion set in. The Council played to his tune immediately, with a collection of gasps and murmurs.

"Drain the fountains. Extinguish the flames. Block up the sky. Dig holes in the ground. Wherever there was a Threshold, we should have it destroyed." Cato paused. "Every. Single. One."

"But then the Gatekeeper can't return," Philo replied, slowly.

"My point exactly," Cato said, turning to the King. "If we destroy the Thresholds. She can't come back. Neither can the General and neither can the Whisp. What harm is there in that? We already know enough: the General opened a Threshold without permission. He is a traitor. Let him rot in the other world where he can't harm your power."

"And what of the Whisp?" Philo asked.

"And what of the Whisp?" Cato parroted back. "We only want to throw it in a jar with all the other Whisps. We have plenty of them. Let it go. Lock it out. Does it matter if it is in a jar or free in another world? The important thing is that it isn't here. It cannot harm us. We can tell the people that our great Thinking King has done what he said he would and rid a whole city of its spirits. Soon we will rid the whole nation and then the world. We can have a great celebration, one even grander than your coronation in honour of your tremendous victory."

The King looked like a plump peacock displaying its grandeur. "A celebration?" he repeated, sounding thoughtful. "Yes, I like the sound of that. Let's destroy the Thresholds."

"Your Majesty," the Queen started. "Dear husband. Don't be so hasty. We only sent the Gatekeeper there yesterday morning. She needs some time. If word got out that we had abandoned an old woman in a far-away world—"

"Word won't get anywhere. We are the only ones who know. And the Thinking King can trust his wise Council." Cato knew he playing a dangerous game, but to him the gamble was worth taking. If it paid off it would cement his place in the King's good favour.

Agrippina protested, "Cato, you are being blinded. As soon as the Gatekeeper returns, we can close the Thresholds for eternity. One more day is worth it. Then we will have our answers. We will know what the General was plotting and who he was plotting with. We will know exactly what he discovered, and we can use his discoveries for the good of the Republic."

"Hear, hear," shouted Philo who then eyed the King, giving him a smile.

"The Queen is right, Cato. We should discover what the General had learnt," said the King. He rose to his feet summoning for a Pandora jar.

The rest of the Council stood with him, except Cato. He needed to make his gamble count. "Then I must be dismissed from your Council and replaced."

The other Council members gasped with shock; the King's eyes grew wide.

"I mean it," Cato said. "I swore an oath to defend the Republic by giving you good advice to think upon. A Republic is formed by wise rulers. We voted you as King to take the decisions based on our wise rule. How can I say I'm defending this Republic if you ignore my advice and listen only to your Queen?"

Agrippina flushed red with anger. "How dare you!"

Cato leant back in his chair and smiled impishly at the King. "Every one of us here thinks it." He turned toward the Lieutenant who kept silent, eyeing the ongoings with interest. "Lieutenant Sulla, would the job of hunting become harder or easier if the Thresholds were destroyed forever?"

"Easier, my Lord," Sulla answered.

Cato gave another impish smile and clicked his fingers. "Exactly. Even young Lieutenant Sulla understands. You are quick soldier. You will make a fine lieutenant."

Cato flashed a grin at Sulla who blushed. Cato turned his attention back to the King. "The General went behind your back, your Majesty, and opened a handful of Thresholds. Not many. Only a handful. But now we have boys falling out the sky and God knows what else stumbling through these open holes. If things can escape. Things can get in." He paused. Letting the silence build.

"We are leaving our city, our Republic, open to attack. We have rid the city of Whisps and Ghasts forever. But what if he wanted to flood the place with spirits from another world? All our hard work would be for nothing. And right now, we are leaving the Thresholds wide open for him. All because the Queen is curious to know what he has learnt. Curiosity killed the cat, and it might well kill us all if the Queen has her way."

Cato locked eyes with the King. He had just made the most important and dangerous speech of his life. If he was going to win the King over, it would have to be now.

The King chewed on his lip, tugging his beard once more.

Cato added in a whisper, "No more Thresholds. No more Whisps. Triumphant celebrations."

The King gestured and a footman approached with a sealed Pandora Jar. Drinking the Whisp that had been trapped inside, he shouted, "Destroy the Thresholds. I want my celebration. It is decreed."

The Council roared in approval.

"But the Gatekeeper?" Agrippina tried to protest.

"The King doesn't care about a measly Gatekeeper, Agrippina," Cato chided, rising to his feet. "Sulla, round up your troops. Kill the boy as soon as you find him and destroy every damn Threshold that the General left open." He smiled. "Now I believe we had a birthday party in progress."

Chapter 12
The Crypt

Will's world had changed again. Moments ago, he was in the cavern with a filthy cannibal and his robot, a place that had seemed so strange and dangerous. Now, he was somewhere familiar and safe. It was a place he recognised—the room of flowers. The green lush room full of bouquets and wreaths. Plants sprouting on every surface.

He took in a deep breath waiting to be rejuvenated by the fragrance. But the smell that hit him was nasty. It smelled of the stinging TCP that his mum used to rub on his cuts and grazes. It smelled of the day a mouse got in the kitchen and his dad scrubbed everything with bleach. It smelled of latex gloves and surgical masks.

It smelled of memories.

"Mum!" Will shouted as he pulled at the flowers blocking his way. "Mum are you here?" He clawed at the plants until he found the worn blue curtain that had hung around her bed. He pulled it back slowly.

And there she was. Covered in vines. Vines that seemed to sprout from her chest and her arms and all over her body. Vines that seemed to feed into her veins. He went to grab them too but as he did, he noticed they weren't vines. They were wires. Going in and coming out of her. Blood hangs in a plastic bag above her head.

"Mum, are you ok?" Will asked, tears in his eyes.

She smiles faintly. Her lips have faded into her pallid face and there are dark circles around her eyes. But she still manages a smile. "You're bleeding. Are you hurt?"

He rubs his nose with his sleeve. "It's nothing, Mum."

From behind him, he hears a shout, *Wake up, Will!*

He looks around and by the curtain he sees a white mist in the shape of a girl. "Not yet," he tells the shape then turns back to his mum—

She's gone. Faded into the nothingness.

"No!" he cries, feeling that familiar deep wretched pain starting to chew upon his soul once more.

Will Wake Up! Wake Up, Will, the girl-the Whisp shouted.

He opens his eyes, but the world is still dark.

You're bleeding. Are you okay?

Will rubs at his nose and finds the small trickle of blood. "I'm okay. It's just my nosebleeds. What happened?"

You passed out, she says, *when the automaton squeezed you. Then they threw us in here and your nose started to bleed. I tried to wake you.*

Will's eyes began to adjust to the dim grey light. He felt his way up to standing against a large wooden door that was fitted into the face of a rock. There was a small set of bars on the door and Will stood on his tiptoes to peer out. The automaton was standing by the door and the wicked old man was munching away on his last grub rodent by the fire.

"Let us out!" Will shouted but the man and automaton didn't move a muscle.

When Will heard a scream come from far across the room, he jumped. *What was that?* he asked the Whisp in his mind.

We aren't alone, said the Whisp.

Will turned to see a small, vaulted room, tightly packed with bodies across the floor. At first, he thought they must all be dead. But quickly his eyes were drawn to movement —an arm grabbing at the air. A leg kicking at its neighbour. A wretch and a heave of someone about to throw up.

They've all been cursed. Every one of them has been infected with a Ghast, said the Whisp. *I've never seen such a horrible sight.*

"What actually is a Ghast?" Will asked.

A Ghast is a spirit, that eats away at your soul. It's a kind of darkness. If a Whisp is a breath of fresh air, then a Ghast is suffocation. It makes life unbearable until eventually, you have no choice but to let it eat your soul entirely.

"You mean it kills you?"

Eventually. Only when it has eaten up every last part of you.

"And they all have that? They can't unbind from it?" Will asked, worried at what the answer might be.

The Whisp hadn't even uttered the first word of her reply when in a cacophonous unison, all of the bodies let out a hellish scream. The sound was unbearable.

Will instinctively covered his ears and shirked backwards. The bodies convulsed with the agony of the scream as if the sound was erupting from them, forcing itself out of their weakened bodies. When it finally stopped, the bodies collapsed back into their shrivelled heaps and groans of pain murmured around the cave.

"What was that?" asked Will.

I don't know, I've never seen anything like . . . the Whisp hadn't finished before the unified scream started again.

One of the bodies nearest Will grabbed at his trouser leg and began to pull herself up. Will instinctively tried to kick her off, but she was too strong.

Her yellowed nails dug into him like claws, and she climbed up his body until she whispered into his ear, "You need to stop talking so loud to yourself or this will never stop." When he looked at her, she sighed, adding, "Come with me."

The woman was dishevelled and dirty just like the grubby man in the cave. He didn't want to trust her, but the screaming was becoming unbearable.

At his nod, she crawled through the bodies not bothering to check if she stepped on someone's hand or stomach. She clawed her way across them.

Will tried to pick his way through, creating a path that avoided the bodies writhing on the floor, but it was impossible. The bodies were packed in so tightly that the crypt was carpeted with body parts.

"Hurry up!" she shouted as she leapt from body to body across the tunnel. The bodies responded to her shout.

The screams were deafening, rattling around the walls. The bodies were a monstrous choir, never once stopping for breath.

Will almost fell as the bodies contorted on the floor. When he eventually caught up with the woman, she was at the edge of the vault. She cupped her hands together and gestured for Will to step up. He placed his foot into the crook of her palms and lifted himself up the wall until he found a deep ledge. He clambered up then stretched his hand down to help the woman, but she had already begun to scale the wall picking out small pot marks and footholds. She climbed with ease, like a monkey in a tree.

When she got up, she walked along the ledge until she found a small hole. It was another tunnel. Will followed, winding his way through the labyrinth until they came to another clearing. He saw a small huddle of about ten men, women, and children all crouched together. They were rocking forward and backwards, swaying like they were in a trance. It was only once he got closer that he heard the deep throbbing sobs of people crying.

The woman stopped in her tracks and whispered, "They won't hear us in here. Those screaming bodies are the ones that the Ghasts are nearly finished with. They like to be left alone, in the silence and in the darkness, the souls are easier to eat that way. Ghasts hate conversation. They hate . . . nnngh!" She doubled over clasping her stomach.

"Are you okay?" Will asked.

"He hates me talking like this," the woman said through gritted teeth.

"Who?"

"My Ghast."

The Whisp recoiled at that.

"I'm infested just like the rest of them. I'm going to be just like them soon. Down in that pit. We all are," the woman said gesturing to the sobbing huddle.

"Are they okay?" Will asked. "They look like they've been hypnotised."

"Some souls have been more eaten than the others," she explained. "The ones you see here are fresh. Recently infected. But the Ghasts still hurt them and they're frightened."

The huddle was trembling. Some darted fleeting looks at the woman. They wanted her to stop talking, Will saw it in their eyes.

"And you?" he whispered. "You don't seem like the rest."

"I've not been down here long. Jackle caught me about a week ago. I think." She strained at her words, clearly fighting for control.

"Jackle . . . Is he the old man with the automatons?"

"Yes, he tricked me. I was on a ship arriving in the city. Smuggled in. My home country had become unsafe. He said he would find me work but—" She screamed in pain and the noise set off another scream from the bodies down below. The huddle gathered closer, some closed their eyes and covered their ears.

Will felt their pain. He wanted to help, with every fibre of his being. He wanted to reach in and pull the Ghast out of her. He wanted to throttle it for causing so much agony.

"He made me write my name upon the cave wall, to abandon it there." The woman continued to fight, each word a huge effort. "The Ghast wants me to forget it. He wants to feed on me. He wants me to just become another husk. Another nobody to feed on. But I won't forget. I won't forget who I am. And I won't forget who put me here. I curse his name, just as he cursed me."

She paused. Her eyes lighting with an inner fire. "He is Jackle the jailer and I'm Freya who should be free."

In the cool light of the tunnel, Will noticed just how striking Freya was. Her red hair fell over her shoulders like an ancient headdress made of the feathers of some rare exotic bird. She looked like a warrior even though her body was painfully thin.

She still has strength in her, the Whisp mumbled, *but it's draining fast.*

"I'm Will, Freya. It's really nice to meet you," Will said and he reached out his hand to shake.

Freya's body convulsed and she stumbled back. "Don't touch me! The Ghast hates a gentle touch."

"Oh, I'm sorry," Will said, withdrawing his hand. "I-I don't want to hurt you."

"You're not like the others down here. I noticed that. Still gentle. Still human. That's why I came for you."

It must have been hard to rescue us from the screams, said the Whisp. *Her Ghast must have fought with her to leave us alone. That must have been so painful. We need to help her.*

"My Ghast hates your Ghast," Freya said. "He's scared of her. He can hear her voice; he can hear her hope and he hates it."

"I've not been bound to a Ghast," Will said. "I've been bound to a Whisp."

"A Whisp," she said, slowly. "All great ideas come from Whisps. If someone can escape from here . . . arrgh . . . you can!"

"Maybe you're right," Will replied. "We can escape together, all of us. Me and my Whisp are trying to unbind. Maybe once we're out of here we can unbind you from your Ghast as well."

Seconds later Freya's body went rigid. Her eyes rolled back into her head and her jaw opened. She began to scream.

The bodies below screamed back.

Freya's body didn't move a muscle but through the scream came a voice, it was a pitch so high that Will had to grit his teeth to keep from crying out.

"Silence yourselves! You will not escape! Not from here! And not from each other! A spirit cannot unbind from another living soul without blood being shed! Death is the great separator! You will wither and die alone or wither and die together! Leave me alone to eat this soul in peace!"

Freya's jaw snapped shut. Her body shuddered and she whispered, "Don't listen to him. Ghasts don't tell the truth. Don't give up your hope. Get yourself free."

Her arm went rigid. She wrestled with it, but the Ghast was too powerful. The hand reached up to grip at her own throat.

She looked Will dead in the eye and shouted, "I am Freya!"

He watched as her grip on her throat tightened. She tried to pull it off with her other arm, but it too went rigid. With one swift wrenching motion, her hands twisted her neck and she collapsed to the floor.

Will rushed to her side, her eyes were closed but she was still breathing; shallow painful breaths. He cried out her name—"Freya!"

Don't touch her, Will, it might cause her more pain, said the Whisp. *I'm sorry. I know it's painful to watch.*

The woman with her eyes closed and the shallow breath reminded Will of another. He wanted so badly to hug Freya and tell her it would all be ok, just like he wished he had done with his mother before . . . But he couldn't then, and he couldn't now.

Freya's eyes flickered then closed once more. The screams from the chamber turned into cackles. A wicked laughter that was twice as painful as the screams.

She's dying, the Whisp explained. *The other Ghasts are enjoying the pain of it.*

The cackling laughter continued to build. It rang in Will's head.

He screamed, a guttural angry scream, and turned his attention to the huddle. They were all crouched on the floor covering their eyes and ears. "Help me!" he yelled at them. "Help me keep her alive!" When they stayed silent, he went over to one and began to shake him, trying to get him to stir into action. The man cried out in pain, but his eyes remained shut.

It's not their fault, the Whisp whispered. *It's the Ghasts inside them.*

"I don't care!" Will screamed as he turned to shake another.

They're frightened. You are scaring them. The Whisp surged into Will's arms making them drop to his side; she stayed there, holding them tight.

Held there in the stillness, tears began to roll down his cheeks.

Freya was gone. Dead, in a cave under the ground. Abandoned. She had fought with her Ghast until it killed her. She had wanted to help him; to give him hope. But what good had it done? He was still tightly bound to the Whisp. He was still locked in a crypt with no chance of escape. And the Threshold key, the only way back to his home, had shattered. Gaby had been caught by Mr. Scroggie, and he still had no idea how any of this tied together.

Will tensed his arms snatching them back from the Whisp's control, but all he could think to do was wrap them around himself as he slumped to the ground.

Will, I know this hurts but Freya used every ounce of herself to summon up that bit of hope. And she gave it to you. You can't let it go, the Whisp spoke softly. *We need to get out of here.*

Will rubbed at his eyes with his sleeve. "How?"

We need their help. We need to speak to them. Find out what they know.

With a scoff, Will turned and looked at the huddle. "But look at them."

It's the Ghasts that are making them like that. If we can get rid of the Ghasts, even for a moment, we might get through to them.

"But the Ghasts seem so powerful. How are we supposed to fight them?"

Kindness, said the Whisp. *Kindness can be a ferocious thing. Freya's Ghast hated it. It's worth a shot.*

Will slowly dropped down to his knees and knelt beside the first man that he had shook. "I'm sorry," he said, quietly. "I didn't mean to hurt you."

The man hissed at him, like a cat who had been backed into a corner. He closed his eyes again and covered his ears. Will turned away.

That was the Ghast, the Whisp reassured. *She didn't like you apologising to him.*

"I don't want to hurt you," Will said, turning back. "I need your hel—" Before Will was able to finish the sentence, the man turned and spat in his face, then went back to cowering.

Will wiped the phlegm from his eye and tried once more. "I am not trying to scare you. I just want to talk. I want to help."

The man pounced, pinning Will to the ground. Will couldn't fight the power of a full-grown man as he bore down on him. The man flashed his teeth and Will winced.

"Wait, please—"

The man bit into Will's shoulder; Will cried out in agony. The pain was intense. The Whisp tried to work with Will, to push the man back, but the teeth dug in deeper.

"Stop!"

After a second, the man pulled back and spat a patch of torn jumper from his mouth. The man's lips were red with blood. Will wondered if the man might eat him alive since he looked like he wanted another bite.

Just as his teeth were about to sink into Will's other shoulder, suddenly the man's body went limp. Will felt the weight upon him as he squirmed to escape. The man's breathing was heavy and slow. He had been knocked out cold.

It was only once he was out from under the body that he saw a woman with tears in her eyes and a rock in her hand.

"My husband," she said, her voice breaking. "Ghast been eating . . . for months. Would never hurt . . . wasn't him. Saw what happened to the girl. Scared him."

Will said, "I'm sorry, I didn't mean to scare him."

"Tell us what you want. We give it you. Then you get away from us." The woman was pleading with Will, still holding the rock in her hand, poised and defensive.

"I need to get out of these crypts."

"No escape. One way in. One way out. Automatons keep it shut," she answered.

The Whisp spoke up, *Ask about the Threshold key, maybe they'll know how to fix it.*

Will reached into his pocket and as he did the lady lifted the rock, ready to hurl it at him. He paused his movements. "I won't hurt you. I promise. I just want to show you something." At her jerky nod, he brought out the broken shards of the Threshold key.

"It's broken," she said.

"So, you know what this is?" Will asked, slowly easing his hand forward to give her a closer look.

"No, can't remember. It's from up world. Been too long." Her body started shaking. "Makes you forget. Can't help. Please leave."

One of the others from the huddle, a small ratty-looking girl, turned towards Will and gingerly edged forward.

"You want to look?" Will asked, moving his hand toward her.

"Get back!" the woman shouted. "He hurt you like he hurt Dad!"

135

They're a family, thought the Whisp, sounding sad. *A whole family haunted by Ghasts.*

"She's your daughter?" Will asked and the woman nodded. "I won't hurt her. But maybe if she knows about my Threshold key she can . . ." He gestured his key towards the girl then edged closer again with his hand outstretched.

"Leave alone!" the woman yelled as she threw the rock at Will. It grazed him on his wounded shoulder knocking him backwards.

The woman collapsed to the ground and began to wail. The girl crawled to her mother and hugged her knees, squeezing tightly.

"This isn't working," Will whispered. "We're terrifying them."

We should leave them, the Whisp agreed.

The problem was, the only way out was back the way they came, past the family. Will carefully and slowly picked himself up then gingerly stepped forward being careful not to make any sudden movements.

As he stepped over the knocked-out man, he said, "Don't worry. I'm leaving."

The small girl lifted her head. "They didn't want to hurt you." Her eyes were wet with tears.

"I know," Will said. His shoulder ached. He felt blood trickling down his back. "I'm so sorry." Instinctively, he reached his hand to her head, touching the top of her hair.

Will. The Whisp paused as she felt her world expand for a second as she bonded with the young girl. The Whisp stretched—it felt good. It felt freeing.

The girl's eyes blinked and her whole face changed, suddenly she was looking at Will without fear, without trepidation. A smile spread across her face. "You need to visit Thales Crickwicker. He can mend your broken key."

Will was taken aback. "Thank you," he said, lifting his hand from her hair.

Oh. The Whisp snapped back into Will's body, like an elastic band that had been stretched too far. Pain radiated through her consciousness.

"You're—" The girl's face was once again consumed with the dark shroud of fear. She watched Will, her beady eyes flicking from his hands to his face and back again.

I just expanded into her. I was bound for a moment with both you and the girl, the Whisp said in awe.

"I know I felt it. It hurt you though. I felt your pain when I let her go. How did all of that happen?"

I don't know. Maybe that's why Ghasts hate a gentle touch. It means I can expand into their territory. She paused, considering. *Try it again.*

Will slowly reached out his hand to the girl's hair once again. But as soon as she noticed, her hands shot out, grabbing his arm tightly. Her teeth gnashed and she went to bite at his finger. He pulled it away just in time, wrenching his arm from her grasp. She let out a deafening scream, forcing Will to retreat.

Neither Will nor the Whisp said anything to each other as Will headed back into the tunnel, returning to the ledge at the edge of the crypt of bodies.

We need to be careful, the Whisp cautioned. *This place is dangerous. Your shoulder is already hurting and that was just one of them. If there are any more attackers, we won't be able to fight them off.*

"Don't worry. I won't touch them," Will promised. "We need to figure out how to get to Thales Crickwicker"

I know where he is, the Whisp revealed. *Some of the other Whisps used to hide under the bridge just beside his shop.*

"Great … Now all we need to do is get past Jackle and the automaton and out of this crypt. Any ideas?"

The Whisp realised that she didn't know what to do. She was a Whisp, it was her job to bring great ideas and bright sparks of inspiration but since she had been bound to Will she had felt that ability slowly ebb. Her brilliance was supposed to be fleeting. It didn't seem to work if it was tethered. Being rooted was unnatural. When she had flowed into that young girl, she had felt it. She had felt her power. But now, back in Will, she realised how contained she was. She didn't want to say it, but being inside Will was weakening her.

I'm sorry, Will. I don't know. If I was free to skip from person to person, I would skip around giving inspiration and learning all the best ideas, but I'm stuck, and everyone in here has a Ghast bound to them.

"Well," Will mumbled, "we can't give up the hope." Lowering himself down into the crypt, he added, "The automaton saved us before. Maybe we can convince him to do it again."

Maybe.

He crept across the floor of bodies, trying his best not to stand on any fingers and limbs that were sprawled across the cold rock floor in his path.

Finally, he found himself back at the wooden door. "Ready?" Will asked.

The Whisp sighed. *It is worth a shot. But remember stay alert. If the Ghast gets inside you – you are done for.*

Will replied, "That won't happen. I trust you." He stood again on his tiptoes and saw Jackle picking at his toenails while the automaton stood on guard.

The Whisp whispered, *Hey, Tin Ears, you can hear me, right?*

The mechanical man didn't move.

Pssst, Tin Ears . . . I got a deal for you. How's about we swap places? You let me into the automaton, and you can come here and get to munch on this little boy. I bet his soul will taste extra sweet. I get to wander out in the open, in the robot, and you can stay in the crypt with all your Ghast friends. Old Jackle won't even notice the difference.

The automaton turned. *I'm listening,* it hissed inside Will's mind.

The Whisp replied, *All we have to do is shake hands. That's why old Jackle's banned it. He doesn't want anyone shaking his hand and a Ghast getting into him by accident. You just reach through the bars now and we shake.*

The automaton looked around and saw that Jackle was still busy digging the dirt from his toenails with a rusty screw.

If your boy is so tasty, why aren't you feasting on him? the Ghast hissed with suspicion.

The Whisp was quick to answer. *I don't like Jackle just lobbing us anyone he can find. I prefer to hunt my own prey.*

The automaton took a step back, sizing Will up through the bars. *I don't trust you,* he stated.

I'm only going to offer the boy once, the Whisp replied. *You only have to shake my hand . . . Unless you want to stay in the tin bucket, feasting on nobody.*

The automaton slowly lifted his giant hand to the bar and squeezed a few fingers through.

Now, I'm going to reach up and shake, be ready to swap places, instructed the Whisp. *But don't squeeze too hard, it's got to be gentle.*

OK. OK. Let's do it before the dirt crumb notices, the Ghast said.

Will reached up and placed his fingers to the cold steel—

The Whisp again felt her world expand as she rushed into the automaton, pouring herself into his cogs and gears and oil ducts. The Whisp immediately latched onto the automaton's free arm. She concentrated hard making it open and clasp at the crypt door's large handle. She made the whole body pull and the door creaked with the force.

The Ghast began to push back against the Whisp's intrusion. She knew she didn't have long until it would regain control.

She pulled at the door with a heave. The wood splintered at the edges and the huge metal hinges began to buckle.

Keep going! Will urged.

The Whisp pulled once more, and the lock snapped.

As the door came away in the automaton's hand, the mechanical man fell backwards with the weight of it, collapsing into the fire. Will fell through the open doorway and the Whisp hurtled back into Will's body.

It hurt even more than last time. It wounded her. It was like having a limb cut off. She suddenly felt all the constraints of Will's body and it stung.

Will felt the Whisp's agony. It took his breath away.

The fire roared and flames spat around the chamber as the automaton's oil ignited. The Ghast inside the automaton let out a high-pitched scream. The bodies in the crypt hollered in return. Jackle who had jumped to his feet to avoid the spitting flames ran to Will and grabbed him by the hair, pulling him to his feet.

"What've you's done?" he spat at Will. "Lil' wretch."

Will's face contorted with the pain. Feeling this, the Whisp seized control of Will's leg and brought the full weight of Will's shoe down onto Jackle's foot.

Jackle howled. "Yous——" He stopped, his eyes growing wide and his face draining of colour. He saw, coming out from the crypt, screaming bodies that advanced towards him.

"You said you'd keep us safe!" one of the bodies screamed as it convulsed towards him.

"You've broken the bargain!" another yelled.

"Broken the bargain!" a chorus of Ghasts repeated.

Jackle was terrified. "No's I's broken nuffin! I's broken nuffin!" He backed off into the chamber. "No's don't eat me!" he shouted as he felt the arms wrap around his legs

The flames of the fire licked the air, the automaton and the wooden door fuelling its ferocity. The place was soon ablaze and hot embers spat along the ground. The Ghasts moved forward, crawling closer.

Bodies began scuttling over each other as they tried to hold Jackle. Will was at risk of being trampled by the hoard if he didn't think quickly. He skirted to the edges of the cavern; the heat was intense and suffocating.

Go! Go!

Will scrambled for the tunnel. He crawled, fast, hearing the screams of Jackle and the bodies behind him.

Chapter 13
A Devilish Bargain

The Gatekeeper struggled to push the flat's door open. The lock was stiff, and the door seemed to be jammed. Once she had managed to shove it open a little, she noticed on the other side there was a mountain of letters and leaflets wedged underneath. She took her cane and reached in to clear away some of the mail.

It was a useful little thing this metal cane, she thought, her little miracle find. She had discovered it, when looking for a Threshold, in the back of a long-forgotten storeroom beside a set of more sporty looking sticks used for hillwalking.

"Hello?" she called out as she pressed the door open. She had not checked on the flat for years, not since the Thresholds were all closed. She wasn't sure if someone else might be occupying it.

She waited for a moment but there was no response. She poked again at the letters, shuffling them to the side to make herself a small path. As she prodded, some of the decomposing letters broke and crumbled. She stooped to examine one that still held together and noticed that her alias was on all the mail.

It was only then, that she took in the room and realised how familiar it all was. The lampshade, the wallpaper, the telephone on the table, still there, all underneath a thin lair of dust.

When the Thresholds were open, the Gatekeeper had lived in this dingy little hovel almost as much as she did in her own home. She had spied on this world, reporting back on all of its quirks and peculiarities. When she was a young soldier, her report had caused a stir in the offices of the Republic. *A World Without Spirits* was the first-ever report she had written. Back then, she had thought that this world was a utopia. A place without Ghasts or Whisps. A whole society where they didn't rely on spirits to fuel their good ideas. The lack of Whisp inspiration hadn't held them back either, their technology seemed to be centuries ahead.

She had been so enthusiastic in her report that it caused a flood of attention. She'd escorted many officials through the Thresholds to see the sights and wonders of Gaia. Many of them stayed with her in this very flat. But soon visiting officials were writing their reports and some concluded that spirits were just as prevalent here, just harder to detect and contain. Others agreed with the Gatekeeper but suggested that the lack of a common enemy had meant that the humans of this world were disunited and squabbled amongst themselves instead. The more reports that were written, the less interested people became in her little outpost. The visitors began to dwindle and so too did her chance of promotion.

In her final years on Gaia, she grew to resent Worldmouth especially. She had no desire to return. The flat had only been kept since selling it would have created more hassle. It would require forging more paperwork and by that time, she wanted to be rid of this world entirely. It wasn't as if the money in this world would have been of any value in hers. She had only kept the key, as a memento, to remind her that she had wasted her life in a squalid little flat—all because she once got too excited and too ambitious.

She would not let her retirement be wasted in the same way . . . At least, that is what she had hoped. But now, here she was back in her old flat as if nothing had ever changed.

She sniffed the air and gagged. Whatever the stench was, it was foul. Gagging again, she held her fist to her mouth. The further into the flat she went the worse it became.

The Gatekeeper remembered her last day here: she had cleaned the place from top to bottom and disposed of any trace of herself. There wasn't a grain of food in the flat that would have rotted. She'd thrown it all out. Dumping her bags and the folder of notes onto the kitchen table, she began her search for the source of the stink.

Starting in the kitchen, she rummaged through the cupboards before moving towards the bathroom to look around the toilet. She had felt around the taps and the pipes to see if there was a leak that might cause mould but there was nothing. It was only when she opened the bedroom door that she found the source of the problem.

It made her heave, and she felt the vomit rise in her throat.

"Artemis. You fleabag!" she exclaimed.

On top of the bed, curled perfectly into a ball, was the remains of a cat. It had been there for some time and tiny flies swirled in the room.

The cat had been given to her as a gift from one of the many experts who had come to this world and thought they might have a chance of romance with her. The men who made those advances where nearly always married in their world, and the Gatekeeper had hated that they thought crossing a Threshold somehow allowed them to break their vows.

Artemis was company, however, and she liked having him around. But, just like the rest of the world, she grew to resent him. She wouldn't have had to cross the Threshold quite so frequently as she did in the later years if she hadn't needed to come to feed the damned cat. When it was announced that the Thresholds were finally to be closed, the Gatekeeper had bundled Artemis into a bag and headed to the nearest motorway. She released the cat in a layby, fully expecting it to be hit by a passing car but it hadn't—it had survived. And not only that, but it clearly had also found its way back here.

"This is a lesson," the Gatekeeper said aloud to the dead cat. "I should not have been so merciful to give you a chance, Artemis. I should have stoned you dead, myself."

She opened the window, grabbed the carcass, and dropped it onto the street below. She wafted at the flies hoping they might also head out the window, but they hovered over the little clumps of fur that still remained.

"I'll sleep in the living room tonight," she declared, closing the door to the bedroom. "If I sleep at all." Her thoughts had been racing all day.

She had expected to be back in her own world by now. She had expected to come and capture the General, who must have, in turn, captured the Whisp. Except now she was embroiled in something much more complicated. The General was dead, and she had captured a Ghast. And she still had no idea of where the Whisp was. Or even where the other open Thresholds might be.

If she headed home tonight, the Council would execute her. She had to find the Whisp, but so far, her investigations had given her no clues as to where it might be. She had pages and pages of notes leading nowhere. She would re-read each and every one tonight, meticulously hunting for any hint or suggestion that she would follow up on tomorrow.

The longer the Whisp was free in the world, the further it would be able to travel. If she wasted any more time, she might never find it. She had only narrowly escaped being strangled by the Thinking King before. She would not be so lucky if she returned without the Whisp.

The Gatekeeper had one other idea that had been brewing inside her head all day. An experiment she had once seen demonstrated by one of the Republic's leading experts on Pandora jars. It was extremely dangerous . . . She really had hoped to avoid it altogether, but she was running out of options.

Heading through to the kitchen, she went back to the plastic bags she had dumped there. She had taken some time to purchase food and supplies from the local shop but when she looked at what she bought, the thought of eating made her stomach turn. The food of this world was bland and inoffensive, plus Artemis' deathly smell still lingered in her nostrils.

Instead, she reached for the small bottle of gin she'd gotten. She unscrewed the cap and swigged straight from the bottle. It tasted just as she remembered it, bitter and perfect. She took another giant swig and reached into the other plastic bag, inside it was the Pandora jar.

Holding the jar towards the light, she twisted it in her fingers; examining it. It was a thing of beauty. Exquisite blue patterns swirled around the pure white clay at the widest point and again at the rim. Strange to think that contained within was a Ghast. That inside something so beautiful lurked something so monstrous.

She contemplated the experiment, trying to recall it precisely.

"Step one, heat," she said before taking one more mouthful of gin.

The Gatekeeper moved to place the ceramic jar on top of the gas stove. She clicked the ignition and the flame sparked to life. She turned it up so that the flame burnt a bright blue under the Pandora jar. Heating it up, would make it unbearable for the Ghast inside. She knew it was working when the jar began to thrum and wobble in the heat. The Ghast was wriggling violently. It was trying its best to escape the pain.

She was scorching it till it could bear no more.

She was reminding it who was in charge.

"Can you hear me in there, you wretched little thing? Does that hurt?"

The jar shook, like a pan of water that had been brought to boil. The Gatekeeper scoured through the kitchen drawers until she found a pair of oven gloves. Putting them on, she wrapped the mitts around the jar and held it in place.

When she couldn't handle the heat anymore, she took the jar and placed it in the sink, turning on the cold tap. When the cold water hit the jar, it fizzled into steam.

"Step two, relief," she said as the jar began to cool. She let the water run, and took one glove off, touching the jar to feel its temperature return to normal.

"Step three," she said almost whispering it into the mouth of the jar, hoping the Ghast heard her through the cork stopper. "Repeat." She pushed the oven glove back onto her bare hand and lifted the jar back onto the flame.

The Gatekeeper repeated the entire process four times. Each time making sure that the heat of the jar would be excruciating, and the cooling relief of the water would last a shorter amount each time. She was bullying the Ghast into submission. She was trying to tame a wild beast.

"Are you ready to hear step four?" she asked. "Step four is my favourite step. Now what was it again? Ahh yes," She gave the jar a little shake. "Step four is—threat."

She took another swig of gin. "I don't need to threaten you, do I? Because you already know I'm in control. This is my old kitchen in my old flat and in the corner is my old freezer. Do you know what a freezer is? It's a sort of ice chamber. It's completely sealed to keep things very cold. If you find yourself stuck inside there, then there's no escape. Not even for a Ghast like you."

She toyed with the jar, slowly turning it in her fingers. How many of these jars must she have held in her life? Hundreds, thousands? They all looked the same once they were inside. She had no way to tell if this experiment was working. No way to know if the Ghast was beginning to give in. But what choice did she have? She had to see this through, now. She took a mouthful of gin, bringing the bottle down onto the table with a thud.

"Here is the deal. In a moment I'm going to open this jar. But you will stay in the jar. Because if you even for a second think of coming near me and feeding on my soul I will not hesitate to put my body in the freezer. I will die inside that freezer and my body will rot. My soul will perish, and you will feed no more. You will be left trapped for the rest of eternity without another soul to feed on."

The jar sat silent and lifeless in her hands.

"Step five—this is the part you will like—the bargain. Do you know where you are? You crossed a Threshold to come here. This is a new world, one without Ghasts or Whisps. And no one, except me, knows you're here. I can leave it like that. I can free you when we are finished, and you will have a whole world of souls to feed on. No

Republic to hunt you. No Pandora jars. Just you and billions of tasty souls."

She hummed. "I can let you stay here; can tell the Council I only found a Whisp. And for that freedom, all you need to do is give me the memories of the last soul you fed on—the memories of General Markus Anthony. If you give me those memories and you stay in that jar, I will take you back to the school. I will even find you your first victim. Someone young and fresh. Someone full of tasty life to gorge upon. How does that sound?"

Still the jar remained silent.

The Gatekeeper placed the jar on the table and frowned. She had no idea if this had worked. The whole experiment was such a gamble.

She had to hope that the bargain, the promise of a world full of souls, would satisfy the Ghast. She could open the jar and unleash hell. Perhaps, she would actually lock herself in the freezer. She remembered the last days with her mother. The suffering. The screams. Her mother's death was why she had enlisted in the first place. She wanted to rid her world of spirits. She wanted no other child to witness what she had seen.

How things had changed. Everything had got so much muddier and complicated. And now here she was trying to do a deal with a Ghast. Promising to feed it. She despised the Ghast, but she despised herself even more for what she had become.

Step six—release.

The Gatekeeper took one last gulp of gin then roared like a wild animal. She seized the jar and whipped the cork lid from its mouth. Closing her eyes, she braced herself to be possessed . . .

Nothing happened.

The Ghast remained in the jar.

She laughed with delight, realizing it had worked. She looked inside but, of course, saw nothing: the Ghast, just like a Whisp, was imperceptible to the human eye. She tentatively reached into the jar with her finger and scraped at the bottom. When she took her finger out it was covered in a black tarry sludge.

"Memories," she said, placing the lid back on the jar. "Thank you for this. I will make sure I find the tastiest, freshest soul in that school. I promise."

Greedy for answers, she took her finger and placed it into her mouth, sucking the black tar down with a gulp. Her eyes rolled back into her head as Mr. Anthony's memories wash over her. From the moment the Ghast crossed the flaming threshold to the moment his life ended.

She began to understand what had happened. She stood in the kitchen entranced by the memories. She played them back and forward, savouring new details each and every time.

The sound of a bell made her jump. Was someone at the front door? No. That isn't it. The bell . . . *Ring*. Pause. *Ring*. Pause. *Ring*.

"Ah. The telephone. One of the worst things about this stupid world," she griped to the jar. She had no idea why, when having the wonder of electricity, Gaia's inhabitants had used it to create an infernal device that interrupts your chain of thought and demands instant attention. This whole world is so bloody rude.

The telephone continued its incessant ringing as she grabbed her stick and hobbled to the hall. She wondered who it might be. She had scribbled the number down and given it to Ms. Sharpe and Inspector McNamara. But she hadn't expected to be called. She had been surprised that she still recalled the number.

"Hello," she said, with a rough bark.

"Mrs. Porter?" said the man on the other end.

"Yes? May I ask whose calling?" she replied, with her weak voice.

"It's Inspector McNamara here. I'm afraid there's been a wee bit of an incident at Worldmouth Academy. A child was discovered in the back of Mr. Anthony's book cupboard this evening. All fine. But she's obviously a little shaken up. Would you be able to see her first thing tomorrow?"

"I think I should see her straight away. I can come right now," the Gatekeeper said. Her thoughts raced. The back of Mr. Anthony's cupboard was the Threshold she had crossed through. The child must know something if she was in there . . . Maybe she has the Whisp?

Her mind spun with possibilities.

"That won't be possible I'm afraid, Mrs. Porter," Inspector McNamara replied, "I've sent her home for a good night's sleep. I'm sure you would agree that's for the best, all things considered?"

"Of course," the Gatekeeper said in her Mrs. Porter voice. "But perhaps I can visit her at home?"

"No can-do, Mrs. Porter. I'm sorry. By the letter of the law, I can't give out personal details of minors to civilians. She will be at school tomorrow. I assure you; you can see her first thing. We won't conduct any more investigations until you have spoken to her. Okie doke?"

"Of course. First thing."

"Can't thank you enough. Won't keep you any longer. Good night now . . ."

"Oh, now one last thing, Inspector. Of course, the address is off-limits. But perhaps the name of the child wouldn't be too much to ask?" Mrs. Porter pitched her voice a little to sound frail and pleading. When he stayed silent, she added, "It's just, I've interviewed a lot of the children today and perhaps I can cross-reference with any notes I might have already taken. In strictest confidence of course?" She was gambling again, hoping the Inspector's fondness for the 'bereavement counsellor' might allow him to bend his rules just a little.

"Well, I shouldn't really—"

"I would like to prepare. Bereavement can be a complicated emotion in a young mind. Any help might allow me to get through to the child. My guidance might help her open up to your officers as well."

". . . Gabrielle Roland Crowsdale. But please, strictest confidence, Mrs. Porter."

"My lips are sealed. Goodnight, Inspector."

Before the Inspector could reply, the Gatekeeper hung up the phone. She rushed to the kitchen and opened the folder of notes, pulling at pieces of paper until she found the right one.

"Gaby Crowsdale," she crooned. "Ahh yes, the insipid blabbermouth; who would have thought it." She took another swig of gin and swirled it in her mouth.

Perhaps she would get some sleep after all.

Chapter 14
Podger's Wynd

W ill opened the secret cellar door and stepped out into the cool night air. He gasped at seeing the wreckage of the first automaton. He remembered how the Ghast had saved him from the Hunters and wondered if it would have survived the flames down below. Everything had happened in a blur. Ever since he got here, he only had time to react. He had been relying on his instincts the whole time but now, in the weak light of the moon, he took it all in.

He had been the cause of so much wreckage and death in this world already. And he had barely survived it.

Don't think like that. We need to keep the hope, said the Whisp. *We need to get to Mr. Crickwicker's. We can still save Gaby.*

Gaby! The school. Mr. Scroogie. It all felt so far away now. So much had happened since then, but it had only been a few hours since Gaby pushed him through the Threshold, trying to save him and the Whisp from falling into the hands of Mr. Scroggie. She had no idea how dangerous this world would be. And the danger above was just as threatening as the danger below. It was still night, and the curfew was not over yet.

Will, we need to be careful, but we can make it if we move quickly.

Will didn't move, still staring at the automaton scraps. *I'm scared.*

Me too. But either we go back down in those tunnels and hide forever, hoping the Ghasts or the Hunters don't catch us. Or we keep moving forward. That's it. That's all the choices we have. I know it's scary but it's all we got.

Will nodded and turned from the wreckage back out of the alley.

Will and the Whisp slipped from one side street to another, carefully picking their moments to move through the darkest parts of the city where the moonlight would not reach them. There were a couple of moments when Will had to lie flat to the ground and hold his breath as a Hunter leapt across roofs overhead.

The Whisp kept whispering that the Hunters would be even more alert after losing him the first time. They would have been furious that he had slipped through their fingers. She knew how to get to Thales Crickwicker's Shop, but they had to be very careful to avoid detection. If they were spotted, they would never be able to outrun them.

Steadily and quietly, they picked their way through the city towards Podger's Wynd. The Whisp felt comforted when she began to hear the familiar clanging of the boats that had docked in the harbour. It meant they were close.

They followed along the shoreline until they found the inlet of water that led back into the city. Tracing back up and along the canal, it wasn't long until they found the bridge.

The Whisp shouted, *Anyone there?*

Will jumped in surprise, surely no one else heard her . .
.

I was checking for other Whisps. No one replied, I think I'm the last. I think the others have all been caught, she said with a hint of sadness in her voice.

Will felt how drained the Whisp was. The connections with the little girl in the crypt and the automaton had hurt her. She had used so much energy to rush into their bodies and just as much when she was pulled back out.

Are you ok? he asked.

But the Whisp ignored the question and tried to refocus both of their attentions on the task at hand. *You see that raggedy little street over the bridge? That's Podger's Wynd. Crickwicker's locksmith shop is in there.*

Will looked at the bridge, it was wide and flat and bathed in moonlight. It rested low against the water and had a split in the middle for the bigger boats to pass through. There was a stubby little wall on either side and . . . he froze—leaning on one of the walls was a Hunter with his electric blue stinger in his hands.

There's no way we can get across without getting caught, Will said. *Maybe there's another bridge further up the canal?*

If there's a Hunter here, it means there will be one stationed on all the canal bridges.

Then we can't get to Crickwickers.

Not unless we get a little wet.

Will retraced his steps, heading to the shoreline until he found a small marina with some long canal boats. *Are you sure about this?*

Yes, the Whisp answered. *Hurry.*

Will lowered himself down onto the roof of the nearest canal boat and made his way along, trying to put very little weight into his steps so as to not make a sound. Once he got to the edge of the roof, he slipped down onto the bow of the boat and then climbed down the rudder until the water touched his feet. Taking a deep breath, he slipped in with a small splosh.

The water was shallow, but it still came up to his chest. It was incredibly cold, and his breath quickened. He fought against his instinct to scramble back to the land and slowly began trudging through the water towards the bridge. Will felt waves push against him; he kept moving, fighting the tide.

You can do this, Will. Keep going.

Shuddering, Will tried to ignore the coldness and the sting of the salt in his wound. He struggled against the weight of his school uniform as the clothes became sodden. The extra weight reminded him of walking home from school when his head had been flushed in the toilet. Who knew all of that would lead him here? To this.

He began to wonder if he would ever get home. Would he ever see Gaby or Sacha or his dad again? The thought was a sore one.

We have got this far, Will. All we need to do is get past the Hunter and into Podger's Wynd. Home isn't far away, I promise.

Will looked along the waterway. He saw the now familiar blue fizz of the stinger in the distance.

We want to cross to the other side now. See if we can find another way up onto the embankment. One that avoids the bridge altogether, said the Whisp and Will obliged, trundling slowly to the other side of the water.

The canal wall was steep and slippery. There was no way he would be able to climb it without the help of another boat or a ladder. He eyed the wall, looking up and down to see if there was anything he might use as a foothold, but it was impossible to see in the faint moonlight.

Will and The Whisp

We are just going to have to feel our way along and hope we find something before the Hunter hears us in the water.

He edged along the wall, occasionally reaching up, trying to judge if he would have enough grip on any of the wall bricks to hoist himself up. He got closer and closer to the bridge—the Hunter had not noticed him yet.

There. By that boat, the Whisp said, drawing Will's attention to the small stone steps that wound their way up the canal wall by a wooden rowing boat tied to a jetty right beside the bridge.

If we distract the guard, even for a moment, then we might be able to get up.

Will dunked his head into the water so that his arms reached to the bed of the canal. He tried to feel for a loose rock or something he might be able to throw but he only found the thick sludgy mud that gave the canal its rotten smell. When he came back up for breath, he was careful not to puncture the surface of the water with a splash. He took a couple of steps forward then went under once more. This time his hand found something like a thick tree root. It was heavy, but he managed to haul it upwards with a heave of his body. The rowing boat swung towards him as he pulled.

It's the boat's anchor ropes. It ties the boat into place when it isn't being used, said the Whisp.

Will made his way slowly towards the rowing boat and felt around its edge. He carefully untied every knot he found until the boat was loose. He guided it out into the middle of the canal and then, waiting for a wave, gave it a shove.

The boat drifted slowly. As it passed under the bridge and out into the open, it caught the attention of the guard. He dropped his stinger in surprise.

"Damn!" he exclaimed, running to catch the boat. He

took the steps down to the jetty opposite Will. The Hunter tried to stretch with his stinger to catch the loose boat—it floated just out of reach, continuing down the canal.

Now! said the Whisp and Will jumped from the water onto the jetty beside him. His belly landed onto the hard wood before he pushed himself up onto his feet.

Out of breath, Will ran up the steps. From the corner of his eye, he saw his movements being mirrored by the Hunter on the opposite bank who had noticed him. The Hunter arrived on the bridge just as Will arrived at the top of the steps.

Will froze.

Run! the Whisp shouted but Will had another idea. He pulled on the giant wheel beside the bridge and began spinning it as fast as he could. The bridge split in two with a groan and began to rise, creating two steep slopes. The Hunter, who had been running towards him, stumbled, falling back onto the bank opposite.

Should buy us some—

The Hunter looked right at Will, tilted his head back, and began to howl into the night sky.

Will! Move!

Will sprinted as fast as his weary feet allowed. He knew that the Hunters would be able to catch up. His wet clothes dripped on the ground creating a trail that would lead straight to him. His only hope would be that Mr. Crickwicker could help, and quickly.

Out of all the buildings on Podger's Wynd, only Crickwicker's rose any higher than two stories. It was a tall, thin building that leaned slightly to the east like it was a plant waiting to catch the morning sun. Will grasped the doorknocker and pushed it hard onto the wood so that the rapping would be heard clearly above the whooping and hollering of the Hunters that echoed through the city and down the wynd.

"Come on. Come on. Come on," Will whispered; he banged the knocker again.

The door opened a fraction and a pair of goggles popped out. Will opened his mouth, ready to plead for help, but before he uttered a word the small fellow swung the door open.

"My goodness, a Whisp! Come in. Come in."

Will stepped through the door, his senses immediately dazzled with an intoxicating array of wonders. The smells were intense, hitting him one after another: the beach after a storm, a freshly picked strawberry, sawdust.

The shop was cluttered with potions and lotions, syrups and serums, and all manner of brightly coloured powders. It looked nothing like a locksmith's store back in Will's world. From the outside, Will had pictured the building having two or three floors but this was not the case. When he looked up there were no other rooms above him. Instead, he saw a huge web of ropes and pulleys that weaved right up to the roof. There were thousands of them tangled and twisted, this way and that. It was impossible to follow, but when he did look closely, he saw that on some of the ropes hung the strangest of things. A bed. A chest of drawers. A battered leather armchair. It was as if the ropes made a spider's web but instead of creepy crawlies, this spider wanted to feast on furniture.

The old man went behind the shop counter and turned a small brass dial on the wall. The ropes above Will's head started to heave, pushing and pulling, until eventually, a grandfather clock lowered right into the middle of the shop.

There was a loud and forceful knock at the door.

The Hunters, a short jolt of fear ran through the Whisp and down Will's spine.

"We're out of time. Quickly now," the old man instructed, as he scurried to the clock. He opened its little wooden door and beckoned Will forward.

Will had to stoop down to get through the little door. He stepped inside, expecting to be crammed into a tight, small space, but it wasn't at all. It was like he had been transported somewhere else entirely. He didn't need to crouch, and the walls were not as close against his body as they should be. The room was vast, more like a giant cathedral than a crammed clock cabinet.

The old man followed him in and closed the door. "Find something to hold onto. This bit is always bumpy," he instructed with a wry smile.

"What—"

The whole room hurtled into the air like a giant elevator. It rocketed upwards, at what felt like to Will, a thousand miles per hour. Will was flung this way and that: first up, then to the left, and then up again. At one point, Will would swear that the whole room did a loop-de-loop until it came to rest with a gentle thud. He pushed against a wall to steady himself, letting his stomach settle.

"They are going to tear my place apart I imagine. Looking for you and your boy, dear Whisp. Don't worry they will never find us here."

"Where are we?" Will asked. "I was looking for Thales Crickwicker, the locksmith."

"Then you've come to exactly the right place. I'm Mr. Crickwicker and this is the inside of the grandfather clock that hangs above my Threshold emporium." Thales gestured with outstretched hands, inviting Will to marvel at the room that they were in.

It was, absolutely, the inside of the grandfather clock,

thought Will. He noticed it still had the rich mahogany wood around all of the walls and in the middle, there was a pendulum, but it was huge. It reminded him of a wrecking ball slowly swinging across the room.

"Pretty neat, don't you think?"

"It's amazing," Will murmured. "Have we shrunk or is the clock massive?"

Thales chuckled. "You know, I've never thought about it that way, I suppose a little bit of both. But my inventions are nothing compared to what you must be able to achieve. You must be a marvellous talent!"

"Uh . . ."

"I mean, to say, it's quite incredible, ingenious. I have never seen such a thing before. A Whisp perfectly melded to an automaton. I've never seen one so lifelike either. Tell me, dear Whisp, did you mould the boy yourself?" Thales came closer to Will and pulled at his cheek a little.

"Ouch!" Will exclaimed, brushing him away. "I'm no robot. I'm human." He paused, frowning. "Wait. How do you know I have a Whisp inside me?"

"No. That can't be right," Thales said, taken aback. "That would mean you had been bound to a Whisp. There must be something wrong here." He shook his head. "How are you tricking my goggles?" Thales took off his thick-rimmed goggles and breathed on them, wiping them with his sleeve.

"You can see Whisps with those goggles?" Will asked, his eyes growing wide with surprise.

"Indeed. And Ghasts. And . . ." He tapped the side of his glasses, continuing. ". . . nope these say it's definitely a Whisp. But a Whisp doesn't bind. It skips and bounces. I don't understand."

"Neither do we. We got bound together by accident. But we were told you might be able to help," Will replied, reaching into his pocket to produce the broken shards of the Threshold key.

"Ahhhhh," Thales said, with a sudden sense of realisation, "you are not from around here, are you?"

Will shook his head. "The Whisp comes from here. She was being chased by Hunters and somehow ended up in my world. And then we got stuck together. And now we are here but we need to get back to my world quickly because our friend is in danger." Will's voice quickened as he realised how much he still didn't understand and how much he really needed help.

"Well, it sounds like a long story," Thales hummed. "Let me brew us some hot cocoa and fetch some barrel berry juice for your wounds, then you can tell me all about it."

"I'm sorry, Mr. Crickwicker, but we really don't have time. Our friend is in serious trouble. We really need to get back."

Mr. Thales pointed to the pendulum as it traced its path across the vast room. "One swing of that pendulum is one second in the world outside. Time moves slower in here. The Hunters will already be in my shop, tearing the place apart. We aren't going anywhere fast, I'm afraid. Besides, it looks like you both need the rest. You're bleeding and wet and it looks from my goggles that the Whisp is injured too. You need to take a moment and heal. Otherwise, you won't be good for anything." He motioned around the room with both his arms. "Please make yourself at home."

When Will just stood there, a blank expression on his face, Thales gestured to a couple of battered armchairs in one of the corners. "Go on."

He's right Will, we both need the rest.

With a sigh, Will shuffled across the wooden floor and

slumped into one of the chairs. His shoulder ached and his body was cold. Tired, he watched the pendulum that moved at a glacial pace. If time moved slower inside the clock, he wondered if it moved slower between worlds as well? He crossed his fingers and hoped that somehow Gaby was still in the school cupboard and Mr. Scroggie hadn't found her yet.

Each swing of the pendulum made his eyes grow heavy—

When Thales came to a stop beside him, Will woke with a start. Rubbing his eyes, he was soon content to sip his hot cocoa and let Mr. Crickwicker dab at his shoulder with barrel berry juice. The balm soothed the sting, and he began to talk. He told the locksmith everything. Right from the moment his head hit that toilet bowl all the way up to finding himself inside the clock.

Thales listened attentively, only stopping to clarify or ask questions about Will's world so that he better understood. Will tried his best to give Thales every detail, but he found it hard to talk about Gaby and his dad and Sacha. He missed them all. He wished he hadn't lied to his family. He wished he had never got Gaby involved. He wished he had done it all differently. When he came to the end of his sad tale, all he thought about was the decisions he had made and how they had led him to so much trouble.

At the end of it all, Mr Crickwicker took a big sip of his cocoa that left a small chocolatey moustache on his lip. He licked it with his tongue and hummed.

"Quite the adventure for you both. I can most certainly help, but not how you might think."

Chapter 15
Crickwicker's Confession

"I've been a locksmith for a very long time. Making keys and locks, like you would use in your world. I had a wife, Liffle Crickwicker. She was a gorgeous woman. Huge heart. Big warm laugh that sounded like a bassoon. She would have loved you." He smiled. "She always had a warm spot for a Whisp. She used to say 'all of my best ideas happened when there was a Whisp in the room. So, there must have been one fluttering by when you proposed, and I said yes.' She used to thank that Whisp every night before bed like a little prayer. I loved that woman and her little prayer."

Thales picked at the broken shards as he spoke, occasionally lifting his goggle to look a little closer.

"We worked together and one-day Liffle went off to a job in the tar lands. I would have gone myself, but I was behind on orders. When she arrived, she found a house with every window boarded shut and the keyhole stuffed with rags. It was a simple task, they only wanted her to change the lock. She went to remove the old one, and the rags fell out and—whoosh, out from the keyhole came a

Ghast. It flew straight into her; she felt it at once." His voice broke. "The people of the tar lands gave her double the money and sent her packing—she had been sent there as bait. They wanted the Ghast to bind to her so that she would take it away from their village. It was a horrible trick to play on anyone. But most of all my Liffle."

Will thought of Freya and the poor souls left down in the crypt.

It must have been terrible for Thales to see his wife like that, thought the Whisp.

Thales continued. "A Ghast is like a weed. The roots of the Ghast spread through the soil of your soul. It feeds on it and dries it out until all that's left is a knotty tangle of weeds and moss. The richer the soul, the better the feast. And Liffle had the richest soul of all. I tried everything to help her. To tend to her. But it eventually got too much, even for Liffle. She left a note. She didn't want me to be the next victim, she wrote. So, she went off to die alone in the hope that a Ghast would never haunt me or the door of our shop again. I looked everywhere for her, but I never found her."

When Thales fell silent, massaging the bridge of his nose with his fingers, Will felt like he should say something, but he wasn't sure what. Before he thought of anything to say, Thales started again.

"That's when the Order of the True Republic started to emerge, promising to take us back to happier times. All we had to do was follow their lead. They had rediscovered the old technology: Just, like in the ancient myths, they would trap the Ghasts in Pandora jars. They said it could rid us of our terrible infliction." He shook his head. "At first, people laughed, called it ridiculous. Ghasts were complicated creatures, they couldn't just be trapped in a jar. But I loved the Republic. I knew how deadly the

Ghasts could be, and I was willing to try anything. I joined the rallies and I marched in the streets. Soon people heard that the Pandora jars were working, in the small towns at first and then some of the bigger ones. Eventually, our whole city turned against our old rulers, and we marched the leaders of the True Republic right in. They were our kings. We wanted them to keep us safe forever."

The older Whisps used to tell us about the times before the Republic. I always thought the people who supported the Republic must have been so evil.

Will felt the Whisp's confusion, she had so many questions.

"Then they asked for more. More power. More money. More anything they wanted. We gave it all to them, happily. Then they made a declaration, across the whole country that said that a Ghast and a Whisp, were one in the same thing and if we wanted to truly get rid of the Ghasts we needed to rid ourselves of the Whisps as well. All they asked for was a few nights of curfew. A few nights where the Hunters could go out into the streets and round up every Whisp and Ghast they could find to stick inside their Pandora jars. That was years ago . . . The curfew never ended."

"So, the Whisp has been chased for years?"

All my life, Will.

Thales nodded slowly. "Back then, most of the people were just so relieved that the Ghasts were gone that they would accept any orders, even if it meant a few Whisps would be captured in the process. But I thought about Liffle; she had loved Whisps. They had been so good to her. To both of us. I knew they weren't like the Ghasts. It wasn't fair to lock them up.

"I found that there were others like me, gathering in secret. Working with the Whisps. Helping them to evade capture. And I joined them," Thales revealed. "We dug tunnels under the streets, but it didn't take the Hunters too long to figure out what was happening. We had to abandon the tunnels and hide the Whisps in other ways. We worked hard. Meeting at night in the back rooms of taverns and shops. My locksmith's shop became an outpost for messengers. Different members of the resistance, from all across the land, would visit Podger's Wynd to exchange codes and cyphers."

Thales dropped one of the key shards onto the tray and picked up his cocoa.

"One of the most frequent visitors was Martha Ulcedi, a great mathematician from Kemet. She was fascinating. I learnt many things from her. All it took was a visit from one of the Whisps we were protecting, and inspiration struck us. She had all the brains, and I was always good with my hands. Within only a few days we had made a new type of door. A door that would allow our Whisps to hide in other worlds. We called them Thresholds."

Will noticed Thales becoming more and more animated at this. His stubby fingers still wrapped around his hot cocoa drummed at the cup making the cocoa slosh over the edge, splashing onto the discarded pieces of the Threshold key.

"Can you repair it, Mr Crickwicker?"

"Oh, my dear boy, goodness no. It's been smashed to smithereens …"

"You can't fix it!" Will shouted, jumping to his feet. "Then we need to leave. I need to find someone that can. It's an emergency!"

"Quiet now," Thales urged. "Listen to them down there."

Will heard only a deep, rumbling, like a constant thunder that vibrated through the floor. "I don't—"

"If those Hunters get you, we will all be dead." Thales sighed. "I'm not telling you this story just to pass the time. I need you to listen."

Will's hands gripped at the side of his chair as he sat back down. *Whisp? Can you find us a way to escape from here?*

No, Will. He's right. We can't go anywhere until those Hunters leave.

Will spoke his thoughts out loud, "What Hunters? I don't hear Hunters. I hear thunder. I'm not scared of a bit of thunder."

"Listen," Thales ordered in a sharp whisper.

And then the Will heard it, and he and the Whisp immediately understood. The rumbling was not thunder at all. It was the shouts and crashes of Hunters stretched to match the swing of the pendulum marking the slower pace of time.

Will folded his arms and frowned.

"You need to understand what you are facing. You both do. Across every world, in every reality, the same four elements can be found: earth, fire, air, and water. With the correct maths and a little bit of work, one of those elements can open a door to the same element on the other side. You jump in a fountain and whoosh you end up in a toilet bowl. Water to water. You go through the air in the back of a cupboard and whoosh, you fall through the sky. Do you see what I mean?"

"I still don't understand what this has to do with us."

"It doesn't. Not yet," Thales said. "I'm coming to it. But I am going to give everything I know. Especially since those brutes are still looking for you." He frowned at a particularly loud rumble of thunder. "Oh, it will take me a century to clean up the mess they are making …" Thales rubbed at where the strap of his goggles sat on his ears.

"Never mind. Never mind. That's all just a cherry trifle

of a problem. You are the one with the real task at hand. Now where were we ... ah, yes, betrayal."

Will groaned, "Please, Thales, the story is fascinating but—"

Thales paid no heed to Will as he continued. "The Republic's Hunters couldn't figure it out. By day Whisps would whip all over the city bouncing from person to person, binding and unbinding, but by night when the curfew came into force, the Hunters didn't find a single one of them. We would attach a sound to each new Threshold we made; one that only a spirit could hear. That way the Whisps always found a Threshold singing to them, no matter where they were. All they had to do was follow the sound and slip into another world. The Hunters were so confused." Thales grinned. "Oh, we would laugh. Our Thresholds had fooled them all.

"Martha had an assistant. Another mathematician, a young eager lad who had been helping her in her studies. He worked day and night using all kinds of figures and formulas to discover theoretical new worlds. She would then give me their exact coordinates and I would make a Threshold somewhere in the city to this new hiding place.

"Over time, the assistant grew jealous that Martha had worked with a little old locksmith to create the greatest invention of our lifetime. He hated all the time Martha spent with me—I never understood why. But his jealousy grew and grew . . . Eventually, he betrayed us. He went straight to the Republic and told them everything. I escaped but Martha was captured and soon they stationed Gatekeepers at every Threshold they found, guarding them day and night. Waiting to capture any Whisp that would try to use it.

"We had made a terrible mistake. With each Threshold the Republic discovered they had a whole new world to explore. The Republican Gatekeepers would venture into these new worlds and report back on any discoveries or new technologies they found. The Republic was getting stronger and stronger.

"The greatest discovery was Amber Elan or that's what we called it. Electricity is what it was called in your world. It powers the Hunter's stingers, sends a jolt of blue through any spirit it touches and makes them visible for a time. With this new weapon, they were fast catching every Whisp left.

Will felt the Whisp shudder as she remembered the feeling of the stinger's pierce.

"With Martha gone, her sister Hypatia called together members of the resistance. Both human and Whisp gathered together deep in the secret cellars. It was decided we had to close the Thresholds, even if it meant the Whisps no longer had any escape. I got to work straight away, trying to forge a key that would seal them shut. But without Martha Ucledi by my side, it was completely impossible to get the maths right. I just couldn't do it. I tried every day. Until, eventually, I got captured myself." Thales paused, adjusting his googles.

"I knew what fate awaited me. Martha's apprentice was now the Republic's General and he took complete control of my incarceration. When he entered my cell, I expected the worst. But even I could not have predicted what he had in store for me. A Pandora's jar placed at my feet and a piece of string tied to the end. The string led all the way out of my cell, to a safe distance. He told me that when he left my cell, he would pull on the rope and the jar would smash." Thales took a deep breath. His eyes haunted.

"Inside the jar, was one of the worst Ghasts he had ever caught or so he said. It would grab onto the first soul it found . . ." He looked away in shame. "And I couldn't bear it. The thought of being tormented just like Liffle. I told him all about the key that sealed the Thresholds shut. His eyes lit up as I talked. I finished with, 'If you take this Ghast away from me, I can give you everything I know. But if it haunts me, you know my mind will become numb and dull and I will forget everything.'

"He was a smart man. Almost as smart as Martha. It didn't take him long to work out my mistakes. The maths was corrected, and I got to work—I made the first Threshold key. The key worked and the General demanded I made more. I pleaded, insisting I could make as many as was needed if only I could get back to my instruments.

"'If I free you, he said then, what's to stop you making more Thresholds?' 'How can I?,' I asked, adding, 'I need Martha or you to provide me with the coordinates. I couldn't find another world if I tried.' He laughed and eventually agreed."

A heavy silence lingered before Thales whispered, "I am not proud of it. But that's what I did. I didn't bargain for Martha's freedom or even to save just one Whisp. I bargained for my own life. My Liffle would be ashamed."

When the thresholds were shut, that is when the hunting really began. Thousands of Whisps older than me were rounded up. Thousands.

Will felt the hurt scorch the Whisp. He didn't know if he should comfort Thales or scold him. "I-I think you were very brave for helping all the Whisps . . . at first. I don't think your wife would have been ashamed about what you did at all. Anyone would have done the same faced with a Ghast at their feet."

Thales supped at his cocoa, sighed and began again. "I was freed from my cellar, and I returned to my store. I got to work, refining the first key with every copy. Shapes within shapes. Elements within elements. Worlds within worlds. Each key looked beautiful, but they were lethal. Once I made enough, the Republic seized the Ether I had been using and my work was done." His eyes travelled to the broken key pieces Will had given him. "The General locked every Threshold I ever created. He was awarded a seat on the Republican Council and became in charge of all the other worlds—General of the Orbis Alius.

"I tried to make up for my selfishness. I tinkered away with this and that. Trying to make new hiding places. Experimenting with all the maths and tricks that I remembered: That's how I made this clock. It was to be another hiding place for the Whisps. But it was too late. Most of my comrades had been captured and the number of Whisps in the city started to dwindle. Until I thought there was maybe none left at all."

The giant pendulum arched over their heads and began its slow swing back to the other corner; the bell of the grandfather clock began to chime the hour. The tone of the bell was enormous, and it made the entire room reverberate. Will held his hands to his ears

When the bell stopped, Thales poured himself another cup of cocoa. The jug was half empty, its contents having been spilt all over the place with the shaking that the bell had caused. Thales didn't take any notice of the mess, commenting, idly, "One in the morning and they are still going. They are bound to tire themselves out soon …"

Tell him to go out and fight. Tell him he needs to make up for what he's done to the Whisps that went before me. Tell him no more stories. Tell him if he can't fix the key then he is no good to us.

"I—" Will stopped and took a deep breath. "Do you know how I can get home?"

"There is a chance, if they have not discovered my

instruments, that I can make another threshold that does not need your key"

"Really!?"

"But—" Thales face paled. "I need the help of your Whisp. I need her inspiration. Like the girl in the crypts. I need her help to remember."

Take his hand. Let me find what he needs. Let's get out of here.

Will outstretched his hand but Thales shirked away.

"No. You don't understand. She cannot search my soul. Not yet. She needs to know what I have done. How I have wronged her. If she sees my memories, I fear she will never help."

"She will help. She is kind and forgiving and—"

Thales eyes narrowed, "Boy, do not speak for her."

Will made to speak but didn't.

The Whisp sighed. *Tell him to go on,*

Will nodded and pulled his hand back to his side.

Thales looked through his goggles, trying to read the Whisp as he continued.

"That was my life. Till about six months ago when I got a knock at the door: it was the General. I hadn't seen him in years. Not since I finished my last key. He had aged, grown out a moustache but I would recognise those glinting eyes anywhere. He had a Pandora jar under his arm, and I thought, this was it. That he'd come back to do what he didn't do before—he was going to unleash a Ghast on me. But he must have seen my horror and said, 'No, no, no. Not at all. You've got it all wrong, Thales. The jar is a gift. A peace offering.'

"He wanted me to study the technology to see how a Pandora jar could truly bind any spirit, Whisp or Ghast, for eternity or as long as it remained sealed. It is quite a marvellous invention, actually. The General went on to explain how he had been wondering, recently what would happen if the jars were combined with the other marvel of our lifetime—the Threshold.

"I have to admit, the idea intrigued me. After some thought, I explained if it was crafted just right it would create a sort of mousetrap. The Threshold would still be a doorway between worlds, any human would be able to cross back and forward as they wanted, but for a spirit, instead of being a doorway, it would be more like a pocket. You would go through the opening and land into the other world, but the spirit would be bound to the earth, air, water or fire … trapped in whatever elemental Threshold you had used. And the spirit would remain there stuck. Possibly forever. He told me there was one left and he wanted to capture it …"

That was me. Thales created the Threshold in the fountain. It was to trap me. He was luring me out for the General!

"So, you built it for the General? After all the Whisps you helped?" Will interjected, feeling the Whisp's pain.

"I didn't plan to, at first. He asked me to keep the trap 'away from the eyes of the rest of the Council.' I thought this was my moment; that I had caught him. So, I planned to play stupid. I'd go along with his plans and as soon as he is left, I'd double-cross him. I would go to tell the Council once he left, tell them how he was travelling to other worlds to capture Whisps in secret. How he was trying to get around the Republic to break the rules. I wanted to betray him just like he betrayed Martha.

"But the General was far too clever. He saw my intent in my eyes and tsked. 'I've not come here empty-handed. You do this and I can give you the one thing, you've wanted the most for as long as I've known you.'

'And what is that?' I asked.

"He said her name, 'Liffle,' and watched me. Waiting. At my silence he taunted me with further hope. 'I can bring her back.' He then began to explain his experimentations—soul bonding, he called it. When the Thinking King was coronated he had decreed that the General should stop wasting all of the Republic's Whisps on his foolish experiments. But all the General needed was one more Whisp. One that would be his alone. He said he knew a *certain technique* that could tame a wild spirit, and make it do his bidding. The Whisp would fill him with creativity and inspiration, whenever he needed it. He was certain this was all he needed to perfect his experiment."

He wanted me to be his slave, the Whisp thought, *to torture the inspiration out of me.*

"Martha had died. She was his greatest regret. He never wanted to be a general—the General. He was an academic just like her and had never wanted her to languish in prison till she died. If only he could bring her back and try again. That was all he wanted. If he could bring her back, then he could bring back Liffle, too." Thales rubbed at his temples. "And what choice did I have? I went to work straight away making these new special Thresholds. These binding traps.

"He got out his charts and asked me which of the Thresholds I could reopen without the Republic noticing. He explained that he wanted the Thresholds to be rerouted to a school to lure a Whisp since young minds are full of imagination and creativity. A school is exactly the type of place where a Whisp would want to go. Together we found four little Thresholds, each a different element, that were dotted in public places around the city that led to Gaia,

"When the crafting of four thresholds was over, I got a message to the General in secret. And that was six months back. It was the last I heard of him. There have been rumours he vanished." Thales looked at Will, his gaze full of regret.

"And now you have shown up, my dear Whisp, after having gone to Worldmouth Academy and binding with a boy. And the boy has the broken shards of a Republican Threshold key. I can't help but think something has gone terribly wrong. And now I think I might not see my lovely Liffle again, after all." He groaned. "Oh, my dear Whisp, how sorry I am for the spot of trouble I have put you in."

"Dear Whisp?" Will snapped. "Dear Whisp! It isn't a spot of trouble; you were going to trick her into being captured!"

"Hush now—wait. Listen." Thales held his finger to his lips. "They have gone."

Will did not move, still throbbing red with anger.

"Well, what are you waiting for? No time to waste! We need to find my instruments." Thales shuffled his stubby little legs quickly across the room and flung a small lever that was built into the side of the clock.

"What are you—"

And the room began to spin.

When they finally landed, the clock door sprung open, and Will tumbled out. The speed of the journey made Will feel nauseous and it took him a moment to realise he was back in the shop because it looked completely different.

It had been decimated. There wasn't a single item that hadn't been broken or overturned. Many of the pulley ropes had been cut and some of the furniture lay smashed on the floor.

Will spun his attention to Thales who was scurrying around a pile of overturned books.

"The General was going to torture her, wasn't he? That's what he meant by; making her 'tame.' You knew what he meant. You were going to let the Whisp be tortured?"

Thales looked up. "I've hurt many Whisps in my life. And yes, I was going to hurt your Whisp too. I'm so sorry."

What does he need me to find? the Whisp asked.

You don't need to do this. You don't need to see those memories. To help him.

Yes, I do, Will. It is your only way home. Our only chance to save Gaby.

Thales had collected a small cloth bundle that had been hidden inside a hollowed-out book. He unfurled the cloth and arranged his instruments.

"If she is willing to help," he said, reaching out his hand, waiting.

"What does she need to find?"

"The coordinates to your world. I cannot remember those numbers."

"Where will she find them?"

Thales gulped. "When I shook hands with the General. He gave the coordinates to me on small pieces of parchment."

"When you agreed to capture the Whisp. Knowing she would be tortured." Will countered, stepping back.

"Yes," Thales spoke softly, dropping his eyes to the floor.

Will, give him your hand.

Will hesitated.

Give him your hand.

Will stretched out his palm and just before they touched Thales whispered, "I am so sorry."

Thales felt a swell of energy, his mind expanding with ideas and possibilities and memories.

The Whisp leapt forward and focused on the locksmith's memories: Pictures of Thales' life raced through their minds. He was a child eating porridge. He was fixing his first lock. Here he was at a friend's wedding. Here he was reading the note Liffle left. Now he was making an escape, smuggled inside a carpet. The moment of awe when the first Threshold he created was opened. The first time he met Martha. And Whisps in jars. Jars in rows, hundreds of them. And prison cells. And screams . . . All of it jumbled together until—

They were reading the coordinates from the General's note.

The coordinates that led to Earth.

That led to Worldview Academy.

Will dropped Thales hand. Thales blinked once, twice, like his eyes were adjusting to the room. He held his arm out to balance himself.

I found it, Will. I found it.

Will heard the weakness in her voice. It sounded distant.

The General, she started. *The Genera—*

Before she could finish the word, her voice faded into nothing.

"I can't hear her inside me anymore," Will whispered. "I think she's hurt."

Thales adjusted his goggles and seemed to look straight through Will's chest. He hummed. "She's in there. But your right; she's very weak. My memories have taken much out of her. Best to leave her to rest. We can take this from here. She's given us everything we need to get you back home."

"Mr. Crickwicker do you think my Whisp will be okay?"

"Yes, I do," the locksmith reassured. "You've helped her survive so far. You must make a wonderful team."

"Do you think we can ever unbind?"

"Well, Will, I have to say never in my life have I seen a Whisp not be able to unbind from a human. There must be thousands of Whisps stuck inside Pandora's jars. But you're the first Pandora's boy. Now can you hand me that thingy-ma-jig over there?"

Thales pointed to a small instrument with an emerald handle. It had a corkscrew blade that reminded Will of the corkscrew his dad would use for opening a bottle of wine. Handing it over, Thales took the instrument and twirled it around in his hands.

Will watched as he knelt at a pile of red sand that had once been in a large basket but was now heaped on the floor.

"Red Silt. Perfect. It's a form of Earth. It will do nicely."

Up until that point, Will had thought Thales looked like he would be a clumsy fellow, with his silly shuffle and his stubby fingers, but he wasn't at all. He had the gracefulness of an orchestra conductor. He used his tools as if they were all part of some elegant dance with his fingertips. He twirled and cut and fiddled and adjusted; every so often he closed one eye to take an accurate measurement.

"People like to think of a Threshold as a boundary. Something you need to cross over. Or get through. But that's not it at all. A Threshold is like poetry. It's points of symmetry. In worlds and universes where differences can be vast, there are always bridges. There are always things that connect us." Thales turned the corkscrew blade within the silt. He tilted his head and listened to each small adjustment, twisting the blade ever so slightly, like a musician finely tuning piano wires. "If your Whisp was awake, she would think it sounds quite beautiful."

Then with another instrument, like an ivory knitting

needle, the locksmith pierced the silt and made one fine slice into the ground. He sat back and placed his tools back into their cloth.

Will watched the silt, unsure of what he was trying to see. "How long does it—" His mouth fell open. He saw the red silt shift and twirl downwards. It sunk into a deep hole precisely where Thales had cut. The hole tunnelled deep into the ground—it looked as if it went on forever, but Will knew that just on the other side was home. He had never missed his dad and sister as much as he did right then.

"Now, I'm going to keep this Threshold open as long as I can before the Hunters find it. You find your friend and then you get back here. When you return, I will do everything I can to unbind you and your Whisp. She should be free."

"Thank you, Mr. Crickwicker."

And with a deep breath, he crawled through the Threshold.

Chapter 16
Memories

W hen Will started crawling, he had been heading downwards but somewhere along the journey, it turned into an uphill climb. Suddenly a hard surface blocked his entry back into his world. He pushed at it, and it swung upwards and away from him. The bright morning sun blinded him for a second and he had to look away. He climbed out of the red silt and into the daylight of his world.

"Yes!" he cheered and punched at the air.

Only hours ago, the chance of being home seemed impossible but here he was. He looked back at the Threshold and discovered that he had just climbed out of a bright yellow plastic bin, labelled 'GRIT.' He had seen them dotted around the school but never once contemplated climbing in or out of one. Inside of this one was now another world . . . he very carefully closed the lid.

He spotted a group of older girls who were staring at him with open mouths. They were looking at him and his school uniform, which he now noticed was shredded. He was also covered from head to toe in the dirt of the crypt.

He must have looked like a zombie coming out of his grave as he crawled out the bin.

Will began to laugh. It was all so preposterous. They had no idea what he had just been through. And they would never know.

He couldn't remember the last time he had laughed, and it came out as big bellyful chortles that he didn't try to stop. The girls watched him a few more seconds before they ran off. This only made him laugh more.

Did you see that they were terrified of us? he thought to the Whisp, but there was still no reply. It brought him back down to earth with a rough bump. He had hoped that crossing back through the worlds would have awoken his Whisp, but his mind was silent.

He was all alone. No one to ask what to do next. No one to help him. He had to find out what had happened to Gaby all by himself. He had no other choice. He would have to find Mr. Scroggie and confront him.

It took Will a moment to find his bearings: he was at the back of the school, on a road that the service vehicles used—a part he hadn't really taken much notice of before.

He thought it must be early because the rugby pitches still had dewy droplets hanging on the grass. He wondered what the most direct route to Scroggie's office would be, and if the school doors would even be open yet and how he would get inside. Then he remembered one of Gaby's stories about the school. She would come to the school early to get a breakfast roll at the dining hall.

'I asked one of them once why they use a traffic cone to keep the door open and they said it was because the kitchen gets very hot. But actually, that isn't really the case at all. It definitely does get hot, but really, it's because some of the kitchen staff like to smoke and they use it to have a cigarette and not be caught. I've not told anyone because I think Ms. Sharpe would fire them if she found out. It's a pretty big secret actually.'

Will remembered how much he had wanted Gaby to shut up at the time and go away. How he had wanted to be able to eat his lunch in peace. That was the last lunch he had in the hall before discovering his spot in the park. Gaby had annoyed him so much with her incessant chatter . . .

He wished, with everything he had, that she was okay now.

Will made his way along the road towards the back of the dining hall and slipped through the propped open door.

The smell of macaroni cheese and warm bread rolls hit his nostrils as he walked into the kitchen. The stainless-steel worktops were busy, filled with ingredients. Some of the chefs were chopping, others stirring big bubbling drums of food. Everyone had headphones in, which made it easy for him to sneak by. The kitchen staff were not Hunters, he could walk by them without any need for stealth.

As he got closer to the doors, he heard the din of voices —the dining hall was busy with breakfast club. There might be trouble. Someone might ask him where he had been or what had happened . . . He balled his hands into fists and pushed the kitchen doors open. He had gotten this far; he couldn't stop now.

A server working on the till, turned around and spotted him. "What were you doing back there?" she asked. "My God, look at the sight of you!"

Will kept his head down and walked past her without responding.

"Don't you walk away from me! What were you doing

in the kitchen? No pupils allowed. Do you hear me? Get back here, you insolent wee sod!"

Will continued to march through the dining hall with his head down but the shouting had made being invisible impossible. Every single pupil in the dinner hall was looking at him. There were bouts of laughter and whispers that Will heard clearly.

"That's Sacha's brother. He's a total freak."

"He must be stinking."

"Looks like he shit himself. With, like, turbo shits."

Will walked through the rows of dining tables until he was nearly at the exit door. Then with a huge clatter, he fell to the floor.

He had been tripped up. A foot had been stuck out at the last second, and he fell straight over it. Stephen McFall and Danny Stobbie's faces peered above him.

"Caught him for you!" Stephen yelled. "Are you going to get him expelled?"

Will got to his feet and made to leave but Danny moved to block his way. Will turned to see Stephen, still in his seat, with a leg outstretched from underneath the table. He was grinning from ear to ear.

The kitchen server had caught up to Will and stood behind him. "Thank you, boys!" she said to Stephen and Danny. Her eyes narrowed on Will. "Now, you. Just what is the matter with you?"

Will shrugged.

"Never in all my years, have I ever seen such rudeness. Ms. Sharpe will hear about this. Name and class?"

"He's William Devine; he's new. He's in Form 2B," Stephen said helpfully.

Will looked away. He didn't care how much trouble he was in. He just wanted to find Gaby. He needed all of this over with because he needed to find Mr. Scroggie.

"Well, thank you again, boys. William," she said his name like it disgusted her, "I suggest you get out of my dining hall. I don't want to see you in here again unless you've come to apologise. Do you understand?"

Will nodded and turned. Danny made a grand bow as Will walked past him.

"And clean yourself up. You are filthy. It's unhygienic. We'll have to scrub down the entire kitchen."

Will pushed open the dining hall doors and headed into the school lobby. He had thought he was through the worst of it . . . until he fell to the floor again. This time he had received a shove from behind: Danny and Stephen had followed him out.

"Don't touch him, Danny! You heard what the dinner lady said, he's 'unhygienic.' Probably covered in shit," Stephen said, and Danny laughed. "In fact, we know it's shit." Stephen continued. "Cause we know what happened. Don't we Stobbie?"

Danny mimed pulling the handle of a flusher and made gargling noises with his mouth.

"My cousin and Danny's brother rule this school. And they will flush your head down any toilet whenever we ask, got it?" Stephen almost spat the words. "You do what we say when we say. And tell your stupid dumb bitch of a girlfriend same goes for her!"

Will felt a rage boil inside of him at the mention of Gaby. He didn't care what Stephen or Danny or any of their older relatives did to him. But Gaby . . . They had always been awful to Gaby. Will felt his skin grow hot. He clenched his teeth and the muscles in his neck tensed.

Danny scoffed. "What's wrong? Have you broken up? Does she not want to kiss your shitty lips?"

They both started to laugh and at that moment Will snapped. He pushed his body back along the ground, bringing both his feet up to kick Danny and Stephen in their middles—

Both of them flew back. Hitting the ground with a howl.

Will spun onto his belly, picked himself up from the ground and ran.

Stephen, his voice muffled as he held his hand to his face, yelled, "You're a dead man! My cousin's going to kill you. You baaastaaard!"

Will didn't care. He was free from them, for now.

The door to Scroggie's office was closed and covered with the same police tape that was on Mr. Anthony's classroom door. It hadn't been there the night before.

Will moved to open the door and heard someone inside. He tilted his head and listened.

"Righto. Everything in here, please. We need it bagged and tagged. All of it, logged for evidence, at least until this whole mess is sorted out. Let's get it done pronto before there are any more balls ups."

Will recognised the voice, it was the policeman, Inspector McNamara.

A thousand thoughts raced through his head all at once. *Why was the Inspector in Scroggie's office? Maybe they had arrested Scroggie? Maybe Gaby was safe? Or maybe they had found her body?*

He half expected an answer, but the Whisp remained silent.

The door opened.

Oh Whisp, I hope you're OK. I hope Gaby's OK. Please let this all be ok.

It took him a moment to refocus, to see that Inspector

McNamara was looking at him in confusion. Behind him were two other officers.

"Well?" he said to Will.

Will realised, while his head had been swimming with thoughts, he had missed the first part of the conversation.

McNamara sighed. "I said this area is out of bounds. Can I help with anything, little chap?"

"Is Gaby safe? Has Mr. Scroggie been arrested?"

"Well, how the hell—? That's a very serious accusation to be throwing around. I am going to have to ask—?"

Will frowned. "Is Gaby alive? Is she safe?"

The Inspector clasped Will by the shoulder. "Never you mind about this Gaby. What do you know about Mr. Scroggie?"

"I will tell you everything I know . . . if you tell me where Gaby is."

"This isn't a negotiation, boyo. You listen to me. *I* am asking the questions. Tell me what you have heard about Mr. Scroggie."

"I just really need to know if Gaby is safe first," Will retorted.

"I'm not telling you anything about anyone. This is a police matter, so its time you did the talking. Who has been speaking to you about Mr. Scroggie?"

Will realized he wasn't going to get any more out of the police. Whatever Inspector McNamara knew, he wasn't divulging it to Will. So, if Will was going to find out where Gaby was, he would need to do it himself.

"It was Ms. Sharpe. She's been telling all the teachers. They've all been gossiping about it." Will saw the look on Inspector McNamara's face as the officer bought his lie.

Inspector McNamara began shouting at his officers: "Right, Mitchell, you're with me. We are off to have some words with Ms. Sharpe about professional discretion and the law. Silversmith, you stay guard at this office, keep everyone out."

Will watched as the Inspector and one of the police officers headed off down the hall. Silversmith stepped out of Mr. Scroggie's office and stood beside Will.

Two down, one to go.

Officer Silversmith looked up and down Will. "You are filthy. Have you been mud wrestling?"

"My friends threw mud bombs at me as I ran across the playing field," Will replied. "It was for a dare."

"A dare?" Silversmith repeated, looking sceptical. "That is some dare."

"Wasn't as bad as the alternative." Will shrugged.

"Oh, and what was the alternative?" Silversmith asked, with a smile.

"You had to go into Mr. Anthony's classroom and pick up something that belonged to him and say his name three times looking at your reflection. Then he will come back as a ghost. All the other kids were doing that one. But I thought it sounded super creepy, so I did the muck bomb run instead."

"They were going into Mr. Anthony's classroom and handling things?" Silversmith asked. "They were going behind the police tape?"

"Yeah, they are all doing it right now. There must have been about ten of us. Maybe more," Will said, with an innocent look.

Silversmith headed up the corridor. Suddenly she stopped, exclaiming, "Jesus Christ!" She reached for her radio, shouting back at Will, "Wait there!"

"Will do," he said, waving goodbye.

As soon as Silversmith rounded the corner, Will slipped inside Mr. Scroggie's office and closed the door behind him.

Will and The Whisp

Not much time until one of those officers figures out I've been lying. Better act fast, Will thought, reaching for the Whisp. He worried that he might never hear her again but knew this wasn't the time to think about that. He had to look for clues. Quickly.

Will scanned the room locking on the small CCTV monitors that were filled with overhead shots of students moving through corridors. The large clock and an old school bell rested below the monitors, Mr. Scroggie's mop and bucket was in the corner, and then he spotted a small cardboard box, no bigger than a shoebox sitting on the janitor's desk. It was marked: *Caution. Evidence. Handle with care.* He couldn't think of a better place to start his search.

Inside the box were neat little see-through bags, like the ones his dad would sometimes put his sandwiches in. Only a few of them had been filled. He picked one up, examining the contents before dropping it back into the box. There was also a memory stick, a notepad, a pair of rubber gloves, a laminated list of after school activities with closing times, an old digital watch, and then—bingo!

Will spotted the key card, the one Mr. Scroggie had stolen the night before. It read, *Mr. Marcus Anthony, History Teacher.*

Mr. Anthony's photograph was printed in a square on the corner of the key card. As soon as Will saw it, it struck him—the resemblance. Thales had described the General as a man with a moustache and glinting eyes. And here was Mr. Anthony with that greying moustache staring back at him. Of course, Mr. Anthony must be the General. That was what the Whisp wanted to tell Will before she faded. She recognised him. It would explain why he had the Threshold key. But it didn't explain why Mr. Scroggie had been hunting through Mr. Anthony's belongings. Why did he want to steal this key card?

It must mean something. Will turned the card over in his hands, examining it. There was a magnetic stripe on the back like a bank card. It looked like the type of card you would swipe in a scanner . . . just like the one attached to Mr. Scroggie's computer . . . the one right in front of him!

He swept the evidence bags onto the floor and started up Mr. Scroggie's computer. The small loading bar appeared on the screen.

"Come on. Come on," Will whispered. He knew the police would be back any second. He looked up to the CCTV monitors, seeing if he could spot them, but there were so many camera angles, and the corridors were still full of pupils. It had made him itchy, not knowing where they were. He had figured so much out; he didn't want to give up now.

BRRRRING—the school bell sounded, and Will worried about his time. Pupils would be filling into classrooms. The halls would be empty, and the officers would surely be on their way back.

The loading bar was halfway across; Will twiddled the card in his fingers,

How had he not thought of it before? How had he not realized that Mr. Anthony was the General when Thales first described him. But then how could he? Thales had described the General as a ruthless killer. Mr. Anthony had seemed to be so kind and fair; he was the only teacher that put Stephen and Danny in their place.

"What do you think?" he said aloud, only to be met with silence.

He had grown so used to the Whisp being with him throughout their journey that her silence now unnerved him. When all this started, he would have done anything to get her out of his head. Now, he missed her. He wished she was here, helping and reassuring him.

As the screen finished loading, the thought flashed into his mind that she might be gone, forever. He couldn't bear to think about it. He couldn't bear the idea that he might have lost not only Gaby but the Whisp, too.

"Please give me something," he said to no one as he ran Mr. Anthony's card through the little scanner attached to Mr. Scroggie's computer.

The details blinked onto the screen—it was a log that listed all of the doors that had been opened by the key card in the last month and the times they were opened. There was a lot of data and Will scrolled down the screen with the mouse, trying to read it all as fast as he could. Trying to see if he could find a pattern.

Mostly it seemed to be opening the doors to the staff room and the history corridors. But Will could see another pattern emerging. Every night, for the last month, Mr. Anthony was in the school and visiting the same rooms, over and over again.

He would start in his own class and then head down to:

Mrs. Duncan's biology classroom at roughly 9:30 p.m.

Mrs. Dernwig's physics classroom at around 10 p.m.

The old wing of the school at 10:15 p.m.

And finally, the gym store by about 11 p.m.

Mr. Anthony had been going to these rooms every single night when the school was supposed to be closed. Since Mr. Scroggie was in charge of locking the place up, maybe he knew about it. Maybe they were in on … something together. Maybe Mr. Scroggie killed Mr. Anthony because he discovered some dark secret in one of those rooms. Maybe that was where Mr. Scroggie was keeping Gaby prisoner.

Will didn't know. But he had no better leads. He was

going to have to check each of those rooms and see what he could find. Hopefully, maybe, Gaby was in one of them.

He grabbed the key card from the scanner and headed to the door, peeking his head out. Noticing the coast was clear, he ran down the corridor and around the corner.

Then a shrill sound of static drilled into his ears when the tannoy system was switched on.

Ms. Sharpe's voice hissed through: "Master William Devine to Ms. Sharpe's office, immediately. Master William Devine report to Ms. Sharpe's office—NOW!"

They had already realised Will had lied. If they would check the CCTV monitors in Mr. Scroggie's office, they would spot him immediately now that the school corridors are empty. While Ms. Sharpe was one thing, Will didn't fancy his chances of outrunning the police.

He needed a distraction. He needed the school corridors busy again. They wouldn't be able to spot him in a crowd.

Will ran along the lobby and to the main stairwell. Beside the door was the fire extinguisher and just above it on the wall, a small red box with a glass pane, read, BREAK IN CASE OF EMERGENCY. Will took the small plastic hammer that was attached to the wall and smashed the glass. He hit the red button and the sirens started to wail immediately.

Fire drills were always organised chaos in his old school. He just hoped that Worldmouth Academy was no different.

Sure enough, the stairwell filled with students, all filing downstairs. There were shouts of joy and shrieks of laughter at the impromptu interruption to their lessons.

One spoke to him as he made his way up the stairs.

"Wrong way, tubby."

Another added, "It's a fire alarm, we're supposed to be going *down* the stairs."

Will ignored them. He knew that this only gave him a few minutes before the corridors would be empty again. Those minutes would be precious.

He bolted down the corridor, almost skidding to a stop as he reached the history corridor. All of the doors had been closed shut and covered with police tape. He beeped open Mr. Anthony's classroom with the dead man's key card and went to the back cupboard, pulling it open.

"Gaby, I—"

It was empty. Gaby was not there.

Disappointed, Will kept moving, up the stairs and along another corridor to Mrs. Duncan's classroom. Again, he bleeped the door open. This time he hurtled into the classroom, opening every book cupboard he found. He searched everywhere Gaby might be hidden. But there was nothing out of the ordinary, just old books and microscopes and the big plant pots with no plants.

He ran to the physics section.

Since he wasn't taught by Mrs. Dernwig, Will ran past the classroom at first. Only on noticing the police tape from the corner of his eye did he stop and turn back. He cursed himself as he realised his mistake—he didn't have time to waste. Again, he was beeping himself in and then, again, throwing open every hiding place he could find. He overturned the bin, in a desperate hope that Gaby might just magically fall out.

He tried hard to understand. To picture Mr. Anthony heading from his classroom to Mrs. Duncan's class to here. Every night. Why? Why, these classrooms. Why would a General from another world be sneaking around these classrooms?

Will looked around and noticed on every desk there

were small gas taps, all attached to the Bunsen burners. They were like little gas candles that every science teacher gave strict warnings about: 'Never turn them on unless instructed, it's very serious. Detention for anyone who even thinks about playing with the FLAMES.'

Bunsen burners create flames . . . Will's eyes widened. Fire.

Mrs. Duncan's plant pots . . . Earth.

These rooms were Thresholds. Mr. Anthony must have checked them every night looking for a Whisp. His classroom had the air Threshold, Mrs. Duncan's the earth, and Mrs. Dernwig's the fire. The old school corridor was where the boy's toilets were located. Where Will got his head flushed . . . in the water Threshold. But that still leaves the old gym cupboard. That room still didn't make any sense to Will.

He took off again, fast. Down the stairs and round to the right. Past the dining room and down through to the large gym hall. His shoes squeaked on the floor as he ran. He noted the CCTV camera in the right-hand corner of the gymnasium. He would be spotted for sure. He was running out of time.

When he got to the gym store, it was also covered in police tape. He used the key to beep it open. It beeped but the little lights flashed red.

"NO!" he yelled, realising they must have deactivated the card. "Gaby!" he shouted. "Are you in there?" He didn't wait for a reply.

There were a set of weights at the corner of the hall, and he ran to grab the heaviest dumbbell on the rack. He carried it with both hands and with a shout, he slammed it into the small key card panel. It broke clean off the wall—the magnetic strip that held the door shut clicked open.

Will shoved the door open with his shoulder and found

that it was being blocked on the other side. Was someone holding it closed? He charged again with his shoulder and the door shunted open another half a foot. He realised that the door had been blocked by a fallen netball stand. It must have crashed to the floor when he hit the wall with the dumbbell.

But . . . No one was in here. His heart sunk.

"Gaby!" he shouted again as he pulled large bags of balls and stacks of hurdles out of his way. "Gaby! Are you in here?" He had to be sure she wasn't trapped.

He clawed his way through, javelins and hula hoops. Climbing over goal posts and punch bags. At the very back corner of the store, he found an old gym horse, used for acrobatics. It had a wide wooden base and a leather top. And on top of it sat a small white pillow and a sleeping bag. Like someone had made a home for themselves.

It didn't make any sense to Will. His head was swimming with confusion.

I don't understand . . .

The Whisp didn't answer.

"Gaby!" Will shouted, pulling the sleeping bag away. Underneath, folded in a neat pile, was a stack of clothes: some white shirts and trousers. And what looked like a Roman toga.

He had seen this before. Or something just like this.

A drop of blood fell from his nose onto the white folded shirt.

His mind started to race.

Will was back in a room filled with stuff and clothes all folded neat. A room filled with flowers. His dad was packing a suitcase with his mum's clothes. His mum had been in the hospital. His dad was packing up her stuff . . .

They had only just said goodbye. They left all the flowers. 'Someone else might enjoy them,' Dad had said.

Sacha is crying on his shoulder at the funeral. Will hears his gran's 'brave little soldier' when Will didn't cry as the coffin was lowered into the ground.

His dad is packing up clothes again. This time into boxes—moving boxes.

They are moving everything. Leaving Mum again. Leaving her in the old house. They are heading somewhere new; somewhere far away.

Mr. Scroggie is shoving a shirt at him. He's dizzy; really dizzy.

He sees the blue electric of stinger. A wet rooftop. Water.

Water is all around him. Like he is drowning. He can't breathe.

He sees his own reflection in the water, like it's a stranger's body.

'Don't ye worry, yer pretty little 'ead. There's toys and sweets and all sorts o' treats in 'ere,' Jackle says as he opens the door to the crypt.

Will sees metal and gears and he can hear whirring noises. Then there are the screams . . .

The General is at the door. He holds Liffle's clothes, smelling them.

These aren't his memories anymore. Will fights. Pushing at the fog, glaring at his reflection in the water.

They're hers. They're everyone she's touched. They're . . .

Will, called the Whisp.

The world is spinning. His mind is being pulled in a million directions all at once.

Will.

Only this time her voice is mixed with another, "Will!"

He's falling.

Will and The Whisp

When Will looked up, he realized Inspector McNamara was there, holding him; cradling him.

"We need a doctor!" the Inspector shouted over and over.

I'm with you, the Whisp promised, and it soothed him.

Will feels her close and he closes his eyes.

Chapter 17
Interrogations

Will woke up looking at the blemished blue sky through a window. White dusty trails of clouds meandered through his vision. He remembered the glaring sun as he emerged from the grit bin and for a second, wondered if all of this had been a wild dream.

Everyone is staring at you, the Whisp warned, and Will turned to look at a sea of faces. Inspector McNamara, Ms. Sharpe, his dad, and a couple he didn't recognise. All were frowning at him.

"Where am I?" he asked.

"You are in the school nurse's room, Will. I'm Nailyn, a paramedic. You had a nosebleed and fainted. But you seem to be ok. Me and my colleague are going to leave you now. Mrs. Soutar, the school nurse is here, and so is your dad, OK?"

Will nodded.

"Rest up and make sure to drink lots," Nailyn instructed. As she left the room, she shook hands with Will's father. She then gave Inspector McNamara a look.

"He's going to be a bit confused, Inspector. Please give him some time."

"Well Will, quite a spot of bother you caused today," the Inspector joked once the paramedics left.

Ms. Sharpe erupted. "A spot of bother! You've vandalised the school by smashing up keypads; we've had the fire brigade out which is thousands of pounds of public money, teaching time has been lost for your fellow pupils, and above all that, ABOVE ALL THAT, you had the audacity to tell the police that I am a liar and a gossip. I am not a gossip, Will Devine!"

Ms. Sharpe collapsed into a padded seat beside Will's bed and started to fan herself with her hand.

"Are you ok, Ms. Sharpe?" Mrs. Soutar, the school nurse asked.

"I'm getting a hot flush. I'm getting all . . . would someone please open a window."

Will's dad leant over him to open the window. Will could tell from one look that his dad was furious. And he hadn't spoken yet, which was always bad.

"Never in all my years, has one pupil caused so much —a flagrant disregard for school property—you're a scoundrel—we could press charges, couldn't we, Inspector? We could sue for damages. I could sue for work-related stress. You could be in a juvenile prison, Will Devine. This was a rampage! A rampage!"

Mrs. Soutar, the school nurse, fanned Ms. Sharpe with a maths textbook.

I think she might be completely crazy, the Whisp commented, and it made Will smirk.

"This isn't a laughing matter, William," Will's dad said, catching the expression on his face.

"Where have you been? I've been worried all night."

"Perhaps it might be best if I have a little chat with

Will and his father alone, Ms. Sharpe," the Inspector suggested before he opened the door.

"I'd rather stay if it is all the same to you. I'd like to hear what the thug has to say for himself. I forgot to mention that, didn't I? Your son assaulted two of my pupils. I forgot to even mention that."

"Really? It doesn't sound like him?" Will's dad said.

"Oh yes. He's a hooligan." Ms. Sharpe was working herself up into a fervour and Mrs. Soutar went back to fanning having stopped and stepped towards the door.

"Ms. Sharpe, I think it's important we take a breath—" Inspector McNamara started.

The room erupted into chaos as the adults bickered amongst themselves. Inspector McNamara kept gesturing to the door and Ms. Sharpe refused to budge, revelling in telling Will's father every last detail of Will's morning. Will's dad wanting to know just how, despite multiple calls to the police and the school, no one even thought to check if he had been there all night. Mrs. Soutar tried to remind everyone, "they really should keep the noise down" because "there will be music lessons going on just down the corridor."

Will took the moment to speak to the one thing in the room that he really wanted to hear from. *Are you ok?* he thought.

Yes, the Whisp replied. *Expanding into Thales just took a lot of energy, I think. I think it's the same thing you felt when the automaton squeezed you and when I woke up. I think it's like fainting.*

I'm glad you're ok. It's good to hear your voice.

You too, the Whisp said. *It seems like there's a lot I need to catch up on. What happened? Is Gaby OK?*

I don't know yet, but I have an idea, Will answered. *You might just need to trust me and follow my lead. Do you think you have enough energy to expand again?*

If it's to save Gaby, then I can do it, the Whisp said.

Good. But before Will explained any more, Inspector McNamara came to the edge of the bed and cleared his throat.

"Now then, young lad, how is your nose? You gave us all quite a shock when we saw the blood, we thought there had been a massacre."

Will instinctively touched his hand to his nose.

"You are going to need to take me through quite a lot of your actions this morning. But your dad said he hadn't seen you since last night. You told him you were with a friend but when your dad tried to call your mobile, there wasn't any answer."

"I'm sorry, Dad. My mobile got smashed," Will answered. "Where's Gaby?"

"Whose Gaby?" his dad asked.

"She's the young trespasser we discovered last night."

"Oh, my giddy aunt! It's all too much," Ms. Sharpe moaned. She then commanded Mrs. Soutar to keep fanning her with the textbook.

"Ms. Sharpe, quiet now." The Inspector shot Ms. Sharpe a look before turning back to Will. "Don't you worry about Gaby; we have that all under control. How about you try and answer my questions, son?"

"I just want to know where you've been Will," his dad pleaded.

Will nodded. "Ok. But first, can I please have a drink?"

The Inspector reached down and poured some orange juice from a jug at the table beside Will's bed into a red plastic cup. When he held the cup out, Will reached for it, clasping the Inspector's hand too with a gentle touch,

"I am sorry," he said, truthfulness in his voice. At the same time, he thought, *Whisp, we need to know everything he knows about Mr. Scroggie and Gaby, now!*

The Whisp went to work. She expanded, rushing into the Inspector's body and headed straight to his memories. Seconds passed as she flew through everything that didn't matter until she found what she was looking for.

Mr. Scroggie's face was twisted more than usual, and he was tugging at a lock of his hair. The Inspector looked at him through the swishes of his windscreen wipers; he knew the look. Mr. Scroggie looked guilty. He looked like a man with a conscious that got the better of him—like he had something to admit.

The Inspector didn't know what the janitor wanted to admit, but he hoped to God it wasn't too serious. He turned off his headlights and the rhythmical scrape of the windscreen wipers slowed to a stop. With a clink and a clunk, he undid his seatbelt and opened the car door.

"I really wasn't expecting to be at this school again tonight, Scroggie. I had just put my bolognese in the microwave."

"I found someone," Scroggie said, still looking sheepish and fidgety.

"I think I better come inside then, don't you?" the Inspector answered and Scroggie opened the school door.

"She's a student. I've got her locked inside my office," Scroggie muttered as he led the Inspector inside.

"You've locked a child inside your office, Mr. Scroggie?" the Inspector's asked, forehead wrinkling.

"Not in a bad way. Not like that. Just until you arrived. Called you soon as a found 'er."

"Have you contacted her parents?"

"I couldn't do that. She wouldn't tell me her name. And anyway, I'm just janitorial services, I don't have access to that kind of information." Mr. Scroggie tugged at the hair on the side of his head again. To the Inspector it was clearly a nervous tick.

"Well, have you called your headteacher, Ms. Sharpe? Someone needs to contact the minor's next of kin."

"I'll do that right away. Maybe when I call Ms. Sharpe, you can go check on the girl?"

"Is she hurt or traumatised in some way?"

"She's scared of me, I think. I keep telling her not to be frightened but I can tell when a kid's scared and she's shivering with fright."

"That might have something to do with you locking her in an office," the Inspector retorted.

They followed the familiar school corridor. As the Inspector pushed the caretaker office door open, his eyes looked down to see—

———

Gaby! the Whisp shouted with happiness.

Within an instant, the Whisp was catapulted back into Will's body.

Well? Is she—

Gaby's fine. Didn't see the whole memory ... Need more ... Touch ... Again . . . The Whisp's voice was small, coming in tiny bursts.

The Inspector pulled his hand away and the cup of juice crashed to the floor. "What was that?" he asked, paling.

"What was what?" Will's dad asked, stepping closer to Will's side.

"Did you hear a little girl shout something just now?" the Inspector asked, the panic in his voice made it go up at the end, till it was almost a squeak.

"We are in a school, Inspector McNamara," Ms. Sharpe snapped.

"No, no. It was like it was right beside me. Like right in my ear."

"My daughter, Sacha, is a teenager and when she's on the phone with a friend, it can be deafening, even from the other room," Will's dad offered. "Perhaps you heard—"

"I'm not a dunce, Mr. Devine. I know what I—"

Mrs. Soutar interrupted this time, "Maybe you would like a little sit down too, Inspector?"

"No. No. No," he muttered, shaking his head. "Forget about it. Would you please get a cloth? That juice has gotten everywhere." He looked at Will, warily. "Will, you were going to tell us about last night?"

"I was going to have a drink first," Will insisted, crossing his arms.

"Well, you spilt the drink all over my shirt. So, that's not going to happen. I need you to start talking now, boyo!" the Inspector shouted.

Will's dad stepped in between the policeman and Will. "Inspector McNamara, this is very serious, but let's not raise voices again. My son lost his mother only a few months ago and he's clearly still distressed."

We need to get the Inspector to touch us again, the Whisp reminded.

We need a touch of kindness though. That might be impossible, Will replied.

He's scared of me not you, said the Whisp.

"I just heard it!" Will shouted. "The girl's voice."

"What?" McNamara's eyes turned into giant round saucers.

"It was weird. It was a girl's voice. Like inside my head. It was like moments from my life just flashed across my eyes and then I heard her voice."

"What is happening here? Is everyone losing their minds today?" Ms. Sharpe threw her arms in the air in frustration.

"Calm down, Ms. Sharpe. There is clearly something very paranormal going on in this school. I suspected that might be the case. Tell me, son. Tell me what she said?" The Inspector came and sat on the edge of Will's bed.

"I think I heard her voice all morning. I think she possessed me . . . " Will whimpered, trying to seem as innocent as possible.

"This might explain it, Mr. Devine. You said it yourself, Will is normally a very well-behaved child." The Inspector wagged his finger, pointing it at Will's dad then back at Will, like he was a detective from an old television show, unravelling the mystery in an instant.

Will's father rubbed at his face in exasperation. "Will is a well-behaved child. He is also a child who has just lost his mother and moved to a new house and started a new school. Psychologically speaking, I think that might make a bit more sense."

"Well, yes. There is that. But there's been a lot of strange goings-on in this school. Possibly demonic! Don't you agree Ms. Sharpe?" The Inspector asked excitedly.

Ms. Sharpe lifted her head slowly. "Well, he's certainly been acting like an EVIL LITTLE DEVIL!"

She suddenly lunged towards Will before Mrs. Soutar pinned her back into the chair.

"Calm down Selma. Remember your blood pressure."

"Oh, for god's sake," Will's dad mumbled and he slumped against the wall.

Will persisted, whispering, "She's in my head now." The Inspector looked at him with anticipation. "She's hypnotising me."

"Look at me, Will, don't go anywhere. Don't let her get

205

hold of you. Look right into my eyes," the Inspector instructed. He held Will's face in his hands, patting his cheeks.

The Whisp rocketed forward, straight from Will's face into the Inspector's hands and then back up into the Inspector's mind. She nudged him out of control and went right back to the memory of Mr. Scroggie and last night.

———

The Inspector and Mr. Scroggie were arguing.

"The girl says she followed you. She says you went into Mr. Anthony's classroom first."

"No. Not true, Inspector. I found her. She was in Mr. Anthony's bookstore. She must have hidden there all night. It's a lucky thing I went and checked. Don't you think?"

"And what exactly made you check, Scroggie? You said you were just following me out."

"Mmmmm . . . it was just like a hunch I had." Mr. Scroggie looked at the floor avoiding the Inspector's intense stare.

"Well, that was quite the hunch. Glad it worked out. We could do with someone with your intuitions on the force."

A big grin came over Mr. Scroggie's face. "Yes. I'd be happy to help." He laughed, adding, "Anytime."

"Of course, now the CCTV is working we will double-check. Just so we can verify your version."

Mr. Scroggie's face fell. He turned ashen grey, like someone had pulled a plug beneath his feet and all the colour drained out of him. He had been caught and he knew it.

"Alright. I went in there first," he admitted with a sigh.

"Lying to a police officer is a serious offence, Scroggie.

I suggest you tell me everything that's going on here right now." The Inspector had switched his tone of voice completely. He was stern and forceful. He had played Scroggie's game for too long and wasn't in the mood for any more deceit.

"I was looking for this." Scroggie produced a plastic card that hung on a thin blue shoelace, from his pocket. It dangled on the shoestring and the Inspector bent down to get a better look at the face that was printed on the side of the card.

"It's Mr. Anthony's key card. I was going to put it back. But I wanted to wipe it clean first."

"For fingerprints?" the Inspector leaned closer, suspecting foul play.

"No. Not like that. Wipe it of its data. The key card logs every room Mr. Anthony would enter and the time of entry. I wanted to make sure when you found it, it would be blank—that's all."

"Tampering with a crime scene is not a small matter. But that's not all though, is it, Mr. Scroggie? The CCTV was working all along, wasn't it?"

Scroggie barely nodded but it was enough for McNamara to know that he would be arresting the man tonight.

"A man died here, Scroggie," he said through gritted teeth. "And you are behaving in a manner of a murderer."

Scroggie burst into tears. "No. No. No. I didn't mean no harm! It was stupid. I made a big mistake. But I didn't kill him. I promise." He forced the words out between sobs and giant sniffs of his nose.

The Inspector didn't say a word. He just continued to stare at Mr. Scroggie, waiting.

When Mr. Scroggie composed himself, a little, he began to speak. "Mr. Anthony was my friend. He came to the school six months ago and we hit it off. The other teachers don't talk much to me. The only time they even say hello is to complain about their bins not being emptied or that something hasn't been fixed right away. Never ask how I was or my opinions on anything. They think 'cause I don't talk proper like them, I'm stupid. But I ain't, this place would fall apart without me.

"Markus was different though. He comes and says 'ello on the first day. We chat and he's a good guy. He then invites me for a drink, at the pub, after school one day. I cancel the after-school clubs and, go. The other teachers are angry at me closing the school on short notice, but Marcus and me have a great night. We talk about politics and history and all kinds of stuff. People around here think I'm stupid. But that's a misconception, just cause I ain't a teacher, don't mean I'm dumb. Markus listened to me. He wanted to hear my opinions on all sorts of things.

"During our drinks, he tells me he is struggling for a place to stay in Worldmouth. He can't find any rooms, and his hotel is expensive. He tells me he even asked Ms. Sharpe if he can stay in the school for a couple of nights. Just until he gets somewhere. So, I tell him, strictly speaking, anything to do with the property of the school is my decision. I'm in charge and I lock the place up at night, and I don't see how a couple of nights would be a problem.

"He hugged me and . . . he's so thankful. He buys all the drinks that night to say thanks.

"Next day he shows up with a big bag full of clothes and toiletries and stuff. I tell him, we have to maybe hide his stuff, so no one will get suspicious. I give him a loan of a sleeping bag that we have packed away with the Scout club's camping supplies.

"He agrees and says not to worry, that he's found the

perfect spot. On the hobby horse at the back of the gym store behind some unused equipment.

"A week goes by and it's the worst week of my life. Every time Ms. Sharpe calls me, or I bump into her in the corridor, I'm certain she's going to say she has found Mr. Anthony's stuff and that I had broken council rules and she would have to fire me. I hated every second. My heart palpitated all week.

"I go and speak to Markus, and I ask him if he's found a place to stay. He takes me out for more drinks, and I get a bit happy with my drinks again. I agree he can stay in the school a little longer. Yet, I feel so stupid the next day. I wish I hadn't agreed but I didn't want to go back on my word and disappoint Markus. He was my best friend.

"It just kept going on and on for months. I worried about it a little less and a little less each day. Till eventually, it became normal. Markus would say goodnight and I would lock him in the school and then I would open up and he would be there to say good morning.

"But in the last couple of weeks, things started to change. His mood was different. He seemed, darker. When I came to say goodnight, he would just grunt at me and slam the door. During the day, I would see him lose his temper at the children. I thought, maybe he's annoyed he hasn't found anywhere to live yet.

"So, I looked in the newspapers and in my local shops and I found some flats nearby that were available to rent. I went to Markus' classroom to show him what I found; I thought he would be happy. But he wasn't. He was really angry. He pinned me up against the wall and said if I tried to throw him out, he would tell Ms. Sharpe that he had seen me with a pupil, behaving very wrongly. And everyone would believe him cause everyone else here thinks I'm just the big dumb janitor. They don't know me well enough to know I would never do that. If he told those lies, I would be in huge trouble. Like worse trouble than even the trouble, I'm in now. I got scared. I left him alone after that. I didn't say hello or goodbye. I just locked him in.

"Then I came in yesterday morning and saw on the CCTV that he was sleeping on his classroom floor. I thought I better wake him up before pupils start to arrive. I go and I knock on his door. Gently because I'm scared he might shout again. And then I find him dead.

"I call the police straight away. Like I should. Then I think when you arrive, when Ms. Sharpe arrives, there will be a lot of questions. And people will find out I let him live in the school, and I will get fired—I don't have anything else. This job is what I've got, and I don't want to lose it.

"I know I've made a big mistake. But I am scared. I show the police officer to Mr. Anthony's classroom before I run down to my office and look at the CCTV. I see Markus is there every night acting very strange. He goes to the same classrooms, and he has his paperweight with him and a knife. Like a small letter opener. He cuts his hand, just a little, with the knife and he lets it bleed over his paperweight. Then he puts the paperweight, into something. Like it's a ceremony or a ritual or something.

"He does this in his classroom at the back of his classroom. He does it in Mrs. Duncan's classroom over an old plant pot and in Mrs. Dernwig's class over the flame of a Bunsen burner. Every single night. And he goes down the old part of the school where there's no CCTV, and finally he goes to sleep in the gym store. I watch this on fast forward. Same thing every night. Like he's been possessed or something. It's creepy, him cutting his hand every night.

"I think, maybe you should know about this. But then I think, what does it matter? Markus is dead, and it's clear he killed himself. What does this stuff matter? The only thing it changes is that it means I'm fired . . . So, I delete it all. I delete all the CCTV recordings. And when you said it doesn't matter much anyway, I think 'phew.'

"Then I remember the key card. And I know going into Mr. Anthony's classroom is a serious crime. Because I know what you said about it being a crime scene and how strict Ms. Sharpe was to the pupils about it all. I think, if I do this, If I get the key card and I wipe it and I put it back, it will all be over. It will all be done, and I can relax. I can just concentrate on my job and never make another mistake and follow all the rules.

"I speak to you, and I turn all the lights in the school off so no one will notice me. I try to sneak into the class and disturb as little as possible. But I can't see a damn thing. So, I go get a torch. And then I see the key card is hanging on a hook on the back of Mr. Anthony's door and I stuff it in my pocket. I think 'phew' again. It's all over. But then I hear a noise in his book-store. I get frightened. Cause that's one of the places where Markus would bleed. But I am brave, and I open the door. And it's a pupil.

"I grab 'er out and she screams like I'm going to kill 'er. I try to calm 'er down. But now I know I've made big mistakes. I've made it all worse. And I've scared the girl. She won't even tell me why she was there in the first place. She won't tell me anything.

"I think about how I'm going to be arrested. Because I tried to cover up my mistakes. And I know I shouldn't. But I didn't hurt Markus and I didn't hurt the girl. That's the truth. I promise yer. Hand on my heart, promise yer."

"Well, Scroggie . . . that's quite a tale but I can't believe anything from your mouth anymore. I will need to check all this out. My officers are on their way, and when they arrive, you are going to go down to the station and go through all of this again." The Inspector made tiny scribbles in his notebook.

"I'm under arrest?" Scroggie asked in almost a whisper.

"Yes, Mr. Scroggie. I am just about to arrest you," the Inspector confirmed, putting the little notebook into his pocket.

Scroggie began to cry again, "Is the girl OK?"

"She's a little shaken up. Mr. Anthony was her teacher. I think she must have snuck in to say goodbye or something. God, I don't know. I don't really understand kids. She'll be escorted home when backup arrives. We'll make sure she sees Mrs. Porter, the bereavement counsellor, first thing in the morning."

Mr. Scroggie presented his hands to be cuffed and the Inspector looked down at his balled-up fists.

"I'm going to need that key card, Mr. Scroggie."

Gaby's alive. The police took her home, the Whisp said as she crashed back into Will's body.

Has Mr. Scroggie been arrested?

Yes, but Mr. Anthony wasn't murdered. He killed himself.

They were the last words Will heard as the energy drained from the Whisp. He reached inside himself to hold onto her to keep her from slipping into a sleep. The tighter he tried to hold her with him the more energy it took from his body until eventually, Will's body slumped, and his eyes closed.

The Inspector shouted for help.

Will's father rushed to his side.

"Will . . ."

Chapter 18
Pandora Jars

Gaby's night had been difficult. Mr. Scroggie had not killed her, but she had lost Will and that felt even worse. She blamed herself for pushing him through the Threshold. She was certain that Mr. Scroggie would kill them, and it was the only thing she could think of doing to save her friend. But now, she was the one that was alive and well, Will and the Whisp, the last thing she saw before the Threshold closed was them falling. Falling through the air.

They could be dead.

Somewhere.

Anywhere.

She might never know what happened to them.

She had lied to the police officer, pretending that she alone had decided to hide in Mr. Anthony's cupboard. She knew she was in trouble and didn't want Will to get in trouble as well. She regretted her decision all night. She had wished that she had told the officer everything. Maybe they could have helped Will. Maybe. Then again, without another Threshold key, how would she show them that at the back of a book cupboard was a portal to another world? Who would even believe that?

When the police dropped Gaby off at home, her mother came to the door and immediately burst into tears. Her mascara streaked across her face. The officer tried to speak but her mother made the usual sign she makes—the one that shows the person that she is deaf, and her daughter is going to have to translate. The last thing Gaby wanted to do was translate a conversation between her mother and the officer.

The conversation consisted of the officer awkwardly trying to include Gaby and her mother wanting the exact opposite. Her mother would speak to Gaby later. Right now, she wanted to know exactly what the officer was saying. She did not want Gaby to put her own spin on it; Gaby knew this. She translated as best she could. No matter how excruciating it was. No matter how much she wished she could explain all the bits the officer was getting wrong.

When the officer said their goodbye, Gaby stepped inside the house and her mum closed the door behind them.

'Mum, I—'

'Gabrielle, we agreed I would confiscate your phone and the laptop. Go get them please.'

'But Mum, I . . . Gaby stopped. She hadn't agreed to anything. Her mum and the officer had come to this arrangement, but Gaby really thought it was only fair that she would get her chance to explain what happened before she was punished.

'Enough! Just go get them.' Her mum turned her back and headed into the living room. This was always how her mum would end the argument. She would turn her back and stop watching Gaby's signs.

Gaby fished her phone out of her pocket and fetched her laptop from her bedroom. She placed them both on the coffee table beside her mum and stood, waiting.

Her mum lifted her head like it was a tonne weight. 'Go to bed, Gaby,' she signed, and her head slumped back into her hands.

Gaby felt her own tears, welling up. She hated seeing her mum like this, but she knew there was nothing she could say at that moment to help, so she turned and headed to her room.

All night she tossed and turned and she didn't get an ounce of sleep because of the worry. She had decided in the morning that she would come clean and tell the police everything she knew. She would try her best to convince someone, anyone, that Will needed help. It wouldn't take them long to figure out he was missing. Someone might believe her. It was worth a shot.

The car ride into school was silent. Her mum gripped the steering wheel with both hands. Gaby sat in the back, her head down the whole way. When they arrived, her mum pulled into the small car park usually reserved for staff— Gaby knew that her mother must be coming in as well.

The school was still the same. Other kids were chatting and messing about. There was no hint of last night's turmoil. People barely even raised an eyebrow as she was frog-marched into school by her mother.

She was greeted at the entrance lobby by Mrs. Porter, who sat on one of the small green plastic chairs, looking rather uncomfortable.

"You must be Mrs. Crowsdale," Mrs. Porter said with a smile. "And hello again, Gaby."

"My mother's deaf, Mrs. Porter. Her name is Simone Roland. Crowsdale is my dad's name," Gaby answered as she signed 'deaf' and finger spelt 'Simone' so that her mother knew what was being said.

At her mum's nod, she signed, 'This is Mrs. Porter, she's a bereavement counsellor. I spoke to her yesterday.'

'Well, nice to meet you, Mrs. Porter,' Gaby's mother signed, and Gaby interpreted before turning to the receptionist. "We're here to see Ms. Sharpe and Inspector McNamara. My mother asked the officer last night for an interpreter to join us."

Mrs. Porter got up from her seat and used her stick to interrupt the conversation, gesturing for the attention of Gaby's mother. "Tell your mother, Gaby, that I've been waiting for you both. I've been asked to speak to you first, without your mother."

Gaby noticed the look Mrs. Porter was giving—the counsellor could be firm when she wanted to be.

The stick was rude though, and the look was even ruder, and it made her mum bristle. 'There's a misunderstanding. I was expressly told to come here with Gabrielle to speak to the police. I've taken time off work for this.'

"There's no misunderstanding. That will still happen. But I'm talking to Gaby first," Mrs. Porter said once Gaby translated. "Ms. Sharpe and the police are quite busy this morning. You do realise your daughter and Mr. Scroggie both left a lot of bother to clean up? Tampering with a crime scene …" Mrs. Porter leaned in for a mock whisper to Gaby, "Did she get all of that. You didn't leave the last part out?"

"I told her what you said, Mrs. Porter," Gaby snapped, scowling.

Her mum signed furiously. Gaby struggled to translate:

"I can lip read Mrs. Porter. Do not attempt to speak to Gabrielle without me. Where is our interpreter?"

"Do you really need one? I thought you said you read lips."

"I have a few things I would like to say myself without my daughter speaking for me. Especially to Mr. Scroggie. Where is he?" Gaby translated aloud.

"That's a matter for you to take up with the police, Ms. Roland. They will be here shortly. Why don't you take my seat, and I will take Gaby? I will bring her back as soon as we've chatted," Mrs. Porter said, gesturing to her seat.

Gaby's mother wrapped her arm around Gaby as if to defend her.

Gaby answered, "My mum won't let me go anywhere without her right now."

Mrs. Porter's eyes blazed like hot coals, perfectly framed by round spectacles. She growled, "Fine then. Follow me."

Her mum didn't budge; Gaby still wrapped at her side.

"We need the interpreter," Gaby reminded, knowing that her mum was not going to negotiate.

"Tell your mother I only want to speak to you anyway. She can lip read all she needs to know. "Usually, bereavement sessions are private. Would she like me to report back to the police how uncooperative you both have been?" Mrs. Porter began walking out of the reception without waiting for a reply.

Her mother eased her arm around Gaby's body and signed, "I don't like this woman."

Gaby nodded as they moved to follow the counsellor. She was surprised by the anger of the old woman. She had seemed so sweet and benign when they chatted yesterday. But Gaby knew, just as well as her mum did, the veiled threat of telling the police that they were uncooperative could cause a lot of problems. The old woman would always win that argument, even if it wasn't really true.

She had assumed her mother had come to help punish Gaby. It was only in the short exchange with Mrs. Porter that she realised her mum might be there to defend her.

Despite the feeling of animosity towards Mrs. Porter, she did want to speak to her alone. It would be easier to tell the truth, the real truth to a complete stranger. Her mum had always said that Gaby had an active imagination. She suspected that's what her mum would think now. Spirits and other worlds? It sounded exactly like something Gaby might imagine. She would have to try extra hard to convince them of the truth.

The school bell had already rung to start the day, meaning the place was virtually empty, with every student in their classroom. The heels of her mum's shoes clicked on the floor, accompanied by the thud of Mrs. Porter's walking stick. They walked the corridors, in silence—Gaby could hardly bear the tension.

When they arrived at Mrs. Porter's makeshift office, Mrs. Porter held open the door for them to enter first. Gaby stepped inside, and her mum followed.

CRACK!

Gaby spun around to see her mum lying on the floor. Mrs. Porter stood above her, a wild look in her eyes. She held her stick like she was brandishing a sword.

"She's still alive. But if you make another sound, I will squish her skull like a bug."

Gaby was too shocked to cry out. Her body trembled and she fell to the ground to check on her mum. Before she could do anything, her chin was lifted by the walking stick. Her eyes met Mrs. Porter's.

"Me and you have a problem, Gabrielle Roland Crowsdale."

Gaby stood with her fists clenched, ready to fight. Mrs. Porter stepped over Gaby's mother and pushed her walking stick against Gaby's throat, pinning her to a small wall. Gaby grabbed the stick and tried to push back but the old woman had a tremendous strength she hadn't expected.

"I think you have something I need Gabrielle."

Gaby could barely breathe, but she managed to wheeze out, "Wh ... wh . . . whaaat?"

Mrs. Porter released her stick and Gaby doubled over, trying to regain her breath.

"I was sent here to collect a Whisp."

Gaby's fear of this old woman was immense but the mere mention of the word 'Whisp,' made her even more terrifying.

"That's right," the counsellor said, her tone vicious. "I know all about your little friend. You can either hand the thing over or I take you back to my world and drag it out of you. Your choice." She paused., looking at Gaby's mum on the floor. "I know what your mother would prefer."

"I don't have her."

"Liar," Mrs. Porter spat, looking ready to choke Gaby once again with her stick. "I wonder, what's the best way to get at it ... Do I bash your skull in or slice your guts open?"

"I'm not lying," Gaby insisted. She fought against the rush of adrenalin. She fought against the urge to scream and run and show all her fear. Instead, she looked Mrs. Porter in the eye and said, "And when you bash my skull in and find nothing inside me. You are going to be the one in big trouble, I think."

Mrs. Porter froze. If the girl was telling the truth ... She grabbed Gaby by the hair and dragged her to the window. Pushing her face down, her cheek pressed against the plastic sill in between the two vases Mrs. Porter had used to make the place seem homely. Or so Gaby had thought.

"Let me go!"

Mrs. Porter grabbed one of Gaby's arms twisting it against her back; Gaby shrieked in agony.

"Shhh, now. Shhh," Mrs. Porter whispered in her ear. "Remember what I said about your mum."

"Do you know what this is?" Mrs. Porter asked when Gaby sucked in a deep breath.

Gaby stayed silent; her eyes fixated on her mum. Wishing she would wake up. Wishing she would come to Gaby's aid.

Mrs. Porter pushed one of the vases, so it was touching Gaby's nose. "This is a Pandora jar. It was meant for the Whisp. But I caught something else. I caught the Ghast that killed Mr. Anthony. Do you know what a Ghast is?" She didn't bother to wait for an answer.

"Thing is," she continued, "if I crack this open the Ghast is going to attach itself to the first spirit free body it sees. It drove Mr. Anthony to kill himself and it will do the same to you. Unless you've got a Whisp inside you that is, then I suppose it might just feed on your mother over there? Please, let me ask you again, do you have my Whisp?"

Gaby stuttered, "N-no."

Mrs. Porter turned her attention to the jar that she had pushed against Gaby's face. With a hum, she leaned into it. "Can you hear me in there, you wretched little thing? I got a nice little child for you to munch on. Young and fresh. I'll even keep her alive for you . . . so, you can munch away the rest of her life. You got it? But first, you get to feast on her mother's soul while I make her watch? Does that sound fun?"

Gaby's eyes grew wide, as the jar wobbled in front of her.

Mrs. Porter laughed "See that? He's going frantic. Begging to be released." She paused, pushing a little harder on Gaby's back. "Last chance, do you want to tell me where the Whisp is?"

Gaby was terrified but she didn't move a muscle. She didn't utter a single word. She only looked at the jar with horror.

Mrs. Porter gave a long dramatic sigh. "Foolish child. Being brave won't help you or the Whisp." She pulled Gaby from the jar and threw her to the floor. "You are going to tell me everything you know. Or I kill her."

At Gaby's silence, Mrs. Porter took the jar and lifted it up as if to crash it down on Gaby's mother.

Gaby screamed, "No!"

Mrs. Porter yelled back, "Tell me where the Whisp is!"

"She isn't here. They've already escaped. Will took her back to your world."

Mrs. Porter's eyes flashed with fear until Gaby saw the rage return. The counsellor lifted the Pandora jar high above her head, ready to crash it down.

There was a shrill buzz and then Ms. Sharpe's voice came over the tannoy: "Master William Devine to Ms. Sharpe's office immediately. Master William Devine report to Ms. Sharpe's office—NOW!"

Gaby sucked in a gasp at the mention of Will's name, which made Mrs. Porter grin.

The shrill sound of the fire alarm began before anymore could be said between them.

Chapter 19
Temptation

W ill awoke once again looking out the window. The powdery blue sky had disappeared behind thick grey clouds. It made the room feel dark and Will wondered just how long he had been out. He turned expecting to see a room full of people but there was one small figure sitting in the corner.

"Mrs. Porter," Will greeted and she smiled at him.

"Good afternoon, William."

"Where is everyone?"

"We all agreed that there was far too much commotion when you are supposed to be resting. The Inspector insisted he and your father take their little debates somewhere more private. Your dad would only leave if there was a responsible adult watching over you. I've agreed to take over and let Mrs. Soutar have a break. It has been quite a stressful morning for her." She paused, leaning forward in her seat. "How are *you* feeling?"

Will tried to sit up. "I'm fine, I think."

"That's good to hear. Do you think you are well enough to manage a little stroll?"

Will nodded and pulled back the covers of the bed, slipping his feet onto the floor.

"A stretch of your legs can do wonders, young man." Mrs. Porter offered her hand so that Will could help her up. He obliged and took her weight as she stood.

When Mrs. Porter opened the door, Silversmith was standing guard outside.

"We're taking a walk," Mrs. Porter announced.

Silversmith looked alarmed. "I'm afraid the boy has to stay here until the Inspector is ready to see him again."

"Is he under arrest?" Mrs. Porter asked, throwing the slyest of smiles to Will.

"No, but—"

Mrs. Porter was firm, cutting her off. "Then you have no right to detain him."

Silversmith shook her head. "He's already tricked us once today."

Tugging Silversmith's shirt, bringing her forward, Mrs. Porter whispered in the officer's ear. "Officer, the father's wanting to file a complaint that the Inspector laid hands on the boy. Don't make it worse."

Silversmith danced on the spot, unsure.

Mrs. Porter spoke once more. "Besides, he's quite ill and I'm quite old. It's not like we are going to go far." She turned to leave.

"Then I'll follow," said Silversmith, determined.

Mrs. Porter spun back around, and with a flash of anger said, "No, you won't. The boy is not under arrest. I'm the appointed bereavement counsellor. Rule 4A section C states the students right to complete confidentiality. We are taking a walk—alone."

Mrs. Porter looped her arm through Will's and tugged him to start walking. Will couldn't help but feel a little admiration for Mrs. Porter's cunning arguments.

From behind them Silversmith muttered, "Crap."

Mrs. Porter gave a small chuckle as they turned the corner. "Don't tell anyone but there is no Rule 4A Section C. I just made that up."

Will laughed. He liked Mrs. Porter and he appreciated the opportunity to escape for a bit.

"Your friend Gaby wanted me to say hello. She has been in with her mum this morning."

Will felt relief pour through him before he felt a feeling he hadn't felt for a long time. He felt safe and reached for the Whisp. *Did you hear that? Gaby! She knows we are home.*

But the Whisp didn't respond. She hadn't woken yet and he was worried for her, but he knew she would awake again. And now that he knew Gaby was safe, and he was back in his own world, the danger was over. When the Whisp awoke they would quietly make their way back to Mr. Crickwicker to unbind them. But they would be patient, only leave when they knew they wouldn't get into trouble, only come back when they were both free.

He walked arm in arm with Mrs. Porter through the school. At the big glass windows of the lobby, she began lamenting the weather. It had been such a beautiful day, to begin with, but now, it looked certain a storm would be coming. She joked next with Will about the state of his clothes and all the trouble he had created.

Will wondered if Mrs. Porter might even believe him if he told her the truth: "Mrs. Porter, everything that happened this morning. It all has an explanation."

Mrs. Porter squeezed his arm a little. "Oh, I know all about your Whisp. Gaby told me. I think I can help. But shhh. We need to go somewhere a little more private first."

Will's hairs tingled. Mrs. Porter knew about the Whisp? She could help . . . A huge grin shot across his face. *Whisp? Whisp? Wake up! Mrs. Porter—she can help us! She knows all about you. She might know how to unbind us! Whisp? You've got to wake up and hear this.*

But he heard nothing.

Pushing his worry aside, he figured she would be even more excited when she did wake up and found out that everything's been sorted.

Will expected Mrs. Porter to eventually double back or circle round the school back to the nurse's office but she veered left down the old winding corridor that led to the smoker's toilets.

"Where are we going, Mrs. Porter?"

"Where it all began, I believe," she said, rummaging in her cardigan pocket to produce an old looking key. "That's what I like about this part of the school. No keypads. No CCTV. It's all done in the traditional way." She unlocked the door and pushed it open then gestured for Will to step inside.

The last time Will had been in here, he had been with the vultures when his head was flushed down the toilet. It had been locked ever since. He hadn't expected Mrs. Porter to lead him here. But she had . . . and it looked like she must have planned it because in the centre of the room, on the tiled floor, was one of her vases.

Mrs. Porter looked around, her expression serene. "I was always told the smell in the gents' toilets were bad. But I never expected it to be this potent. Shabby too. Look, all the paint is peeling off the walls. Still, it will have to do." She shrugged. "Sit down."

"On the floor? Beside . . . your vase. Why is it here?" Will asked.

"Yes, on the floor. I know it's a tad unusual but this whole situation is rather odd, isn't it?" Mrs. Porter smiled.

Will crossed his legs and sat down on the floor beside the vase.

Mrs. Porter lifted her cane and struck at one of the bathroom mirrors until it shattered.

Flinching in surprise, Will gasped. "What—"

"Ssh." She bent down and grasped at one of the shards with her fingers. She pushed the tip into the back of her other hand, testing it, before nodding. "Sharp enough, I think." She tossed the shard to Will who caught it in his hands.

"I would have preferred a knife, but we need to improvise," Mrs. Porter commented. "Prick your finger and let a little spot of blood trickle into that jar and your Whisp is gone.'

Will looked at Mrs. Porter. "Really?"

"I know. It's simple. But that's all it is. A drop of blood freely given will bind or unbind any Whisp. That's one of the secrets that Mr. Anthony discovered. One small cut and you are free."

Will could hardly believe it. It did seem simple. So simple.

"How do you know all this Mrs. Porter?"

"Mr. Anthony wasn't the only visitor to this world. Now hurry, we don't want to get caught. Those police officers will never believe us."

He toyed with the shard against his finger. It was sharp. It would easily prick him. "But what happens to the Whisp?"

"Well, this little jar takes care of her." Mrs. Porter gesticulated at the vase with her cane.

"That's not a vase," Will realised, gripping the shard a little tighter. "That's a Pandora jar. But aren't they used to trap Whisps?"

"You're a quick learner, Will Devine. One drop of blood and your little menace is out your life for good."

"My Whisp doesn't want to be trapped. She wants to be free," Will said, hoping Mrs. Porter would understand.

"She's not *your* Whisp. She's not *your* anything, Will. She's supposed to be in the jar. It's where she belongs.

"I really don't think she would want to be trapped in the jar," Will countered, dropping the shard.

"She needs to be trapped, Will." Mrs. Porter's voice trembled with anxiety. "You have no idea how precious she is. We can't let her escape. If she fell into the wrong hands, it will be disastrous."

Will looked down at the jar. Mrs. Porter seemed so certain that this was the right thing to do, but he couldn't shake the apprehension he had. He wished he could ask his Whisp what she wanted, but she was silent in his mind.

"She's incredibly powerful," Mrs. Porter said. "It would be very selfish to keep her locked up inside you."

"I'm sorry," Will started, looking Mrs. Porter in the eye, "it's not my choice to make. The Whisp has passed out. We need to wait for her to wake up and then we can ask if she wants to go in the jar. I shouldn't make the decision for her."

Mrs. Porter sighed and cocked her head. "We don't have time. The police officers are going to come looking for you. You are going to get expelled; probably sent to another school. This is my one chance to help."

Will picked up the shard again and saw the reflection of himself in the mirror. He looked weak. He didn't look like he had a powerful spirit inside his body. He looked like a boy who wanted it to all end. A boy who desperately wanted to go back to his normal life. But he knew somewhere deep, deep, inside of him there was a Whisp and right now he had to protect her.

"I'm sorry I can't do it, Mrs. Porter," he said, and returned the shard to the floor.

"I didn't want to tell you this. I didn't want to promise something that might not be possible." Mrs. Porter gave a heavy sigh before using her cane to come down onto her knees beside Will. "I think we can bring your mother back to life."

Will looked at Mrs. Porter and blinked. Had she really just said she could bring his mother back to life? How was that even possible?

"Me and Mr. Anthony are both from the same world as that Whisp, Will. In my world, Mr. Anthony was a terrible man. He was the General of a great army and had killed many people. But there was one death that haunted him. When he was a young man, he fell in love with his teacher, but she had fallen in love with someone else. He grew jealous and he hated the thought of her with anyone but him. And that's when he did the most terrible thing imaginable—he tortured and killed the woman he loved. And he regretted it ever since. All he ever wanted was to bring her back."

"Martha Ulcedi," Will whispered. "Mr. Anthony loved her, but she loved Mr. Crickwicker."

"You know the story?" Mrs. Porter asked with amazement. At his nod, she shook her head. "You have discovered so much already, Will. You're a bright boy. You must know that Mr. Anthony had figured it out. He figured out how to bring back the dead. To bring back loved ones just like your mother. All it will take is a simple sacrifice."

The counsellor pointed at Will's chest, continuing. "The Whisp, Will. We would need to sacrifice the Whisp. She flies around bouncing from person to person giving inspiration to all that need it. But that's not her power. That's not her *true* power."

Mrs. Porter looked into Will's eyes, and he felt his own

burn. He was flooded with memories of his mum. All the pain and anguish of his grief was overwhelming him.

"Do you know where these words come from —'In*spir*ation?' '*Spir*it?' 'SPIR?' SPIR is a Latin word. It means breath. As in to breathe, to have life. That's the secret that the General discovered.

"It's been staring us all in the face, this whole time. These little Whisps have the power of life. When they touch you, they bind with your soul for just a moment. But your soul is already bound, it's linked to everyone you've ever loved—that's what Mr. Anthony figured out. They can bring back the dead."

She paused. "Mr. Anthony had wanted to bring back the dead and he thought one little Whisp would be worth the sacrifice. I can't be certain, but I know what it is like to lose your mother. I know the pain it causes. Don't you think it's a chance worth taking to see your mother again?"

At that moment Will wanted it more than anything. He wanted one more chance to see his mum smile. One more chance to hear her hum off-key. One more chance to receive a kiss on his forehead before she left for work. He wanted it so much that it hurt to think that it might be possible.

Mrs. Porter picked up the mirror shard and took Will's hand in her own. She drew a thin line across his palm with the tip of the shard and a moment later the line was crimson with blood. "A drop of blood freely given, Will," she said, softly. "Let it trickle into that jar and I promise you as soon I have figured it out, I will kill that Whisp and bring your mother back."

Will closed his hand into a fist and the blood dripped onto the tile floor. "Kill," he repeated as the full meaning of the word settled into his mind. He pulled his hand back, shifted away. "We can't."

"That's what a sacrifice is Will. For something to live. Something has to die." Mrs. Porter opened the lid of the jar and held it towards Will.

Will's mind was alive with noise. Memories of his mum. Memories of the room. Of flowers. Of her funeral. The hot stinging pain of his cut hand throbbed in time with each replayed memory. Everything was all swimming in and out of focus and he battled with the decision in front of him.

It's ok, Will. It's time to say goodbye.

At once his mind went quiet. He knew it was the Whisp speaking; he recognised her voice. He felt her stir awake and she immediately understood at once the fate in front of her. But then he heard the words again and they echoed somewhere deeper. Somewhere in his soul.

'It's ok, Will. It's time to say goodbye.'

And he saw her face. He saw his mum say those words and felt a kiss upon his forehead.

Will withdrew his hand and stood; Mrs. Porter glared at him.

"Don't you miss your mother, Will?" she asked with venom in her voice.

"I do. But I can't let you take the Whisp, I'm sorry." Will retreated, heading for the door when Mrs. Porter spoke.

"I wouldn't leave just yet, William. I've brought some insurance."

Mrs. Porter got to her feet and pushed open one of the toilet stall doors with her cane. The door squeaked open and that's when Will laid eyes on her—

Gaby! the Whisp shouted in Will's mind as he rushed towards his friend.

"Not so fast," Mrs. Porter said, blocking Will's way, holding her cane like a drawn sword.

Will paused but never took his eyes off his friend. She had been bound to the toilet seat with skipping ropes. They were round her arms and chest and her mouth had been gagged shut with a bean bag and Sellotape. "What have you done to her?"

"Nothing yet." The edge of Mrs. Porter's lips curled into a small vindictive smile as she spoke. "But that jar at her feet contains a Ghast. I'm sure you must know what that means. The one in this particular jar is exceptionally vicious and it's very hungry. It's not fed on anyone since Mr. Anthony."

Will tried to sidestep Mrs. Porter, but she was nimbler than she had made out. She swung her cane till it rested on the top of the jar at Gaby's feet.

"Ah. Ah. Ah. Don't want this little jar to tip, do we? No fast moves. No little accidents. Otherwise, Gaby's soul is as good as dead."

Mrs. Porter played with the jar, the cane gently tipping it till it was on one edge before bringing it back down to balance. "Mr. Anthony wanted to catch her. He opened those Thresholds and every night he dropped a little of his freely given blood into each of them, hoping that the Whisp would come through and bind with him. But the Ghast got there first, Will. It fled through the Threshold and right into Mr. Anthony's soul and he couldn't unbind with it. He lived with it torturing him because he had hope that eventually, the Whisp would come . . . And it did. It came right through that Threshold and into the water in this very bathroom. But when he got here that night, he discovered it had already gone. Only a trace of it was left behind. It had bound to someone else."

When he looked away, she sighed and continued. "It had bound to you, Will. And that's when Mr. Anthony gave up hope. That's when Mr. Anthony realised he would never find his Whisp. He would never bring Martha back from the dead. He could never undo what he had done. And so, he let the Ghast devour him. He let the Ghast take away his life. All because you stole his Whisp. You killed Mr. Anthony, Will. You took away his hope." She tsked. "Are you going to let Gaby be eaten up, too? All for your precious little Whisp?"

Gaby was frozen with fear like a statue that had been shattered and put back together with the skipping rope that stretched across her body. Only her eyes were alive, sparkling with tears. Will's cheeks flushed red with anger, and he glared at Mrs. Porter, horrified at the cruelty she displayed.

Her smile curled into a scowl.

"If you want to save your friend, I'm going to need you to give me *your* Whisp. Right now." Her voice cut with spite as sharp as a razor blade.

Will turned inward hoping that the Whisp might have one final flash of brilliance. One moment of genius inspiration—

I'm so sorry, Will.

She and Will both knew that Mrs. Porter had outwitted them.

Will looked at his bloodied hand and the empty jar sitting in the middle of the bathroom floor. He bent down to pick it up. The clay was cold in his hands. "I need a moment," he said softly, "to say goodbye."

Mrs. Porter struck her cane to the floor in frustration. "Fine. But be quick. If the police come in here, I will make sure the Ghast comes out of that jar, I promise." She gestured to the next toilet stall and Will pushed the door open with his cut hand, leaving a streak of blood that trickled down the door.

He sat down on the toilet seat and pulled the stopper out of the jar in front of him.

Will, the Whisp said, *thank you.*

Will held out his hand over the jar. *I'm sorry.*

He squeezed his cut hand into a fist and plunged it into the jar. He felt the blood trickle down through his fingers and when the first drop hit the base of the jar his body began to shake. He felt her essence pour out of him like he had opened a giant hole in his heart.

Mrs. Porter looked on. "Done?" she asked after a moment.

Will shook his head, whispering, "Not yet."

He held his hand in the jar a little longer as bits of the Whisp and Will pulled apart. She had been interwoven with Will for so long that every part of him was affected. It hurt, but as much as it hurt him, he knew it hurt her more. She wasn't expanding this time. She wasn't filling up; she was shrinking down. She was being squeezed until every last drop of her was locked inside the dead vacuum of the clay.

Mrs. Porter snapped with impatience, "Now?"

Will shook his head, his face clenched from the pain.

Based on her slight smile, Will could tell she enjoyed watching him struggle and squirm. She took a Threshold key out of her cardigan pocket and toyed with it.

"One more thing," she said, "which of these toilets did the Whisp come from? Gaby only said it was from a toilet bowl. She never mentioned which one."

Will couldn't speak, the last of the Whisp's spirit was flushing out of him and it took every ounce of energy he had. And his nose began to bleed, tracing a crimson line down from his nostril onto his lips.

There was a knock on the door and Mrs. Porter tensed.

"This is the police. Anyone in here?" came the shout.

Mrs. Porter bolted to the door, taking the door key from her pocket and locking the inside bolt. "Make a sound, and I'll kill you both," she whispered, glancing over her shoulder as the door was pushed on from the other side.

"It's locked," a male voice muttered.

"Police! Open Up!" came another shout.

Mrs. Porter spun and grabbed Will's face, squeezing it between her fingers. "Where is the water Threshold?" she spat.

Will stuttered, "F-farthest-t . . . le . . . l-left." His head rolled back; his vision narrowed, the blood from his nose rolled down into his throat and he tasted it on the back of his tongue.

"Get the rest of that Whisp in that jar," Mrs. Porter ordered, propping the jar between his legs so it wouldn't fall over before she rushed to the furthest toilet and plunged her Threshold key into the water.

The door shuddered under another knock.

If the police caught her there would be no way to explain Gaby's kidnapping or her mother who was likely still knocked out on the floor upstairs. She would be detained, and investigations would be opened. She would never be allowed back to this school and therefore the Thresholds. She needed to get the Threshold open so that she could snatch the jar and jump away—now.

Her hand plunged deep into the toilet bowl, and she moved the key around hoping to feel the door open.

The police banged again. It sounded as if someone was trying to force the door open with a stiff kick or a shoulder. The sound echoed around them.

Will felt the last of the Whisp go, felt his consciousness come out of the jar and back into the room. He blinked and pulled his hand from the jar.

I'm so sorry, he thought as he placed the stopper into the jar, sealing her inside, but he knew she would not hear him now.

A drop of blood fell from his nose to the floor and as he looked down, he noticed, at his feet, another jar—not the one that contained the Whisp.

The second jar.

The one containing the Ghast.

It took him a moment to realise what had happened. Then he grinned.

In the moment that Mrs. Porter left to open the Threshold, Gaby had carefully lowered the jar to the floor and rolled it between the stalls to Will.

Will did the same now, putting his jar down on the ground and rolling it under the wall of the bathroom stall. He saw Gaby stop it with her feet and carefully, using both legs propped it up so that it was in the exact same position as the one that contained the Ghast.

Quickly, Will picked up the Ghast jar and held it in his hands, pretending nothing had changed. The door to the toilets' clattered and banged.

"Police. Open this door!"

Mrs. Porter frantically ran to Will's stall, grabbing hold of the stall door having abandoned her cane on the floor. "My left or your left she shouted?"

"My left," Will said and held out the jar.

She snatched it and crashed again into the toilet on the far side. Her Threshold key plummeted into the water, but the Threshold didn't open. "No!"

"Police." A pause. "Mrs. Porter is that you? Mrs. Porter!" came the reply from outside the bathroom door.

"It's not working. Those bastards have destroyed the Thresholds." Mrs. Porter got to her feet, her arm now dripping wet with toilet water, her eyes wild. "How did you get back to this world, Will, which of the Threshold gates are open?" She grabbed the shard of mirror glass from the ground and held it threateningly towards Will.

Will looked at the sharp point of the mirror and back to Mrs. Porter.

"Grit Bin. Behind the Dining Hall. It's a new Threshold Mr. Crickwicker made for me."

"Will? Are you in there? Will?" someone shouted.

"Grab me that fire extinguisher!" Inspector McNamara snapped.

Mrs. Porter eyed the small narrow frosted window on the far-away wall. She dragged Will to it, using his body to balance herself. "Quick boy, help me up."

Before he could react, she had already climbed on top of him using his back as a step. She hammered her forearm at the glass until it swung open. Scrambling towards the fresh air, she wriggled her old, plump body out of the window, holding the jar like it is a small baby she is trying to rescue from a fire. She writhed her belly down the wall outside and squeezed and twisted to get her backside out—Will watched her wide eyed.

The door crashed inward, and the police burst through.

Officer Silversmith reached for Mrs. Porter but only managed to hold onto her shoe.

With a last twist and curse, Mrs. Porter crumpled to the road and hobbled off around the school with the jar in her hand.

McNamara yelled, "Catch her!"

Officer Silversmith took off back out the toilets' door.

Will snatched the jar from Gaby's feet.

"Don't!" shouted the Inspector "That's—"

Will hurled the jar across the bathroom and it shattered against the already broken mirror. Glass and clay cascaded to the floor in a hundred tiny pieces. He heard a whispered, *Thank you,* skip across his mind like a stone skimming on water. And he knew she heard him thank her too.

Will pulled at Gaby's ropes until she was free. They smiled at each other as he did this. Their eyes stung red with tears that were for every emotion and no emotion all at once.

The Inspector held back watching the two children hug and he looked at the scene with utter confusion. "What in hell happened in here?"

Chapter 20
A Present for the King

C rickwicker's locksmith shop had been abandoned.

Thales had reasoned the best way to ensure his new Threshold remained open was to make it seem like anything of value had already been lifted from the shop and that Thales, in fear of his life, had gone on the run. This was, of course, another one of his illusions. A great trick that would deceive even the most astute of Hunters.

He had, in fact, loaded a great deal of his shop's contents and his life's works into his old grandfather clock. He then proceeded to bash the clock in with an old hammer to make it seem like it was just a knackered piece of furniture that had been broken when the ropes across the roof had all been slashed and cut down. Thales then carefully propped the grandfather clock onto its side, positioning the keyhole perfectly to keep an ever-watchful eye on the Threshold, in case Will or the Whisp managed to return.

Time moves slowly inside the grandfather clock, so Thales had been watching for what had seemed like days on end, when a strangely dressed elderly woman sidled her way out of the Threshold, clasping a Pandora jar close to her bosom. Thales was so excited to see the Threshold in use that he wanted to immediately jump out and greet the strange new arrival, but something about her made him hold back. She had a look in her eye—a hungry look, like a famished wolf that had just clenched its jaw shut on some unsuspecting prey.

The Pandora jar was most certainly the prey . . . Thales felt defeated. Maybe Will and the Whisp had been caught. Maybe this old woman had the Whisp in the jar at that very moment. Maybe he should burst out and give her the fright of her life and wrestle the jar from her claws. Then again, as he adjusted his goggles to see better, it didn't look like a Whisp in the jar. No, he thought, that was a Ghast she had in her grasp.

Maybe Will and the Whisp were safe. They were quite a team after all.

———

Mrs. Porter limped out of the shop and onto Podger's Wynd, which was teeming with the life of an early morning. Tradesmen and sailors all turned to stare at the unusual sight of the Gatekeeper in an otherworldly red cardigan and yellow blouse.

"What are you looking at?" she snarled at one sailor as she made her way down the street. She was looking for the first Republican guard she could find. It didn't take her long to spot one, looking hapless and lazy, keeping sentry watch on one of the many bridges that spanned the canal.

He was entirely startled by Mrs. Porter's approach.

"I am a Porter," she said. At his dumbfounded stare,

she repeated, slowly, "A Porter . . . A Gatekeeper for the Thresholds of the Republic."

The young man stood still, staring with his mouth open. "What are you wearing?"

Mrs. Porter tugged at her cardigan trying to straighten it. "That doesn't matter. I need—"

"Are you from a circus? Or a street performer?"

"I'm a retired military veteran of the old war," she said, exasperated that she had to give more explanations. "I outrank you by several positions, little boy. I was charged with executing a clandestine operation under a direct order from the Thinking King and his Council. I have returned in triumph, and I demand to be taken to the palace at once."

At his continued silence, she tilted her nose higher towards the sky, trying to give off the impression that she was an imperial master of the realm.

"Of . . . course, mistress."

Mrs. Porter immediately corrected him. "It's Gatekeeper."

"Mistress Gatekeeper," the guard said with a nod, and the Gatekeeper rolled her eyes. "Only thing is. I'm under strictest instructions myself. I cannot leave this bridge till another of the Republican guards can relieve me of my position."

"I overrule that command. Escort me to the palace gate at once."

The boy seemed perplexed at the dilemma. He tapped his finger against his lip. "Beg pardon, Mistress Gatekeeper. But if, as you say, you were under the order of King and Council, then shouldn't they be expecting you? Can't you just walk up there yourself? Why do you need me?"

The Gatekeeper couldn't answer with the truth; to say,

'Well because they tried to lock me out. They destroyed all the Thresholds and so they won't be expecting me at all.' There wasn't a chance that a palace guard would let her into the courtyard, never mind the Council chambers, to explain her triumph. Not without a Republican soldier to vouch for her.

Frustrated, she grabbed the boy by the ear and twisted it. "I've had a long day," she said with her hot breath against his face. "Don't disobey me."

———

The Gatekeeper didn't speak another word to her escort as they walked, using the time instead to concoct exactly what she would say to the Council, to ensure that they understood how hard she had worked and how deserving she was of some great reward for her efforts. Maybe, if she played her cards right, she might get the old General's place on the Council herself. Then she would discover who had convinced the Thinking King to destroy the Thresholds and ensure they were punished for the misery they put her through. She daydreamed about all the cruel tortures she would inflict. She relished all of the lethal inventions she had created in her mind so much that the long march to the palace gates passed quite quickly.

When they arrived, her guard proved totally and utterly useless other than as a sacrificial lamb to the slaughter. The palace guards did indeed try to bar her entry, but she spoke with enough command and authority that they eventually sent word to the King. She then sauntered into the palace and left the boy stuttering and stammering as he was interrogated for more information.

Not waiting for permissions to be granted, the Gatekeeper walked through the great halls retracing her steps until she was at the door of the Council. Two guards in the royal blue togas moved, barring her entry with their spears. She gave a long hissing sigh and stood tapping her foot on the marble floor. Eventually, the door swung open, and Philo stuck his head out.

"Guard, send word to the palace gate, they are to bring the wretched old Gatekeeper up immediately."

"She's already here," the Gatekeeper replied with a smirk and brushed the spears aside, stepping in the doorway.

When she came here before, she was intimidated by the whole thing. But now, returning in triumph, she realised she had the status to belong in this great room.

She gave a faint bow to the Thinking King, who sat in his throne at the other end of the table, and before she was even asked, she launched into her great address:

"I bring you a gift, your Majesty. As you instructed, I went into the world of Gaia, and I did what all the Hunters in this great city did not. I captured the last Whisp in our capital. It is inside this Pandora jar at this very moment. I discovered the General's wicked motives, and I learnt the dark secrets of the science he discovered. I killed the man, myself in hand-to-hand combat. He was a traitor to the Republic, and I had to wrestle the Whisp from his great grasp—but I did it. I then discovered that the Thresholds had been destroyed. But as the Republic's humble servant, sworn to my duty, I worked tirelessly to forge a new Threshold and make my way back to this chamber with the spoils of war!"

She held the jar aloft and was met with stony silence.

The Queen spoke, "Sorry, I didn't quite follow. Did you just say you murdered the General?"

The Gatekeeper took a small step backwards, wondering if she had overplayed her hand. Maybe she shouldn't have lied. But she could hardly say she had found the General dead and left the Ghast that killed him locked away in another world, ready at any moment to come back and wreak havoc. She decided to double down.

"Yes. He planned to kill the King. He was a traitor."

"Well, then thank goodness for you." The King bellowed, "Thank goodness! Because if you could open another Threshold then so could the traitor."

The Queen seized her opportunity. "Yes. It was very unwise to have destroyed the Thresholds and think that the matter was dealt with."

"Still," Cato started, trying to deflect the Queen's attack, "we can reflect on all of our past decisions at some later date. This really changes nothing. The great celebration can still go ahead. Our city is rid of its spirits."

"Yes," the King roared, and held out his greedy fingers, wiggling them in the direction of the Pandora jar. "The last of the Whisps. It must be a mighty powerful spirit to have evaded our capture for so long."

"Oh yes," the Gatekeeper agreed, hurrying around the table. "She is the mightiest I've ever known. She will be sure to give you great wisdom and inspiration."

"Then I shall drink her up immediately," the King replied.

"Maybe she will inspire you to give me a humble promotion as a reward," the Gatekeeper suggested as she slid the jar into the King's hands.

The Queen laughed. "Good for you, Gatekeeper, don't let this opportunity for reward pass you by. There is a spare seat at this table. Indeed, there might even be another space free by the time this day is up."

The Gatekeeper glanced to see the Queen stirring her drink with her finger, all the while looking straight at Cato. He in turn gave the Queen a deathly stare, but the King paid no heed to any of it. He was too busy with the jar, fumbling with the lid in his thick fingers.

He pulled the lid off and brought the jar to his lips—

The King's eyes burned, and he felt his spine shiver as if someone had poured cold ice into his veins. He gasped in shock at the realisation of what had just happened and pushed himself back from the table. "I-I . . ."

The Queen stood. "What's wrong?" she asked with alarm.

The King began to spit and cough. "It's a Ghast! Get it out of me." He gagged. "My God. It's a Ghast!"

"No! You're wrong!" The Gatekeeper said, panicked. "It is definitely a Whisp."

Cato sprung to his feet and pointed his bony finger across the room at the Gatekeeper. "Another traitor!" he cried. "Seize her."

And the Gatekeeper felt the sudden jolt of a stinger, rip through her body as she collapsed to the ground.

Chapter 21
Winter in Worldmouth

W ill and Sacha were doing a strange dance in the living room, twirling and twisting around each other as they tried to untangle the fairy lights. There had been a lot of laughter as they unpacked the Christmas box, the last of the moving boxes that remained. They remembered their mum's love for the tackiest decorations she could find. The multi-coloured light up nativity scene that inexplicably played Elvis songs was a particular favourite of hers.

When their dad came back in the room, Will saw that he stayed in the doorway, watching them for a while without saying a word. He laughed when Sacha tripped over another tangle and Will snorted at her cry of surprise.

"Well?" Will asked, turning to look at him.

"The new Inspector who has taken over the case is very nice," Will's father replied. "But there's no new evidence. No one checked her credentials when she arrived at the school, and the phone number she gave was for a flat that was abandoned years ago. It really does seem like Mrs.

Porter just vanished." He sighed. "Good news is that the new Inspector thinks they have got everything they need from you and Gaby so there won't be any more interviews."

"Great!" Sacha exclaimed. "That's great news."

Will nodded. "I really have told them everything."

His dad ruffled his hair. "I know, son. Still, I hope they find her."

Will looked away. He knew she would never be found again, but he thought it best not to tell them that. There had been a lot of attention to the case in the newspapers. A mysterious woman who had posed as a bereavement counsellor was allowed to sneak inside a school, kidnap two pupils and assault a parent. It had been the talk of the county for a couple of days and then some other story grabbed the headlines and Worldmouth Academy tried its best to move on from the whole affair.

The press attention had died down completely, much to Will's relief, only to flare up again at Halloween when Inspector McNamara gave a sensational interview to a national newspaper saying he believed that the kidnapper might have been an evil poltergeist. He was sure something supernatural happened as Will was seen entering the classroom on the CCTV but when Mr. Scroggie discovered Gaby, Will had vanished.

Will claimed that Mr. Scroggie had just not spotted him, and he crawled out later in the night only to find the school was locked. The Inspector pushed hard for a psychic to come and inspect the school and said as much in the newspaper interview. He was made to take some time off after this and a new Inspector was assigned the case. Will felt a little guilty but was glad the scrutiny would be over.

Will and The Whisp

After the events in the toilet, Will and Gaby were taken in an ambulance to the local hospital to be checked over. It was there, in exchanged whispers, Will and Gaby had agreed it was best to keep quiet about the Whisp and the Ghast and the other world.

The Whisp, free from the jar, had left after checking on them in the hospital. She told them how excited she was to explore the new world she had found herself in. Will, saddened by her departure but relieved that he was the only one in his mind again, tried to settle into his new home and new school as best as he could.

There was no way he could go unnoticed any more though. Will and Gaby had become like celebrities in the school, with children trying to pry details out from them. Will and Gaby didn't speak about it though. They just smiled politely and tried to carry on as normal. Gaby convinced Will to join a couple of clubs and he began to make friends. Movie club was his favourite. He left the bridge club after only one game.

The only times Gaby ever uttered a word about it was to assure concerned parents that her mum was doing much better. And there was the time when one student had said Mr. Scroggie had been sentenced to life in prison. She had looked at Will, shook her head, and then had very quietly but firmly, told the boy that while Mr. Scroggie had been sentenced, it was only to community service and that the police liaison officer had told her mother he was, in fact, now working as a park keeper.

Will got used to the stares and whispers. He knew he would always be seen as different, but that was OK. He had his friends, and he had his family.

The school was, of course, awash with radical theories and stories of what happened, none of them even close to the truth. Some kids thought that Will had figured it all out before the cops and broke into Mrs. Porter's secret lair in the boy's toilet to save the day—just before she was going to kill Gaby. No one ever came up with a good reason as to why Mrs. Porter would want to kill Gaby though. There was one conspiracy theory that Ms. Sharpe had been the mastermind behind it all, fuelled by the fact that after the whole debacle played out in the press, Ms. Sharpe announced she was taking early retirement and suddenly headed off to the Mediterranean.

The vultures had said that Will and Gaby made the whole thing up; that Mrs. Porter had been set up. When Sacha heard this rumour, she started a petition to ensure that, as a punishment, the vultures were publicly disinvited from all house parties that the senior pupils might have. Will was quite proud when Sacha told him everyone in her year signed the petition.

Sacha had, Will thought, been pretty incredible through the whole ordeal. Their dad had a lot on his plate protecting Will from countless police interviews and media attention. So, it was Sacha who got them to sit down one evening to really talk about what happened. Will insisted he had stayed in the school the whole night and had never really meant for it to happen. His dad was happy to leave it at that, but Sacha pushed on.

She was the one that got Will to finally open up about feeling lonely and bullied and how much he didn't like his new school. She was the one that insisted they have one night together a week as a family doing something fun. And every so often, during the lunch hour, Will caught Sacha out the corner of his eye checking in on him, making sure he was with friends and having fun. He never told Sacha he saw her do this but knowing that she did gave him a cosy feeling.

"Hey space cadet, are you even looking for the angel? We can't turn the tree on without Angel on top."

Will smiled. "Sorry Sacha I was lost in my—" He stopped speaking, feeling a small tug in his heart as he reached into the Christmas box and pulled out four matching jumpers, each knitted with a pattern of gingerbread men and candy canes.

He remembered these jumpers, vividly. His mum had insisted they all wore them for Christmas Day; their last one together. She had slept through most of the occasion but had been awake for presents in the morning and during their meal. She laughed at Dad's overcooked attempt at a Christmas pudding and made sure they took as many pictures as possible. Will found her jumper and held it to his nose—any smell of her was long gone; all he detected was the smell of the pine needles that had found their way in the box.

"I suppose the jumpers will be too small now," Will's dad commented, his voice a little strained.

Sacha sat beside Will, grabbing her jumper. "We can squeeze into them."

"Maybe you both could." His dad patted his belly and they all laughed.

"She would like that," Will said when the laughter faded, "all of us in our jumpers again."

"She would." Will's dad looked away and rubbed at the bridge of his nose. "This was her favourite day of the year, putting up the Christmas tree."

"It wasn't because of the tree," Will said, softly. He reached once more into the box, pulling out the porcelain nativity scene. Hitting the button at the bottom, a music box version of *Jailhouse Rock* began to play.

She would like it here, he thought, and smiled.

Will looked out the classroom window, watching the rain drizzle down the glass.

It's funny, he thought to himself, *it's supposed to snow at Christmas, but it never really does*. He imagined a snowflake fluttering to the ground below, quite caught up in this dream, when something pinged off his head.

"Oww," he muttered out of instinct rather than pain. He turned around and spotted a little nub of a rubber eraser on the floor. He noticed Gaby was already scowling at the culprits—Danny Stobbie and Stephen McFall were grinning at him in the back row.

"Ignore them," Gaby whispered.

Nodding, Will turned back to the sheet in front of him. Mrs. Duncan had given them a puzzle to solve for the last day of term. They had 15 minutes to arrange a menagerie of animals and plants into their correct order in the food chain. Bonus points would be awarded to anyone who spotted the animal that didn't fit, and a further five points would go to anyone who identified where in the world this particular ecosystem was found.

"Stop chewing," Will whispered to Gaby. He learned over the past few weeks that she had a habit of gnawing the end of her pencil whenever she was thinking. "You're like a beaver." He smirked.

"I'm really stuck," Gaby whispered back. "Any idea where this ecosystem comes from?"

Will shook his head. He had given up on winning any bonus points today and had mostly been gazing out the window.

"One more minute, my little eco-warriors." Mrs. Duncan was in a bouncy mood and clearly ready to move on with the rest of the lesson. She told them at the start of class that she had a diagram to explain the sheet and most likely would go into great detail about every little thing. She began to countdown the last ten seconds when Will heard a small voice inside his head.

Oh, that's the American Prairie. I visited a ranch there.

Will quickly scribbled 'American Prairie' on the answer sheet. *Whisp?*

Hi Will, came the reply. *Thought I'd come and say hello.*

Will couldn't hide his delight; a huge smile spreading across his face.

Mrs. Duncan spotted it right away and came to stand beside his desk. "Well, it looks like William Devine is confident of his answers."

"American Prairie," Mrs. Duncan said, reading Will's paper upside down. "Very good." She gave him a wink then headed towards the front of the room.

"I thought you said you didn't know the answer." Gaby whispered when Mrs. Duncan turned her back to bring up her diagram on the smartboard.

"She's back," Will said.

"Who's back?" Gaby asked, not catching on.

Mrs. Duncan turned around and waggled her pen at the duo. "No conferring," she said. "You don't want me to deduct your bonus points, Mr. Devine."

Will straightened in his chair and folded his arms to show he was giving Mrs. Duncan his full attention. But as soon as the teacher returned to the whiteboard, Will tore a piece of paper from his jotter and started to scribble down a note:

The Whisp gave me the answer. She's come back to see us. She's been around the world!

Will folded the note and slipped it onto the floor and used his foot to shuffle it to Gaby's desk. She bent down to pick it up but froze. Will followed her gaze to find

Danny giving her a slimy smile as he slowly raised his hand.

"Mi-suss-Duncaannn," he called with the preening sing-song tone he used when he wanted to suck up to a teacher.

Danny's going to tell on us, Will thought and the Whisp snickered.

That's what he thinks.

Mrs. Duncan turned slowly. "Yes, Daniel?" She looked somewhat annoyed that he had interrupted her flow. She had just begun to talk about a new favourite subject of hers, coyote hunting techniques.

"I just wanted to say you look simply radiant today. Your outfit really suits you."

The whole class erupted in laughter and Mrs. Duncan, a little taken aback by the remark said, "Well thank you, Daniel. You're looking wonderful in your uniform, too. Now may I return to my lesson?"

Danny's face had turned as red as a tomato; he gave a little nod.

Mrs. Duncan tries to return to the subject of the coyote, but no one is paying attention.

"What did you say that for?" Stephen whispered to Danny nudging him. Danny shakes his head, unable to give an answer.

Will is trying not to laugh while Gaby is staring at the whole scene with her jaw wide open.

The Whisp chuckles. *That was a new trick I learned. Turns out you can inspire people to do all sorts of crazy things.*

Will snorted and his shoulders started shaking trying to hold in his laughter.

When Gaby finally reads the note, she turned to Will, grinning.

Going back to stare at his paper, Will sighed. *I've missed you. Where have you been? Who have you met? There's so much to catch up on.*

I agree. I want to hear all about it. Let's chat at lunch.

A minute passed before Stephen's hand went up. "Mrs. Duncan," he called out, "you have the most splendid smell today. Is it a new perfume?"

The class again descended into hilarity and Mrs. Duncan blushed. "Well boys I wasn't expecting quite so much affection this morning. Maybe save it till Valentine's Day and you can write it on a card. Save us all the embarrassment."

The Whisp laughed, settling back into Will's mind. *Thought I'd help inspire some manners into those boys.*

Will quickly covered his face to hide his amusement.

When lunch finally rolled around Gaby, Will, and the Whisp headed to the local park to talk in private. The Whisp jumped between them as they exchanged their stories first. The Whisp wanted to hear every last detail of their lives from when she had left them.

"Yeah, we are kind of like celebrities now. When my bridge club plays different schools, *everyone* knows who I am. Even the schools from outside the region."

Will added, "It's all some people want to talk about. It's kind of annoying actually. But we never tell them about you. We thought that was the safest thing to do."

Next Will and Gaby marvelled at the Whisp's stories, too. In the space of a few short months, the Whisp managed to bounce from person to person, travelling around the world. She'd seen incredible sights and managed to help people with some amazing breakthroughs. She inspired some scientists from Canada with a very bright idea about nanotechnology. She helped some environmentalists win a court battle to save part of the rain forest. The Whisp even visited the prime minister of Great Britain!

"That was you?" Gaby spurts out between bites of a sandwich, "That was a really good idea. I read about it in all the newspapers."

Yeah, all the economists loved it. But I'm not so sure how long a smart idea will stay inside that particular brain …

They chatted and chatted and nearly missed the school bell altogether.

As Will and Gaby gathered their things to head back to class the Whisp said to Will, *I'm going to explore the school, see if there are any teachers that might need a helpful thought or two. Can we meet up when the day is finished? There's something I need to tell you both.*

Will passed on the information to Gaby and they agreed to meet up with the Whisp behind the school cafeteria when the end of the day bell rang.

The last bell rang for the day and the school cleared out quickly as excited students headed home for the holiday break. Will and Gaby squeezed through the busy hallways, heading for the cafeteria. The rain was still pounding down hard, so they huddled under the cafeteria doorway for shelter.

Not waiting long, Will and Gaby were chatting about their last class when they noticed the ghostly form of a girl about their size, standing before them in the outline of the water.

"Is that you, Whisp?" Gaby asked and the Whisp melted away to bind with Will.

Can you take Gaby's hand? I want to talk with you both at the same time.

Will reached across and intertwined his fingers with Gaby, giving her hand a squeeze at her look of surprise.

The Whisp expanding through them both: *I've come to say goodbye. I need to go home. Your world is wonderful and safe and full of brilliant, beautiful people. But the more I've travelled the more I've realised I'm not needed here. I need to go back. I was the last free Whisp in my city. Your world is already full of Whisps. Mine needs me.*

"What do you mean? You're the only Whisp we have ever met," Gaby asked, pitching her voice higher to be heard above the rain.

I thought so too . . . at first. But when I started to explore, I realised that there are Ghasts and Whisps here, too. They are even more hidden than I am. But they are all over this world and here people manage to unbind from their Ghasts all the time.

"How?" asked Will.

Hope and Kindness, the Whisp replied.

I keep thinking about that Ghast we sent back into that world with Mrs. Porter. I keep thinking of Freya and how brave she was trying to help us, Will. We left all those people down in that crypt, being eaten by those Ghasts. I can go back with everything I've learned. I can help fix things."

"We are coming then," Gaby declared, aloud. "I left Will and you in that scary place once before. I'm not leaving you to go there without me again." She crossed her arms. "Those Ghasts are going to fight you with everything they've got. You are going to need help."

You both belong here with your families. I belong in my world with mine.

Gaby frowned. "But——"

You are both so brave and fearless, but this is something I have to do alone. I'm going to free all the Whisps from those terrible jars and then we are going to free all those humans from their terrible Ghasts.

Will rubbed at his eyes, the rain hiding his tears. "Don't go," he said, but he knew that the Whisp's mind was already made up.

I need to. If I can come back and see you, I promise I will, the Whisp said. *But if the threshold is still open, I have to go back.*

Will and Gaby stepped out into the rain and walked hand in hand, to the grit bin where they lifted the lid. It was filled with the tiny red stones, and it didn't for one-second look like at the bottom would be a completely different world but there was.

It's still open . . . I wish you could hear how beautiful the Threshold's song is.

"Please keep it open. Come back if you ever get into trouble or just want to see us. We will look after you," Gaby said, wiping at her eye with her sleeve.

Thank you. I would never have survived this world without you. Both of you. Goodbye.

"Goodbye Whisp", Gaby said and slipped her hand out of Will's. She stepped back and Will knew she was giving them both a space. A last moment bound together.

Will wiped at his eyes, hands fisting at his sides. *I've missed you so much. Ever since you left, it is felt like a piece of me is missing. I don't want you to go away again.*

You're right, Will, a piece of you did go missing. I took it with me. And a piece of me stayed with you. It's that way forever now.

But you still have to leave, right? All I get is that little piece.

She sighed. *That's all we ever get.*

And Will knew she was right. Because deep down— deep, deep down inside him was a voice, an echo of a voice that would last forever.

Goodbye, Whisp. Be safe.

Goodbye, Will.

Feeling the Whisp leave him, Will closed the lid and hugged Gaby in the pouring rain.

"Come on," she said after a moment, "we don't want to get locked in the school grounds. I've heard that can cause a lot of trouble."

Will smiled and they began to walk home.

Acknowledgments

My biggest thank you in the world goes to Emma. Emma is my real-life Whisp. She is the extra source of strength I need when I feel weak. She is the extra source of belief I need when I am in doubt. She is my best friend, the most wonderful cheerleader and the most patient of critics. She is the brightest spark, and she keeps my soul smiling even when I feel scared of my ghasts. She is the best team-mate for life that you could ever wish for, and I will never be able to thank her enough.

My mum and dad. They have believed in all of my most crazy dreams, plans, and projects. This book wouldn't exist without them. And come to think of it neither would I.

Craig and Julie, a fab brother and sister-in-law who read early drafts and asked the right questions that helped me understand how the Whisp and her world worked. Also, my nephew Travis, his imagination is even more wild than mine, so he is a great inspiration.

My super sister, Lynsey and her lovely family, Richard, Carter, and Harrison. I would thank the pets too but if I did that the acknowledgements would be longer than the book!

Victor, for his insightful and encouraging feedback. Dawn and Irving too, for their kind-hearted support.

Mr Ferguson, because one good teacher can change a life and Dr Rahim, because one good doctor can save it.

Team Tortoise, my creative family for which I will

always be grateful. Everyone I've ever created a show with has pushed my imagination and helped me become a better storyteller. Special mention goes to Alex and Arran, whose compassion and kindness has meant everything to me as I embarked on the journey of becoming a writer.

Final thanks go to everyone at Creative James Media who gave *Will and The Whisp* a beautiful place to call home.

About the Author

Ross MacKay lives in the village of Aberdour in Scotland with his wife and young son, Noah.

Ross previously worked in theatre as the artistic director of Tortoise in a Nutshell. His productions toured all over the world. His shows have received numerous prestigious awards including a Scotsman Fringe First for New Writing and a Critic's Pick from The New York Times.

In 2020, Ross was the recipient of the William Soutar Award for Poetry and a Tom McGrath Trust Maverick Award. He has been commissioned to write poetry for libraries in Fife, to open a festival in Perth and for two books published by Tippermuir.

Ross' first picture book, *Daddy's Bad Bed Day* will be published in 2022 by Curly Tale Books. The book has been created to help young children with parents with poor mental health. Research for the book has been supported by numerous children's charities in Scotland.

When Ross isn't writing or making shows, he spends his time in his inflatable kayak, trying to steer it as best he can. He loves gardening and is currently engaged in a fierce battle with a collection of snails who seem to love the rhubarb and potatoes just as much as Ross.

Lightning Source UK Ltd.
Milton Keynes UK
UKHW011029021022
409753UK00002B/44